THE
ENTROPY OF
BONES

THE ENTROPY OF BONES

AYIZE JAMA-EVERETT

Small Beer Press
Easthampton, MA

Small Beer Press
150 Pleasant Street #306
Easthampton, MA 01027
smallbeerpress.com
weightlessbooks.com
info@smallbeerpress.com

Distributed to the trade by Consortium.

Library of Congress Cataloging-in-Publication Data

Jama-Everett, Ayize, 1974-
 The entropy of bones : a novel / Ayize Jama-Everett. -- First edition.
     pages ; cm
 ISBN 978-1-61873-103-6 (softcover : acid-free paper) -- ISBN 978-1-61873-104-3 (ebook)
 1. Martial arts fiction. I. Title.
 PS3610.A426E58 2015
 813'.6--dc23
                        2015010352

First edition 1 2 3 4 5 6 7 8 9

Text set in Minion 12 pt.

This book was printed on 30% PCW recycled paper by the Maple Press in York, PA.
Cover illustration by John Jennings (jijennin70.tumblr.com).

To the fam. I don't take a step without you.

To Jumoke, 'cause you're still my brother.
To roadie, 'cause you're always my little girl.

Table of Contents

Chapter One
The Time I Choked Out a Hillbilly

Last time I'd been this deep in the Northern California hills I was on a blood and bar tour in a monkey-shit brown Cutlass Royale with Raj. Now I was distance running from the *Mansai,* his boat, to wherever I would finally get tired. From Sausalito to Napa was only sixty or so miles if I hugged the San Pablo Bay, cut through the National Park, and ran parallel to the 121, straight north. About a half a day's run. Cut through the mountains and pick up the pace and I could make it to Calistoga in another three hours. From downtown wine country I'd find the nicest restaurant that would serve my sweaty Gore-Texed ass and gorge myself on meals so large cooks would weep. The runs up were like moving landscape paintings done by masters, deep with nimbus clouds hiding in craggy sky-high mountains. Creeks hidden in deep green fern and ivies that spoke more than they ran.

Narayana Raj had taught me in the samurai style. You don't focus on your enemy's weakness; instead, you make yourself invulnerable. My focus was to be internal. In combat, discipline was all. But in the running of tens of miles, that discipline was frivolous. My only enemy was boredom and memory. Surrounded by such beauty, how could I not split my attention? Nestled in the California valleys, I found quiet, if not peace.

I also found guns. Halfway between Napa and Calistoga, the chambering of a shotgun pulled my attention from the drum and bass dirge pulsing in my earbuds. The woods had just gone dark, but my vision was clear enough to notice the discarded cigarette butts that formed a semicircle behind one knotted redwood. Rather than slowing down, I sped up and choke-held the red-headed shotgun boy hiding behind the tree before he had time to situate himself, my ulna against his larynx, my palm against his carotid. He was muscular but untrained. Directly across from him was an older man, late thirties, dressed for warmth with one of those down jackets that barely made a sound when he moved. His almost Fu Manchu mustache didn't twitch when he pulled two Berettas on me. I faced my captive toward his partner.

"Wait . . . ," Berettas said, more scared than he meant to sound.

Drop them, I commanded with my Voice. The gun went down hard. I used the Dragon claw, more a nerve slap than a punch, to turn the redhead's carotid artery into a vein for a second. When he started seizing, I dropped him. To his credit, Beretta went for the kid rather than his weapons. I continued my run, mad that I'd missed a refrain from Kruder and Dorfmeister.

As an indication of where my head was, I confess to not thinking about the scrap until a week later. Finishing the run, swimming ten miles a day, keeping the *Mansai* in shape, and avoiding my mother at the other end of the pier as much as possible, covered the in-between time. Even when I went back up the same route for my big run, the redhead was an afterthought.

It was only when I hit Calistoga, almost desperate for my calorie load for the run back to the Bay, that I had to deal with the consequences of my chokehold. I liked hitting up the nice tourist joint restaurants for grub when I was sweaty, and paying cash for double entrée meals. The place smelled of wood and fire, but most of the fixtures were constructed out of industrial iron and brass. Servers dressed in white shirts and black slacks prayed the heavy-fingered piano player's jazz standards would cover the clang of their dropping silverware on the brass tables. Most patrons came in dressed in custom suits and designer dresses. Me, I've always been a sweats 'n' hoodies girl. Usually I was the most out-of-place-looking person in the spot. But not that day.

I was devouring two orders of BBQ oysters, fries, and half a broiled chicken when a bear-looking man walked in. Seriously, he was 6'9", three hundred pounds of muscle with another twenty-five pounds of fat for padding. He was local. I'd seen skinnier versions of his face in the area, long in the cheekbones, bullet marks where eyes should be. He wore a large red flannel shirt and Carhartts fit for a bear. But what stood out was his facial hair. It made a mockery of any other beard I'd ever seen. His hair started on his head and covered every part of his face, from pretty close to his eye sockets to well past his collar line. It seemed almost bizarre that a mouth existed under all that fur. But it made him easy to read. As soon as he saw me, the hair moved into a smile. All the waitstaff and bartenders seemed to know him. It wasn't until he sat at my table facing me that I saw any relation to the redhead in the woods. I'm not usually one for weapons, but I palmed my butterfly knife on the off chance the bear tried to maul me in public.

"What do you weigh in at? One hundred and twenty pounds? Sopping wet?" he asked after it became obvious I wasn't going to stop eating.

And you care because?

"I'm just wondering where all that food goes," he said with a laugh. "What? You one of those bulimics or something?"

Mind not talking about gross shit while I'm eating? I snapped.

"Apologies. Didn't realize you were so sensitive."

The waitress delivered a slice of key lime pie and a glass of red wine so casually I knew she'd supplied the same to him dozens of times before.

That's going straight to your hips, I said while shoving a handful of fries in my mouth. He laughed for a while before he could take a bite of pie.

"I knew this teacher, Filipino chick or something. One of those goody-goodies. Worked at a private school in Frisco. Coached soccer, taught all day, would drive up here and take dirt samples all around my vineyard, acres and acres. All for her thesis. She never broke a sweat." He looked at me like I was supposed to get it. I kept eating.

"Turned out she had this hyperthyroid condition. Made her super strong, super fast, sped up her metabolism something fierce . . ."

Like a superhero, I said, laughing and chewing my chicken.

"Exactly," the bear growled back. "Only if she hadn't have gotten it fixed, it would have killed her."

Believe me, I was listening for the threat. I stopped eating and stared the bear down. To his credit, he didn't blink. But he didn't keep eating either.

I get the sense you're trying to tell me something, I said after I pulled my arms under the table.

"Then you misconstrue me entirely, young lady. I'm filled with nothing but questions."

Better you ask straight away, then.

"Was that you that choked out my nephew not nine miles from here while his uncle stood by and watched?"

Your nephew the sort to chamber a pump-action on a jogger while she's minding her own damn business?

"It took him two days to fully recover."

But he recovered. I leaned back in my chair, spinning my knife to my wrist, ready for whatever came next. The waitress poured another glass of Syrah.

"My brother, the one with the mustache, said he'd never seen anybody adjust to a threat as quick as you did." I nodded. "He's been in Kosovo, Iraq, Afghanistan. But you impressed him. My nephew took a different path. Did six years in Angola—the prison, you understand, not the country. Another three in San Quentin before he got smart about his game. You got the drop on him, and he saw you coming. Now you eat like a horse, but aside from that you don't say much, seem tough as nails and can obviously handle yourself. Type of business I'm in, I can't help but ask if you're looking for work."

First time I met Narayana the entire pier was being threatened by snakes. Some idiot independent filmmaker decided he wanted to make a sequel of a movie that he didn't own the rights to. He was shooting it "guerilla style," meaning without a script, a proper crew, or a clue. Oh yeah, and it involved snakes on a boat. The majority of houseboats on our Sausalito pier were like the one I grew up in, more house than boat. You'd have better luck finding alcoholics and '80s radicals living off the grid in those forever-moored houses than a sailor or anyone with a hint of grit in them. So when the pock-faced twenty-something filmmaker's snakes escaped after a drunken wrap party, let's just say things got chaotic.

Screams of panic didn't rouse my mom from her drunken snoring back then. But I got curious. Not yet fully dark and all I could see were squirming shadows darting to and fro on the dock, in the bushes, out of people's boats, falling in the water. Some of the snakes were thinner than a pencil and lightning quick; some moved so heavily across the port they seemed to dare you to touch them. Folks were grabbing their children and pets and locking themselves in their boats or trying to run past the snakes to get off the pier. I turned to go back inside when a coil hissed at me.

It was a hooded cobra. Don't ask what kind, I wouldn't be able to tell you. I just know it was banded, tan, and hissing. It stood between me and the walkway that went down to my houseboat. I tried backing up but in doing so I dragged my foot, a sound that agitated the snake. It raised its head a little more and hissed in a lower tone than I thought it would. What freaked me out more was that I thought I heard my name in its hiss.

5

I didn't have time to focus on it. From behind me, a man five inches shorter than me and two shades darker appeared. His arms were so muscular and veiny they looked like a knot of rebar. But they were as skinny as his legs. What little hair he had was a deep red and mostly near his temples. He wore an Ice Cube Predator shirt and carried a large metal trash can. I couldn't figure out which one I should be more cautious of: the snake or the man. He didn't give me a choice.

"Hold this," Narayana told me as he took the lid and handed me the can. With circular steps that never left the dock, the tiny man pushed lesser snakes out of his way with his foot until he was able to squat at arm's length of the coiled cobra. What noise, cold, and chaos had been all around disappeared in the distance as I watched this stranger speak in angered tones to this snake in a language I almost understood. After a while, he seemed to get frustrated. So he slapped the snake. Hard. The snake hissed lower, I swear almost speaking. He slapped it again. It opened its mouth in time with the tides, methodically quickly.

Again, Narayana slapped its head. I didn't see it strike. I didn't see it move. But Narayana did. Faster than a bullet he raised the trash lid. The snake's mouth made a harsh thud against it, but before it could fall to the deck, Narayana grabbed its head with his other hand. He stood with it as the snake's body, more than double his length, flopped and fought. But it was useless; his rebar hands would not let go. He held it close to his face, staring in its eyes, and spoke to it in a thick accent.

"I'm free. Tell your masters." He threw it hard in the trash can and slammed the lid on top. If he noticed me, he didn't say anything as he grabbed the can from my hands. But I couldn't forget him. Not ever.

✳

The bear's name was Roderick. His brother, Dale. His nephew was Matt, though I'd call him Shotgun forever. Together they ran a failing vineyard on one part of their property and a pot farm on the more secluded side. The side I'd been running through. They could have had a bed and breakfast on the property if they wanted to. It was gorgeous in that it was both spacious and hidden. Terraced rows of vines were what you could see from the road, but behind their three-story ailing farmhouse, dense tree growth hid acres of cultivated marijuana growing in clusters.

Roderick and Dale gave me a tour of the lands early the following week. They explained their situation as the gusty valley winds pushed earth and water to our backs. We paced rows of deformed vines of grapes as Dale spoke. Roderick would only reach his hands out and caress the plants like sickly lovers.

"We've got a plague of nymphs," Dale's half-humorous voice trickled out from under his mustache. "They are these almost invisible baby insects. They live in the roots and pervert the growth of the vines. Somehow they've encouraged the growth of this invasive tuber. Every time we think we've chopped it all away, the nymph-tuber combo comes back. They, well to be honest, they're destroying us."

"Fucking organic certification," Roderick mumbled, kicking one of the many deformed pale gray vines out of his way.

"We don't know the cause," Dale snapped at his brother. "We just know we can't use any inorganic pesticides to combat them. That's how we came across our secondary income stream."

Neither one said much more until we arrived at a giant red and gray barn with two massive doors far out of view of the freeway.

"It used to be a slaughterhouse for sheep when our grandparents bought the property," Dale said by way of explaining the sign on the door: "Sheep's tears." I ignored it, more captivated by the smell. Inside the barn was a good 50 x 70 feet filled with rows of marijuana plants and PVC pipes. Huge floodlights hung from the ceiling and the plants glistened, refracting light like they were made of green crystals instead of whatever the hell makes up weed.

"What do you think?" Roderick asked.

I think your nephew better get that shotgun off me unless he wants to get dropped again, I said as I inspected the plants.

"God damn it!" Roderick yelled toward the roof. "Matt, you get your ass down here and apologize before I crack your fool jaw my damn self."

Dale came to my side just as his brother mounted the stairs.

"Upstairs is the nursery. Originally we were going to use the oil from the plants as an insecticide. It's been used for centuries as a . . ." I just looked at him. "Ok, so that was probably some wishful thinking Roderick and I used to get started. But then Matt got out of lockup with all these connections."

"I'm sorry I aimed at you," a shamed Matt said quickly as he came down the stairs. He said no more and instead rushed over to a large cistern and started misting the plants.

I'm not a smoker, I told the three of them later at the brass restaurant, which Dale was a part owner in.

"Can't be with those lungs," Shotgun Matt quipped.

I mean I don't know any more about your product than what you've told me today. My mom would burn a blunt occasionally before she had her come-to-Jesus moment, but the bottle was more of her thing even then.

"We're not asking you to grow the stuff." Roderick the bear smiled.

"We need protection," Dale said. I could see Shotgun's ego shrinking up under his nut sack as I smiled.

Say more, I whispered, looking at Shotgun.

"Look, we got Mexican problems." Shotgun spat out quickly so as not to offend the kitchen staff. "We've got ninety acres of farmland. Those plants you saw today are just one strain. We've got five patches hidden throughout the property. But these damn Mexicans keep coming through and stealing our crops. That's why we were out in the woods when you came on us. Not only do we have to fight back bug blight on the grapes and tend to the others, we've got to scare off Mexicans."

How do you know they're Mexican? I asked, sipping tea.

"Huh?" Shotgun was confused. "What? I thought you were some kind of Asian or something . . ."

Yeah, Mongolian and Black. I'm not taking offense. You're saying Mexican. All I'm saying is you know how?

"Who else would steal a man's weed?" Dale smacked him in the head hard before I could react. Roderick put his calm voice on before speaking.

"Jail will do horrendous things to a man's sense of reason. Look, we're not looking for bodies. We don't want a war. But we're fighting for survival, literally. This year's grape harvest is down thirty percent. Last year it was fifteen percent. Without those green buds, we'd have already gone under. All we need from you is to do . . ."

What I do best.

I've always wanted to sing but when I was born I couldn't even cry. My mouth made the shapes, my heart mourned. But there was no sound. I should have been able to speak. I was healthy. I could hear fine; sure, I've always been light for my age, but it's not like I don't eat. My mother says I hit my social markers a little late. I was shy. That's the understatement of the decade. I wasn't shy, I was terrified. All it takes is four kids chasing you around a schoolyard trying to get you to do the one thing you can't do to cancel all thoughts of education as a safe refuge.

I was on the boat experiencing what can only be described as multiple slow-motion mule kicks to my lady parts when I first got my Voice. My mother was not one to hold back anything so she told me what to expect with menstrual cramps. But her words did nothing to prepare me for the persistent Muay Thai jabs to my womb, or the splitting headache that was threatening to vibrate my teeth out of my mouth. Even the slow swaying motion of the ocean against the docked houseboat was enough to make me nauseous. I thought my body was going to split open, I thought something was wrong with me; this wasn't the way it was supposed to be. I knew all of this period drama is pretty typical, but then there's the added dimension of not being able to speak. Not being able to scream it out, or even cry it out. I wasn't about to gain a voice just so I could complain about my period. Or so I thought.

"Girl, what you need to do is calm down and take this pill," my mother told me when she came into my room, hazel eyes already flushed with irritation.

You don't understand how much this hurts, I screamed in my mind.

"Shit, girl, you think this is bad, try childbirth. Now take this damn pill."

Think you could bring me some damn water since I can't stand up?

"That's the only 'damn' I'll be allowing from you today. Pull it together, Chabi. This is just the beginning of your womanhood," she said as she left my room to get some water at the kitchen upstairs.

That was the first day I ever spoke without using my lips. I couldn't really reflect on it, or even understand what happened until the pain meds kicked in, but even then I thought I was dreaming it.

It wasn't until I was at school a couple of weeks later that it happened again. The fact that I couldn't speak somehow meant that I belonged with kids that couldn't hear. At the Marin County School for the Deaf I was a star among the students for being able to hear and still sign; I still found it the most oppressive environment in the world at age twelve. It didn't help that I was the darkest, poorest, most four-lettered signing child that had ever crossed their path. My mother's frequent temper tantrums on school grounds coupled with her inconsistent payments didn't do much to endear me to the administration. There wasn't much Mom could do about it. She worked as a hotel receptionist from the day my father left her. I had a three quarter scholarship; guess they didn't have a lot of half-black half-Mongolians on their brochures. But that quarter was a bitch to get around for Mom. The hotel where she worked paid well enough, but the only place in the Bay where we could afford a two-bedroom was the houseboat, permanently docked and forever in need of repair. The end result: a mute, dark-skinned Asian-looking scholarship kid among the wealthiest white deaf kids in California. Tween social relations being what they are, compassion was a hard currency to come by. Even deaf bitches from San Rafael can throw shade on the playground. So when Callie Mills decided to trip me while playing a game of volleyball I wasn't planning on doing any more than signing for her to fuck off. But I face-planted hard and nearly broke my nose. The pain and the anger triggered that Voice again.

Touch me again and everybody here will know why your dad shows up with a different chick every week, you skank whore, I thought-said-projected-felt, getting up from the ground and staring at her. Callie began putting her hands to her ears with a look of revulsion, almost unconcerned with me, and then stopped. She saw my gaze hadn't shifted, and so did everyone else. Then the tears came. When you're deaf and crying, it's hard to be comforted: you can't really read what people are signing to you behind a shield of tears. I didn't care at the time. My nose was still bleeding. So I added fuel to the fire.

And you better stop telling people the only reason I'm here is because my mom gives the dean head or I'll break your fingers. That was it, my first fully intentional "sentence" someone else heard. Her tears turned to panic screams as she threw herself on the court and began ripping at her ears. No one cared about my bloody nose after that. In fact, no one would look at me after that.

✳

The job itself was beyond easy. The two weeks of waiting would have driven most people crazy, or, more to the point, drove Shotgun Matt nuts. His uncles demanded he follow my lead and I needed only flash a disconcerting look if he ever challenged my authority and the former con stepped in line. I surveyed the land and walked the five fields of marijuana a few times in silence before I found the only spot on the property, about one hundred feet behind the nursery, where I could either see, hear, or feel each of the plots. Unfortunately for Shotgun, it was near a nest of deformed nymph growth that smelled . . . particular.

It looked like a mushroom decided to molest a grapevine, and the grapevine was fighting back. Every time Roderick and his brother hacked at it, the growth just spread its fleshy purple, green, and white phalanges out farther into their property. Left alone it grew in a semi-circular pattern around a huge boulder, creating an almost throne out of the stone that gave off the scent of crushed grape, mashed mushroom, and some foreign incense. It worked for me but I think the smell drove poor Shotgun crazy. It was a constant reminder of how and why his mostly legit family was growing criminal crop.

If that wasn't the cause for his lunacy, maybe it was my stillness. My routine was to hang at the *Mansai* until around three p.m. Then I'd run the seventy-ish miles to the farm. I run faster at night so I'd usually make it around 12:30. Dale would just be coming off his guard/tending shift. A large plate of food would be waiting in the nursery: usually a full roasted chicken and mashed potatoes. After a genuine effort to get me to share more about myself, Dale's fatigue would get the better of him. To keep him quiet I'd take the jacket and sleeping bag he offered. But it was my katas that kept me warm and alert. By two in the morning, I'd be so energized and focused that a once-over of each weed plot on the property took a total of ten minutes. Then I'd sit on the nymph rock, focus my breathing, still myself, and train myself to notice the exact moment when night turned to dawn.

That would be when Shotgun showed up, namesake in one hand, microwaved breakfast sandwich in the other. I knew my senses were sharp when I recognized the ping of his loose muffler a quarter a mile down the freeway. Frustration would set in the second he was done tending to the plants. He seemed surprised to not be allowed a headlamp to read. He didn't know how to just sit and wait.

"In his defense," Dale told me after he took over his nephew's shift, "he was locked up for a while. I think the young man has had enough of waiting."

I've had enough of excessive sighing and tantrum page turning, I said, looking down from the rock to where the older man sat. His dark plaid jacket was only slightly zipped so I saw the strap of his holster. His weapons of choice, the twin Berettas, were constantly with him.

"I'll do my best to make up for my family's inadequacies, my lady." Only a gay man could flirt with a woman so casually. But it was his measured reasoning I appreciated above his flattery. Dale sat quiet, always awake, and always alert. But he was never excessive in his concern. His nephew carried a shotgun and held it like he was under enemy fire. Dale concealed two weapons with illegal hollow-point rounds but would only reach for them if he knew it was time to bring the pain.

I sat and imagined the stories of the nymph growth. I'm not prone to fancy but the growth fascinated me. I'd looked up the word "tuber" and eventually Wiki-trolled my way to the term "rhizome." The idea of an underground growing mushroom/potato that could have been growing for hundreds if not thousands of years resonated with me. It made the idea of trees, growing upwards searching for a sun they could never reach, seem arrogant. The rhizome stayed underground, quiet, growing out instead of up, growing with what-ever was around it instead of pulling from around it to break through the very earth. Here was an unseen, quiet changer of fortunes that represented massive amounts of power. If I sat long enough, still enough, it encroached on my lap. If it was truly as pervasive as

Roderick swore, then it ran underneath all their property, spreading in its haphazard fashion, choosing other growth to interact with at random. I felt/imagined the white thin tubers interacting with the roots of the large spruce Dale rested on early one morning. In that connection, the growth knew all there was to know about Dale: how he'd been discharged from Naval intelligence because a hated subordinate found him in bed with his lover. How Dale evened the score by guaranteeing the subordinate would never advance beyond the rank of yeoman. How he worked in private intelligence in Yemen, South Korea, and Pakistan for five years until he realized the information he was securing was open to anyone willing to pay. Anyone. How he left it all, bought into the restaurant in his hometown, and worked this vineyard with his hunter/hippy of an older brother and tried his best to care for his dead sister's kid.

The knowledge came without asking and was in no way verified. But it was felt, like when I got a kata right or when I was in perfect running stride. I didn't even focus on the man; the knowing came just by keeping my senses open, like the knowing of the weed stealers.

Seven on the ridge two and a half acres away, I said after almost two full weeks of sitting. As expected, Dale was up with both Berettas in hand before I even knew what I was saying. I witnessed the statement coming from my non-mouth with my Voice in the same time that Dale heard it.

Wait, I told him as I stood. Call your brothers in now and we've got war. I've got this.

"You've got seven, possibly eight guys?" he asked, already following behind me as I ran in the early morning light toward the southeastern field.

If you stay quiet, yes, I whispered.

I cut into the dense pine that hid a half-acre of weed plants and disappeared up a tree before Dale could protest. I heard his feet shuffle on the soft ground as I did my first Tarzan leap from one tree trunk to another. But Dale did right and took cover where he was.

By my ninth jump I'd perfected my technique so I didn't shake the receiving tree at all.

The marijuana plants were planted less in rows and more in concentric circles, navigating around all sizes of sage bushes, berry patches, and large pines. Shotgun was partially right: three of the seven were Mexican; the rest were white. Locals, if their accents were to be believed; all of them had guns. I waited until Dale came in range with his weapons before I made my move. That gave them time to spread out. They were disciplined thieves, snipping buds in teams of two. It was only good fortune the terrain was with me. With all of them desperately snipping, no one noticed my descent from the massive sequoia. I choked the first one out in between clippings. His partner only noticed a prick on his neck, then he was out. I signaled to Dale to grab their guns, then moved to the next two, who harvested closer to a thick raspberry bush out of view from the others.

I let the large Mexican see my fist and when he raised his thick Adam's apple to speak I shoved it into his mouth. Falling on his knees caused such a thud his partner had to look over. All he saw was my head-butt causing three grand in dental bills. The last three were closer now. It would have been easier to play it straight but I wanted the challenge. I gathered three stones, half palm sized, and launched them in the thieves' direction. All three hit, but only two went down. The last, another local, twirled, confused by his own pain and fallen friends. I pounced on him quick, covering the distance between us without regard to sound, and finally choking him out with a hush.

All good? I asked Dale as he came up from the berry bushes holding the guns of the others. His breathing was even but his eyes were wide. Before he could say anything I went around salamander-smacking the small of the thieves' backs, keeping them both paralyzed and unconscious. That snapped Dale back into business mode and he began searching wallets.

*

"Walking up hills both ways again, huh?" was what my mom said when she heard about me getting kicked out of school. I didn't help my case by telling her I wanted to go to a normal school. I couldn't figure out how I was "speaking," but it was all I ever wanted and I wasn't trying to question it. I did my best begging impression to Mom in her room, the loft section of the houseboat. She was seeing what I was trying to demonstrate to her. Namely that somehow I was speaking. I could see her trying to logic out what was happening, why I'd been going to the deaf school in the first place, but every time she got close to an answer, her deep red forehead would smooth, her forever light-purple-stained lips would cease their endless dance, and her chest would relax. After that, whatever acknowledgment of my former state disappeared. It was like she never even knew I was mute in the first place. She looked . . . into me, trying to see what was missing, what she couldn't understand. I would've tried to help her, honestly. If I had any clue myself.

"You want to go to public school, you've got to learn how to fight." To her credit, Mom grew up in East Oakland in the crack era. For her, public school and fighting went together like wine and bottles.

Got it. I knew the perfect teacher.

Narayana began taking notice of me after the snake incident. He'd taken on a bit of hero status around the pier. I was just one of his rescues. He'd gone into people's houses with a machete and diced snakes. Apparently he also had some violent words with the "director" as well. But it wasn't his violence I was after. It was his eyes: eyes that could stare down a cobra and not flinch. I caught a glimpse of that stare and I wanted to adopt it.

He'd only spoken to me one time since then. Mom was looking at a DUI, and while she was able to avoid Marin's finest, her seat belt and car door got the best of her entangled and suspended as she tried to get out of the car. I heard her in the parking lot attached to the port, a good two hundred feet from our front door, screaming and cursing up a storm. I went out to help her and had to deal with her wild swings and violent sobs. At the scrap of grass in the middle of the cement parking lot, probably intended to be something more than a place for houseboat dogs to shit and piss, Mom's meaty breast slipped out of her dress. I tried to help but then she fell. I was able to get her to her feet again, but was losing her when Narayana appeared, again out of nowhere, and grabbed her other side. She struggled against him, but only for a second. He dragon-clawed her, but in a gentle way. She seized for a second and then passed out. I didn't have voice at the time to say anything. Instead I watched as he took all her weight and carried my mom back to the house. He put her in the bed without a word. It was only when he left that he spoke, voicing his phone number, and waited until I nodded acknowledgment.

"Ever again, you call. No one talk? I know you. I come." And once again, he was gone.

There's a feeling you get when someone really hears you, you know? You can do all that eye contact, attentive body language stuff, but if you're not paying attention, people really know no matter what you do. I seemed to be able to force that attention, to make people pay attention to me. And that attention was so strong, people understood what I was saying, thinking . . . something. But when I tried to use the phone, the illusion failed. It felt like a mental trick played on me by the world.

I ran out the house in my Crocs and the clothes I slept in, a pair of jean shorts and a gray wife-beater a size too big. I ran over to the *Mansai*, the authentic old-school twenty-five-foot hunk of junk with more power than a small brown man was supposed to be allowed to have in this country. Narayana terrorized the clueless and novices alike in the S.F. bay with that ship when he first docked in our harbor, but after a few months he seemed happy to just have its menace on the waves as a potential threat.

, The afternoon cold was beginning to roll in but Narayana stood on his deck shirtless with the snake-destroying machete and sliced paper-thin sheets of watermelon, not nicking the deck in the slightest. He thought weighing more than one hundred and ten pounds was a sign of American gluttony and on his 5'3" frame, he was probably right. Even though he rubbed cinnamon oil on his arms and legs every day, his skin still seemed slightly ashen to me.

Cool, I said once I realized what he was doing.

"It's practice," Narayana said amiably, right before he did some wild overhand right swing with a machete, and delivered a pancetta-thin slice of watermelon this time to my nose. "I have little caramel downstairs. In between slices tastes good. You want?"

The slice was in my belly before half his sentence was done. Narayana just laughed at me.

My mom says I can go to regular school, I said tentatively suddenly frightened of what would happen if Narayana stopped "hearing" me.

"And why shouldn't you?" he said after another slice. I looked up in delight to see him judging the slice with his eyes closed. He let the edge of the blade roll up and down the light green of that watermelon with his machete, never far away from him. That blade was sharp, but the machete was nothing special, just a farm implement. With that blade, he recorded every ridge, bump, and crease of the fruit. And once he memorized those indicators, Narayana once again chopped a leaf of watermelon off the fruit with an overhand right and would not nick his deck. Only this time his eyes were closed, and he sent the slice directly into my face. I caught it half with my hands and half with my mouth. The fruit was almost gone by the time he opened his eyes.

But she says I can only go if I learn to fight. He was halfway through another blind swipe when Narayana froze and broke posture entirely.

"Why me?" he asked. I took his help onto the deck and looked at the man as though he were feverish.

Um, not a lot of Indian men I know spend their afternoons chopping fruit with machetes. Or call it training. He smiled and sat on his ever-present cooler. It was attended to with religious fervor, never to be absent of its holy sacraments of Jack Daniel's and Coca-Cola. Sometimes I think those two ingredients were the only spices to his life the United States offered Narayana.

"But why do you want to practice for what I am practicing for?"

Because no one fucks with you and you don't even know it. I have never seen you nervous or out of your depth. Ever. I still remember when that group of yuppies almost crashed into you out by San Rafael and how you went all pirate and jumped on their ship. Yeah, that right there. I gotta learn how to carry myself like that.

"You want to hijack ships?" he asked in earnest. My mom told me he used to be a pirate. I thought it was a joke until I looked online and found out booty was still getting plundered and cannons were still being fired on the open seas. Only now it was the poor, the desperate, and the insanely brave who dared become pirates. I saw Narayana differently after that.

No. But I want people to know I can and will in a second if the situation calls for it. I want to be like you.

Something about the reflection of the light from his blade to his face made Narayana look menacing in that moment. He saw me flinch and let the machete down on the deck gently. He turned and went to his ratty green-and-yellow lawn chair and poured himself a Jack and Coke. He offered me one, but I declined. That earned me a little more respect in his eyes. Still, Narayana sat and watched the sun go down behind San Francisco before he said anything in English.

"You do what I say? Everything. Anytime. Never a 'no' from you to me. You become mine. I lend you to your mother. If she's drowning and I'm drowning, you save me. I don't recommend this path for anyone, being under me. Go find a dojo, something like that. They teach you how to fight good."

That I had to think about for a second. Was good good enough?

What's the difference between some dojo guy teaching me and you? Like what's your style? You do kung fu? Tae kwan do?

"There is no name to what I know," Narayana said, taking a long sip from his cup. "Kung-fu, your muay Thai, these arts teach you how to break bones. What I do breaks the memory of bones. People do not heal from the wounds I inflict. There is no humanity in what I teach, only fire and sharp flexible pain. I travel the world for sixty-eight years, and this is the only discipline that makes me humble before it."

Get the fuck out of here. I laughed. My mom was thirty-three. Narayana looked maybe five years older than her.

"The practice," he said, showing off his taut skin.

Chapter Two
The Practice

Each brother had a different idea of what to do with the pot thieves.

"Blow their fucking brains out," came from Shotgun, of course. He always had a reason to be pissed. In this case, it was the identity of their thieves. If not friends, two of the white guys were at least drinking buddies. He almost kicked one of their heads off as soon as he saw the man passed out and covered in early morning dew.

"You kill them?" Roderick asked me.

I could, I offered. Figured you had more options if I delivered them alive.

"Dumbass brought his driver's license along," Shotgun joked as he rifled through what Dale had pilfered.

"Fair point," Roderick said, turning his gaze back to me. Dale's silence was unsettling his brother, but Roderick couldn't understand why. He'd only heard of what I could do. I realized Dale was the only one who'd seen me do my due that close and not get touched. The only person except Narayana.

"So we disappear them. Leave people wondering," Roderick stated, slipping on massive black gloves and a steel grimace.

Thought you didn't want war? I asked casually, not moving as he approached the big Mexican.

"Won't be war." Roderick reached in his lumberjack jacket and pulled out an axe that could only be hidden by his frame. "They'll be a question mark."

Shotgun started hiccuping seizing so hard he fell over face forward. We all stopped. Dale was the first to realize his nephew was laughing. Finally, the older man spoke.

"You want to be serious for a god damn second? Might be helpful!" Roderick shouted.

"I'm sorry." The redhead giggled as he stood with a piece of paper pilfered from a thief and walked toward his uncle. "But you got to see this."

We waited until Dale read it, then watched as he fell into hysterics as well. Fortunately, he retained enough composure to speak.

"It's a medical marijuana card."

Roderick laughed so hard I could actually make his mouth out underneath the beard. After another minute he prepared himself to butcher his enemies again.

"How long can you keep them unconscious?" Dale asked me loud enough to interrupt his brother's murder chop. The other two looked at me with a newfound confusion

I don't know. About a day and a half. After that it's probably easier to kill them than keep them alive. The Dragon's kiss to the back of neck supposedly worked even when someone was already unconscious, but it was a one-time strike.

"You have a plan?" Shotgun asked.

"I'm thinking Chabi's right. We disappear these offenders, more will come. Chabi came through covert style. Not a one of them saw her clearly. To them, they came to do what they've done dozens of times before. Only this time . . ."

"Only this time what?" Roderick asked impatiently.

"Exactly. We get to decide."

"You ain't trying to punk them or something?" We all looked at Shotgun, who felt stupid as soon as he asked the question.

"I wouldn't fuck these morons with my worst enemy's dick. But you're picking up some of what I'm laying down. If we can humiliate and confuse them, then our land will be . . ."

Scary, I volunteered.

"Exactly."

We did end up stripping them. At 2:30 the next morning, after Dale, Roderick, and Matt were seen at their usual spots, we dropped the weed thieves off, naked, in an alley near the St. Helena golf course, bound together by torn strips of their own clothes, knotted so tightly together they had to call for help to get free. I heard one guy went back to Mexico, one of the white kids joined the military, and another started taking community college classes. The rest drank their fear away for months. None of that mattered for me. I was stuck on the smiling faces of Shotgun and his uncles. I hadn't been around their type before; criminals, no doubt, but not bad people. Just willing to do whatever was necessary to protect what mattered: family.

Dale demanded that he drive me home. I'd stayed long past my usual hour. Of course I could've run home but he'd been holding his tongue around me since the attack. Dale had been both close and cautiously distant, like he had something to say but didn't want his family to hear. His black Monte Carlo was at least eight years old but smelled new. It purred like it was just off the showroom floor and almost lulled me to sleep. We rode in silence until we got to highway 1 by the coast.

"I had a friend. He was in Kosovo when all that madness started. He was on the ground counting bodies, if that means anything to you."

Not much, I said trying not to be too rigid.

"Let's just say it left a mark on him. He came back to the Bay about five years ago. Did the citizen soldier thing the best he could, but a few drinks deep and he's putting the hurt on someone. Usually it was someone who had it coming. The bigger the better. He just didn't have fear anymore, you know?"

Yup, I said, smiling inside.

"This one time, he tells me about going to see some fights. Illegal, off-the-radar type. Tells me this little girl, fourteen, maybe fifteen walks in the cage like she's walking up to a fast food counter, not a care in the world. This girl, according to my friend, disassembled grown hard men like toys. Said he's never seen anyone move as quickly as her, as precisely. First time I saw you in the woods with Matt, I got a sense of what he was talking about. But yesterday morning, the way you took those men . . . I understand why my friend felt fear when he saw that girl fighting."

I only did what you asked. I didn't want him scared of me. That image of his brother and nephew grinning, toasting, laughing.

"I know. I know. I just didn't know anyone could move like that. Not you, I mean anyone. Any person . . ."

I wanted to tell him about Narayana's training and the body discipline that was addictive to me. But as we pulled into the parking lot I caught movement from inside the *Mansai*.

I jumped out of the truck before it stopped rolling and jumped the small gate that separated the parking lot from the dock, even though it was unlatched. I moved across the long rectangular patch of grass faster than I ever did before, abundantly conscious of the possibility of Narayana. I knew it was him. I had no idea how I felt about him being on the ship . . . until I saw it wasn't him.

Standing at the entry to the cabin, it took me a second to see the man that he barely was. Light skinned and skinny. A wisp of a trench coat with a giant anarchy symbol spray-painted on the back of it. He was the culmination of every bad fashion choice from the '90s. Under his black bandanna was a face both familiar and confounding. He rummaged through my things, distracted, annoyed, but comfortable. I would make him regret the violation.

Who the fuck are you? I used my Voice on him. But it was like shouting into a windstorm, the usual . . . resonance I got from most people simply wasn't there.

"I'm looking for the tools of my trade, that's all." The bastard only barely paid attention to me. He was ignoring me. Me?

I jumped the last flight of stairs and came for him cleanly, squarely with the Retiring Flame—left elbow strike, exhale, right side kick, hips forward, inhale, spin on the front leg to get the full power of the hips into the back leg. I aimed at his neck. As I moved I checked for counterstrikes and reversals, the whole nine. The hit was going to be clean. But I missed. There was no neck, only air. I don't know how I did, only that I missed. Where there should have been an unconscious fashion misfit, there was just the sound of wind. But he had moved. I caught his attention.

"What the fuck are you?" His breath was slow, like low tide moving from shore.

The wrong one to fuck with, I barked. But when I charged him, again in perfect form for Descending Rooster—inhale, C-step, right elbow strike to the chest, left punch to solar plexus, knee to the groin, exhale, stand with three-fingered strike to the eyes prepared to see a blood-filled hole where his right cheekbone used to be, he disappeared, literally, before I could reach him. Not only from sight, but from memory as well. I felt his presence slipping out of my memory so clearly. I could do nothing to fight it. When Dale came down the cabin steps, guns drawn, no more than a minute behind me, I could not for all the coinage in the world tell him what I'd been fighting.

At twelve years old, in black khaki shorts and a gray wife-beater, I found myself walking into that disaster with a funny-talking diminutive Indian. If his half-English half-ramblings about his days during the pirate wars were any indication of Narayana's stability, his driving skills made the same point. He pushed his rusty Cutlass Royale to ninety like it was twenty-five and treated other drivers the way he treated other people: they were to look out for him, not vice versa.

I went with the old Indian to Gringo's Last Chance at Heaven Bar and Grill in deep El Sobrante, or El Slob, as most folks called it. Just off of San Pablo Avenue, the bar was the last of its breed in the gentrifying neighborhood. It offered no hipsters, no baristas, no mixologists, and no one under the age of fifty. Imagine a one-room bar where the two-decade-old reject pop music is loud, the toothless caesarean-scarred chicks are easy, and the broken bottle fights are bloody. Now add a Montana rancher amount of buckshot into the walls, age everyone by forty years and rid them of any decency.

"Now, Raj, you know . . ." The bartender started as soon as he saw me.

"AH AH AH," Narayana barked like an epileptic dog as he approached the bar. "You know Marko."

Marko shook his head then sized me up before speaking again. "He your uncle or something?"

Something, I said, climbing on to a stool.

Sweet pussy! Narayana shouted after taking a shot of whiskey.

Jesus! I said.

"Never drank here." Marko laughed. "I'll tell you this for free, little girl. Whatever Raj is selling right here, pass on it. You don't want what's coming your way."

Gotta learn to fight.

"Why?"

I'm going to public school. It sounded lame even then but it was all I had.

Narayana, last name Raj I learned that night, drank, smoked cigars, swore, and played pool like a shark. One-ball Willy, the local hero of this degenerate posse, was about to turn himself in for a three-year involuntary manslaughter bid and this was his good-bye party. I didn't even ask how Narayana knew him. I just kept getting nervous when they'd sigh and look over at me sipping on a Coke. Every now and then the Indian would just point at me and scream "Sweet pussy!" It would have been funny if not for the toothless and unwiped patrons who actually took him seriously, patrolling by my perch near the bar and taking deep whiffs of the air, or even trying to touch my leg. I shooed them off but the drunker they got, the more they tried. Finally Narayana, who in my mind was too drunk to stand, found a seat next to me.

"Nine drunk, two high. All horny. It's them or you." Marko's sad look as he went out the back door, Narayana's stunningly sober voice, the wolfish grins of three of the men—these all let me know Narayana was serious. Before I could panic, he was gone. Narayana had offered me up as a parting gift for the soon-to-be convict.

I didn't freak. Despite the toothless smiles and the vague threats, I stayed calm. My goal was to put my back to a wall and . . . what? Call someone? Who? I had no idea. My Voice didn't carry well over cell phones. But even if someone were available, who would that someone be? Mom was most likely passed out or at work. What numbers I could remember became inconsequential as I tried walking to the bathroom, pretending that every eye in the place wasn't on me. But a fat man with a gray bandanna tied around his head jabbed his pool cue at me, and all of a sudden, they all came.

I tried to get away but they were on me fast, pushing my face down into the felt-topped pool table, as a balding guy's fat fingers tried to undo my belt to slide my shorts off. I tried to climb over the table, but the fat man kicked my legs wider apart, then laughed. Something inside of me said, *You're going to get raped now.*

Something bigger inside of me said, "No."

As salty fingers tried to shove a pool ball in my mouth so I wouldn't scream, I vowed to get free and kill them all. Only seconds were afforded me; the drunk fatty couldn't deal with the delicate clasp of my belt. I stopped pulling on the man's arms that held me from across the table and looked in his eyes, not for pity, but for seduction. Either because of or in spite of my tears, he took the bait and tried to readjust his sweaty palms. I lost no time. I spit the pool ball into my hand, freed not a moment earlier. Just as the asshole behind me was touching my underwear, I slammed the bald one's head with the pool ball. I shot up, straightening my back as he did, and head-butted the man behind me.

Something switched in me at that point. No rage or panic dominated. Rather the polar opposite. A deliberate and dispassionate calm overtook me. An appraisal of my situation, including my assets—scared but unharmed; weapons—one pool ball; as well as environment—only two, maybe three attackers, the rest onlookers, all drunk or high, all full-grown men—took half a second. I nodded, imagining a way to survive.

"Little bitch! You broke my finger," Baldy shouted, shucking off his tattered leather jacket to the floor. His partner in crime joined him, ignoring his own bloody nose.

Apologize now and I won't break anything else, I say. Something about my calm and the Voice connected with Baldy. An approximation of regret danced on his lips, inarticulate, but nothing came out. His friend shoved him with an elbow and I knew that an apology wasn't coming.

I played softball for two years. Pitcher. Fairly decent aim. So I can't lie and say I didn't mean to brain the one who had been behind me with the pool ball. When his partner fell to the ground, unconscious and bleeding out of his ears, Baldy panicked and came for me. He broke out a blackjack and swung at me hard. I jumped on the pool table and let his drunken adrenaline-filled body go off balance. As soon as both his knees were on the ground, I jumped on his head and began pummeling the back of the man's neck with the cue ball. I didn't stop until the white ball turned red.

Now who shoved that pool ball in my mouth? Everyone pointed to my first victim, a diminutive Latino who was now twitching and puking on himself on the floor.

Word of advice, I said before I opened the door. Next time you see a girl about to be raped, don't stand around clapping. Makes you all look like subhumans.

I walked out to see Narayana and Marko smoking hand-rolled cigarettes. Marko looked relieved until he saw the bloody cue ball in my hand. Narayana didn't even bother to take his eyes off his cell phone until I got close enough for him to hear my labored breathing. Then he got upset.

"I don't train dogs."

What? I asked, totally confused.

"Dogs pant. Warriors breathe. You pant like dog."

They almost raped me!

"Panting help you stop that? Crying? No. Only three things help surviving: strong, smart, quick. All need breathing. Learn to control your breath."

No one's trying to rape me now, so fuck your . . . I think what happened was Narayana swept my legs out from under me, and while I was falling, he collapsed the antenna of his flip phone on my solar plexus. I came to with Narayana on top of me, his extremely sharp nails scraping the sides of my trachea gently.

"You fuck my nothing. You want to train with me? This is training. You want to spar? Tournaments? Go someplace else. Here? Me? This is where it starts. Respect for me, serious injury for your enemies. You don't want? I take you home; you never speak again to me about training. But you want to train? You show respect."

"Raj, I'm gonna have to take One-ball Willy to the hospital," Marko said as he exited the bar I hadn't seen him enter. "For the love of . . . Raj, if you've got to kill her, can you do it someplace else?"

Narayana stood up like he just finished tying his shoe and threw a bundle of fifties to Marko. I stood, checked myself for injuries, and got in his car. He pushed me over from the passenger side and made me drive. I was about to tell him I didn't have a license, then realized he didn't care.

I knew I'd be on his deck early the next morning, ready for whatever training he had for me that day. I knew I'd do whatever he told me, handle any challenge he put my way. Because I knew that whatever Narayana Raj was preparing me for, it was far more important than high school.

The Green brothers kept up a push/pull relationship with me. I'm sure Dale went back and told his brother and nephew about my freak-out and subsequent amnesia. He saw that it was real, my forgetting, but with only a minute or two behind me, my slightly labored breathing, and my earlier calm, he couldn't figure out if I was insane or not.

I wondered if, minus Dale's presence, I'd have remembered anything about that night at all. I remembered being tense and the ebbing of a tide of anger. But if Dale hadn't come down the galley with guns drawn, I doubt I'd have evidence for the unknown event.

I became . . . irritated. I couldn't shake my sense of frustration and violation. Well, that's almost true. The Green brothers and Shotgun had me come back to the farm for a month or so just to make sure if there was any retribution I'd be on hand. If it was charity or genuine concern, I couldn't tell. But I didn't care. I got to sit on the nymph rock again. It gave me the sense of connectedness that surpassed senses, frustration, and irritation about the event hole in my memory and the Narayana-shaped hole in my life. It wasn't like my missing elements disappeared when I sat on that rock, rather it just placed it all in context of the lives and deaths of everything on the Green brothers' property and beyond. I felt small; my problems smaller.

After five weeks, Roderick gave me $30,000 and gently asked if the family could have some solo time. We both knew he couldn't keep me away by force. Lucky for him, the request hurt enough for me to disappear.

They didn't have my number. I didn't have a phone. All I had was the *Mansai*. I gave my mom $10,000 for no other reason than I could, and went back to practicing my katas and training.

I watched fall turn into another winter then spring again doing nothing more than exercise, downloading the newer transmissions of jungle, drum and bass, and dubstep, and training. I'd made a commitment to never go back to the emotional spot I was in when Narayana . . . left. That required not just physical discipline, but mental as well. Being able to handle anything coming at me wasn't enough. I had to be able to see what was coming. That meant being around people.

One thing about growing up mute, you get used to listening, observing. My habit was to take the ferry from Sausalito to Fisherman's Wharf and imagine takedowns and defenses on everyone on the boat. Sometimes for fun, I'd steal a wallet or two, then return them. I'd watch for folks who trained in some art of another. You can tell, and it's not by muscle mass or gear. Gym rats with flaming skulls on their shirts and tons of attitude only needed a two-finger strike to the throat to go down hard. The ones that really trained would never let you get that close. Their gait is different. They have a confidence, a situational awareness that can't be aped. The little polite Greek guy on the ferry, the one that took the tickets and the riders' attitudes with the same civil disinterest, he trained. Probably most of his life if his balance was any indication. I only saw him in action once.

I sat upstairs, outside on the back end of the 120-person ferry. Tourists dominated my section mostly and the Greek had to tell everyone to hold on and to keep their snot-nosed ankle biters in line. But one of the children was loose and a German tourist was drunk with a bottle in his hand. The ship rolled a bit, like he had been warning, and the kid found his head in the tourist's ass. Everyone but the Greek and I were laughing. The German lost his balance and was about to go overboard. In his panic, the German reached out and grabbed the kid. I stood to go help but the Greek was already there. His right hand struck the German's wrist right at a nerve cluster causing him to release the kid. The Greek sidestepped the kid and slipped his left hand under the neck of the German and pulled him

31

into a seat before his feet left the deck. It could have been a choke; the Greek could have been a lot harsher about saving the man's life. But he was relaxed, calm, like he'd done it a thousand times before. The German got mad. He threw the bottle he'd been holding at the Greek. The Greek caught it, took a swig, and walked away.

The Greek was practiced and trained. Narayana had trained me in a different way. If it was me, the German would have been in a wheelchair practicing how to speak again with only three teeth.

Assessing threats from tourists at places like Fisherman's Wharf and the ferry made me realize no one was interested in hurting me. So instead I'd walk, listen, eat, and watch. At first I enjoyed it all—the subtleties of a mother tying her kid's shoe, a brother lifting his drunk sibling's face out of a garbage can, a crew of high school girls only two years younger than me running to grab a bus. It all looked clean and healthy. Stable.

Then I'd catch a look at my hands or my feet or my clothes. My uniform was sweat pants, black zip-up hoodie, skintight Gore-Tex gloves, and black and silver running shoes when I wasn't barefoot. Body fat was such a distant memory I thought anorexics were fat. I looked like death in training. My mother would now only leave food and prayer at the ship, like I was some dangerous animal. Narayana never taught me how to be depressed. But he did teach me to dance.

Chapter Three
Combat dancing

Sophomore year I started combat training. Freshman year was all about conditioning and observation. Narayana did things like make me take salsa lessons to learn how to work in tandem with another body. Then he'd say something like "What I train is the opposite of salsa." He had me kayak from Sausalito to San Francisco and then had me do 300 push-ups in under five minutes. If I slowed or started crying because of the pain, he'd ask how I was helping myself with all that noise. And of course, more dive bars with horny old men so trained to fail it was hard for them to do anything else. After the fifth one, I think it was in Ukiah, the captain started timing me. I knew I was doing better in his eyes when he stopped leaving the bar. Raj no longer knew the owners of the bars, and occasionally he'd fight by my side. It was in those moments that I realized how much I still had to learn. Say what he wanted about salsa, Captain Narayana Raj danced though those bars like he was choreographing a broken bone ballet, causing strokes with a stroke, cuts with right crosses and hemorrhages with heel strikes.

Early sophomore fall, after Narayana spent the summer making me train like a striker but would only put me in soccer clubs and games if they let me play goalie, I got the first sense that I was on a timetable. I sat at a singular wooden table at an Indonesian restaurant on the outskirts of San Francisco's Tenderloin district, laughing at the lost hipsters that strolled by.

"You have eighty-nine percent blockage rate," he said after sipping from a large bowl of fish head soup.

I'll work harder, I said half in jest. Word around was that former World Cup strikers were trying to find me to take their shots.

"The time for that is past," the captain said regretfully. He was on his sixth beer. Quickly his tone turned to its testing resonance. "I make you goalie. Why?"

To get me used to getting in harm's way. Same with the bar fights. He'd never told me. He never told me anything. The Raj took it on faith that I could put things together.

"That's the aggressive side of what I teach you. The tiger part. Now you know, the tiger tries to eat you . . ."

Break as many teeth as I can before he devours me. I smiled, remembering a story he told me about a boy in an Indian nature preserve who broke every hard calcium pocket out of a Bengal tiger's mouth using nothing but a stick while protecting a sick elephant. I didn't know shit about Narayana's past but I knew that boy was him.

"But there's another way. Who can beat the tiger?" I didn't even bother trying to answer. "The cobra. Quick strikes, evades. Every blow brings death. Entropy prevails." He finished his soup with a loud slurp then got to work on the fish head. I kept my head in my chicken skewers and steamed rice until he spoke again. "Tomorrow I show you how to stop the memory of bones."

By six a.m. that Sunday I had cleaned my house, his deck, made my mother breakfast, run my fifteen miles with that damn gallon water vest strapped to my chest, and gone though every kata-choreographed movement he'd ever taught me. They weren't for fighting, he told me. No one finishes anyone with a kata in a fight. They were to teach your body its options.

It took another twenty minutes of deep breathing to calm myself, which was about how long it took the captain to come on deck. The sun was threatening to make an appearance but the Bay's fog was protesting. Seawater tried to take to the sky and ended up on my hoodie and the recently swept deck. Narayana emerged from below deck, oblivious to my cleaning efforts and the temperature. He carried with him a full human skeleton, bleached white, and propped up with a large wooden dowel attached to four wheels.

As Narayana snapped the wheels into locked positions, he made his dismissive hand signal, which meant "calm down," despite me not saying a word. I grabbed one of the plastic chairs and watched.

Where'd you find a skeleton? I asked.

"I made it," he said almost sadly. I believed him. "Want to feel? Real human bones." I shook my head and waited. He wore his Ice Cube shirt. When he stretched his arms over his head, his shirt barely moved. His sweats were so big I couldn't imagine his little toothpick legs in them. But they did carry him to the other side of the ship after he made sure I was paying attention.

Then the captain started to dance. That's the only thing I can call it. It looked like Balinese stage dancing, complete with low bending pauses, noncombative finger posturing, and facial gesticulations. I almost laughed. But the form looked perfect. He moved even closer to the skeleton, dancing and facing it first, then me, then backwards, then off the deck, and finally back to the skeleton all in perfect time with his dance. He faced it in a low squat, his legs twisted beneath him. For the length of one exhalation he was still. But just as the first ray of authentic sunlight fought its way through the early morning bay fog, Raj struck, twisted, and stood. He was so quick, it was only the feint of movement of the locked wheels that let me know the skeleton was being touched. The creak of the deck let me know he had twisted; the slack of the Ice Cube shirt alone betrayed the movement of his arms. I didn't think it was possible to stand as quickly as he did, let alone strike out. I was astonished before he invited me to inspect the skeleton.

Every bone, from toe to finger, either had a hole in it, a clear fracture, or an ugly splintered break. Every. Bone. Eye checking Raj's fingers gave me nothing; they didn't have bone residue on them.

The obvious occurred to me: in all those bar brawls Narayana had been holding back. Even the skull had a three-inch-wide perfect hole in it; the missing piece caught below the shattered cheekbone rattled with the morning breeze making a sound that almost shook my calm.

What about the spine? I whispered, inspecting the carcass, noticing the rigging and fishing line threaded where joint and gristle should be.

"Pressure from tenth and twenty-sixth blows put tension on the spine. Hairline fracture first four vertebrae right side. Six and seven should be pulverized."

How? I was terrified and fascinated. I never before wanted to bow to him.

"Sit." And we did, letting the fragments of the skeleton fall to the deck as the ocean breeze saw fit.

"In everything two spirits. Life, breathing, movements. Death, no breath, no movement. Always pulling and pushing against each other. There is a little death in everything. Not just skeletons. People, books, sounds, ideas. A little death. You find the death of memory, an idea. It does not exist anymore. Yeah?"

No, I said honestly, so far past confused it physically hurt. He sighed hard, grabbed a beer and tried again.

"The first arm. There is memory of it in every arm, yes? How the arm is supposed to be?"

Like Adam and Eve's first arm? The Raj flicked his bottle top at my eye so quickly I almost didn't catch it in time. What do you want? What the hell is the first arm?

"Listen, girl." His voice went tiger. "You want salvation? Listen to Adam and Eve. What I show, teach . . . is different path. No salvation, only preparation for war against the Gods. You want it? Bury Adam and Eve."

I gave him a bow he could never see. I was never a church kid anyway.

"There is body and there is idea, concept of memory, of body. There is Chabi, you, here now. Stubborn, strong, cold in the morning air. But there is idea of Chabi in her mother's head, yeah?"

Ok, I said playing slowly with the bottle top.

"If I stop the idea of Chabi in her mother's head, is there still Chabi?"

I wanted to say yes. There was my voiceless Voice, my inability to make sound congeal with my skill at making my "concepts," "ideas" known. Whatever it was, I knew it to be more powerful than any physical voice. I trembled at the idea of my Voice being stopped, being locked into myself and non-communicative again, and I trembled. I knew the real answer.

Chabi, the daughter, yes. But me, the person, the flesh and bones is still alive, yes?

"Yes, but less so than before," Raj said, stretching his arms high above his head. "And enough less, no Chabi as daughter, no Chabi as student, no Chabi as fighter, then there is no Chabi, yes? Timing, it's always timing. If I stop your mother's idea of you before you are born, no you? Maybe another child, but not a Chabi, yes?"

Enough people forget about me, I can't function, get it? If Mom never thinks to have a daughter, I don't exist, ok. So what? You can't make your opponent forget they have bones.

"No! Too hard for you. Just make skeleton forget first."

Ok, I said, understanding nothing. How?

"Entropy." I got up from my chair and walked to the bow to look over the dock waters. Small ducks sat calmly on the waves that carried them out from the Bay. I could sooner fathom what they dreamed about than I could decipher what Narayana was talking about. What the hell is entropy, Captain?

Narayana drank a little more of his beer until the bottle was half empty. With a flick of his wrist he sent it flying four feet above him with such force and at such an angle that no liquid escaped it. He stood and caught it with a finesse that kept the beer still.

"When explosion happens, energy pushes. When push is over, entropy grows. The pauses, points, stress area, the descent of all things. This is entropy." Before I could comment, he spun the bottle in the air again. Only he didn't catch it as it lost speed and the beer sprayed everywhere. I barely caught it before it hit the deck.

"Find entropy of bones, then you strike the skeleton like me."

Ok, I said, trying not to ask again simply how. Instead I went to particulars. The dance. How does that fit in?

"You take the life, the energy you have? You put that to the entropy of bones? Bones have no chance. Physical form, especially human bodies, are bad at making new balances between entropy and energy. Memory, the function of the bone, is the first to fail. You want entropy? First you find your life sounds."

Chapter Four
The Little Kid

It took a few hours for me to find the type of club that played my music, but late one April night well after dinner hour, I made my way to a Moroccan restaurant off of Shotwell Avenue in S.F.'s Mission district. I'd caught sight of a flyer advertising the realest in dubstep and grime to be found in San Francisco at this address. With no guidance from Mom, I bought a pair of jeans that lied to the world about the presence of my ass and a deep red faux-satin shirt. The woman at the mall downtown didn't understand why I wanted a trench coat to go with the get-up any more than she could understand why I wouldn't want new shoes. She said since I had so little, it was important to show it off as much as possible. I tipped her for the advice anyway.

When I walked into the makeshift Moroccan club at 11:45, a DJ was making some U.K. vocalist stutter behind world-shattering beats and the world was good. It was less than eighty people, all three to fifteen years older than me. None of them trained, a few want-to-be fighters posing as partiers. With the tables cleared, the small stage set up with red and blue lights, and a sound system too big for the space, the little club seemed efficient in its purpose. This was a scene for those who eschewed the scene. This was a club for those who liked music.

I danced. Like I was a kid again, like I had the security of knowing my pirate future. Like I was ready to break the memory of bones,

I danced. The DJs spun just for me and folks cleared floor space to let me work it out, or maybe that was just how it felt.

When I stopped to drink water, piss-drunk man-boys came close. Once they looked in my eyes they gained distance. I don't think they wanted me. After they pulled down the speakers at two in the morning, I left. But I knew I'd be back.

Now I had a pattern that resembled a life. Training daily, fifty-mile run or thirty-mile swim every other day, and clubbing Thursday through Sunday. Two months into it and I'm at 330 Ritch, a club that looks more like a cathedral than a dance space. I look past the Filipino homeboys, the black hipsters, and the white dreads to the DJ. He was one of those slight looking Latinos with a dirt trail of facial hair on his upper lip. He rocked an old school Eek-a-Mouse yellow T-shirt and had mini flashlights attached to the arms of his glasses, one casting blue light, another red. Another DJ might have been able to carry the look, but the constant head movement conveyed insecurity more than anything. His beats were tight, if a bit academic, mixing current U.S. hits with their Jamaican dancehall remixes. But when I saw him wipe his hands on his pants, his music instantly became irrelevant. I knew the DJ.

Narayana had put my body through every contortion the Geneva Convention had declared illegal and now he was giving me an intellectual challenge. Through his deformed English, his inflection and syntax, I understood that when he said memory in relation to bone he meant the form a bone takes. It made sense in a way. Every time we bend our backs to not trip on our faces, we're thankful our bones have enough give and take not to snap. Raj found a way to interrupt the physical recall of bones to their original shape, their memory. Every bone required a memory of sorts.

Whatever terse truce my mom and I had established over the past year was tested when I came home with Raj's skeleton to study.

"No!" she snapped as I tried to slide by her. She was putting on her work uniform prepping to leave. "There's no way you're bringing any of that voodoo mojo shit into this house."

There's no magic here, Mom. I stood genuinely perplexed next to the skeleton trying to figure out how she got such a notion.

"Believe that and you're a lot dumber than you look," she said, sliding her thick legs into light tan stockings. "And what the hell happened to the As and Bs you were supposed to be getting in school?"

And then what? I asked, pissed.

"Then college. That's what!"

You gonna tell me what classes to take as well? She stopped rubbing lotion on her arms and tensed her body. Rather than thinking, I reacted. I cleared my hands and head, focused on her hips for movement, set one foot back prepped for a low kick, and raised my guard.

She would have been an imbecile to come for me. Mom had never taken a martial arts class. She'd never seen me in action but it was clear I was not going to tolerate any mother-daughter slap action. Still, that woman was never good at holding her tongue.

"There can only be one woman in this house. You so grown, maybe you can find some place to hide your skeletons."

The arrogance of my youth allowed me to forget my mother's threat less than five minutes after her departure for work. I sat with that skeleton in my room all night just staring at it and remembering Narayana's grace. Public school, my previous obsession, was a distant priority compared to the perfection of the entropy of bones now.

At night as the lazy waves of the San Francisco Bay pushed and pulled my room, I fantasized about the end of high school. Narayana would finally take me to his home, to whatever island Indian pirates call home, and I'd learn the final secrets; how to move like poetry, to find the entropy of bones. I'd learn to be like him. Like so many things between us, I never spoke about it with him. There was an understanding. I was his but he was mine as well. And for me to truly possess him, I'd have to understand not only who he was but also where he came from.

Raj would say as much from time to time. He'd be drunk on the Bekseju and I'd hazard a question like "What part of India are you from?" He'd chuckle internally then breathe deep, like he was about to tell a funny story. Never did, though, just kept his anecdotes to himself. Maybe he thought soon I'd be eighteen, a legal adult not beholden to anyone. I slept that night comfortable in the knowledge I'd soon know all Narayana's secrets.

Mom had pretty much stopped drinking. Surprising what that can do to a body. She smiled more, her skin cleared up, lost weight, even went to church on a semi-regular basis. In some ways it made living with her easier. Education was not one of those ways. When she came home early that morning, she was still angry.

"You plan on going to community college?" she asked me gently yet directly as I prepped for school.

That's ok? I asked, falling into the living room couch. Mom sat perched in the kitchen upstairs. From the sound of the folding paper and the question, I knew she was looking at my grades. They aren't that bad.

"No they aren't. Your French teacher even said your comprehension and recitation was excellent," she said as though she'd just discovered the fact to be true. "But they aren't good enough to justify me putting you up past eighteen."

Huh? I asked, too tired to comprehend.

"I'm saying, come your eighteenth birthday I'm giving you all the money I saved for your education. Don't get excited. It's only about seven thousand. But you can't stay here anymore."

I wanted to say "That makes sense" or "That's fair." Or even "I don't care. I'm going off with Narayana anyway." But the shock of her compassionate boundary made me press the issue. I poured all my vague and silent power into one statement.

You know you want me to stay. Without seeing her I knew the sentiment registered on that nameless substrate where my Voice was heard. The echo of a calling back from her nameless place hit my heart. Her mouth said something different.

42

"More than anything I want you to stay," Mom said after descending the stairs to sit next to me. "And if you decided to dedicate even half of the energy you put into that old withered man into your studies, I'd let you. But I know you, girl. You've got more loyalty than sense."

What's that mean?

"It means I failed seriously as a parent letting you spend so much time with that old man all this time."

Nothing's happened, Mom.

"Oh, I don't think he's trying to get some from you. Not anymore. But I know if he wanted it, you wouldn't even know how to say no to him." I went numb realizing how right she was. "No, he got your mind now and a woman should never give a man all her mind. Maybe if I'd said more about your father, you'd know that. But I can't spend the rest of my life apologizing for my failures. I've got to get on a righteous path and like I know water is wet, I know that Narayana is not righteous."

I'll be out on the last day of school. I retreated into my room and left her to Nina Simone's "Sinnerman" playing in her room.

By the time I was at Marin High the next day my mind was obsessing on the skeleton again, but there again, distraction. This time in the guise of a thoroughly green teacher trying to "reach" the class. Most teachers had an understanding regarding my participation. It would always be unsatisfying. Best for both of us to just not call on me. But not this dreadlocked black woman with a southern drawl.

"And what about you, Chabi?" she asked, smoothing out a dress that was a bit too casual for a classroom. "That's a beautiful name, by the way."

The entire class turned to look at me, some of them acting like they'd never seen me before. It took a second to get out of my hyper reflex fright mode before I could respond. It was the first time anyone had said anything about me was beautiful.

Thanks, I murmured in my silent voice.

"So what do you want to do when you graduate?" the teacher pushed.

Be a pirate. All but two people in the class started giggling.

"Like in the movies?" she said, still not smiling, but now more concerned than anything.

No. Those are old pirates. Now, it's Indonesia and Malaysia, Somalia and places like that. Broke cats are taking on multibillion-dollar cargos with RPGs and machetes. The paydays are big.

"And that's what you want to do?" the teacher said cautiously after a class-wide observation of silence for the loss of my sanity.

Well, I hear it's kind of hard work on a woman. Not physically but like the guys will always test. Plus most sailors think having a woman on a ship is bad luck. So I was thinking maybe setting jobs up, driving getaways, something along those lines.

"Well, Chabi." The teacher smiled as a way to disengage. "I think you were meant for more."

Inside I grumbled. She didn't even know I wasn't speaking with my mouth. How could she know what I was meant for? I was kicking myself for opening up and trying when an elaborately folded paper airplane landed perfectly on my desk. It was from the skinny Latino boy I thought of only as the Little Kid. I unfolded it and read, "I heard they make hella money. Who gave you the idea?"

I wrote "My father," crossed that out and wrote "Narayana" then crossed that out. I was about to write "Neighbor" but then just became overwhelmed and said a silent "Forget it'" to the Little Kid. And he did.

That had been happening more and more. I'd been influencing folks around me. Mostly to leave me alone, or forget they saw me. They were minor incidents just as easily chalked up to others being absentminded or forgetful, except for that intimate non-verbal linking I'd feel for a second right before they forgot about me. It was enough to let me know I was doing something.

THE ENTROPY OF BONES

The Little Kid was short with a nose curved like an anteater. His face was long and his mouth was small. I wasn't a big grinner but he was a frowner, forever with his head down and his headphones on as he wandered through the hallways of Marin High. He dressed like he didn't care about clothes and was quickly proving himself both smarter and weaker than the entire class. When he saw me that day outside on the lawn, I began to realize how smart he was.

"That idea about pirates is hella smart. They need people on land to negotiate for them and everything. Where'd you get the idea?" he asked as I walked by. No hello, no greeting of any kind. I eye-checked him. He'd forgotten the note. For him, this was a new idea.

Saw something online, I said and waited, still standing over him as he ate his cold cut sandwich alone.

"I read an interesting article in *National Geographic* about the global rise of piracy. I could send you the link if you wanted."

I grumbled mentally. Who the hell reads when they don't have to? The words "smart people" came to mind. So I asked him, You know about entropy, Little Kid?

"We're the same age." He stopped eating and looked at me with different eyes when I said "entropy." I let my silence speak for me and like all high school geeks, Little Kid couldn't help but throw up everything he knew.

"So it's kind of like when the force in the universe, like it's cooling. The whole universe started with a big bang, right? Well, that explosion pushed everything, like every atom ever, out across the universe like an infinite number of directions. But after that initial explosion things begin to just slow down. Entropy is the measure of that trend towards coolness."

I sat next to him in order to think. Handfuls of grass distracted me as the notion of a cooling universe dominated my mind. A wannabe Latino gangster walked by ready to accost Little Kid. I smiled kindly. He kept walking.

"Thanks," the Little Kid said.

I disregarded it completely. So ice is closer to entropy than fire? I asked.

"Well, kind of, yeah, I guess. When people talk about entropy they're usually talking about energy, though."

What's the opposite?

"Of what?"

Of entropy. The yin to the yang?

"Oh." I had stumped the brain enough for him to grab his juice box. "Not really sure. That's more philosophy than anything I know."

I let him know the answer just before I left. Creativity.

The Little Kid is all grown up, I said after getting past club security such as they were. The kid looked up at me first in confusion, then comprehension, and finally something approaching sympathy.

"Oh my god. You're ok?" He threw his arms around me like some '50s movie starlet. I let my stillness and silence do the shuffling off of Little Kid.

You ok? I asked after he readjusted and checked his next tune.

"I'm good. Good. DJing. I'm at Stanford. Cultural anthropology. And you know . . . Shit, Chabi, what happened to you?"

I was sick. I got better. It wasn't that much of a lie. I owed him some version of the truth. I'm here. Come find me when your set is done. That's what I told him. But then I got scared of him asking why he could hear me perfectly when the speakers were turned up to twenty. So I wrote him a note with my email saying we should hook up and gave it to another wannabe hipster DJ. The kid was from the past, from the bad time. I knew I owed him. But I didn't owe him right then and there.

The next day we grabbed a coffee in downtown Oakland near his mom's sandwich shop. The last time I'd been there was the riot. In my memory, I had been a minor hero there. I couldn't tell what he was seeing when he looked at me but it wasn't what I saw in the mirror. The Little Kid viewed something that scared him but he did his best to stay calm.

Didn't figure you for the humanities, I told him, as I sipped on my hot water and lemon.

"I get my science in," he weak-smiled me. "I'm looking at the connection between music and language in the brain."

Ok, I said, trying to not sound confused.

"It's really interesting. We're finding out about these primitive languages that are almost onomatopoeic. Me, I'm looking specifically at the way tonal languages convey emotional states in pronunciation as well as in music."

Despite my best efforts I must have looked bored, because he stopped talking about himself.

"Chabi, the last time I saw you, you were devastated."

Someone important to me disappeared, I found myself saying as I held back minor sobs.

"That's not what I mean," the Little Kid interrupted. "I'm seeing you here and now, upright, walking around, even doing your version of smiling. But you still seem wrecked."

I had to use my Voice to convince him I was ok. But even then, he begged me to have tea with him every time he came up to Oakland from Palo Alto. He was too sweet to deny.

I swam the seventeen miles home from Jack London with the question in my mind of what the Little Kid saw. It'd only been two years. Had I changed that much? Visions of a walking, talking skeleton plagued me so much I took a break at Angel Island. I'd gotten used to people being concerned for my Bay swims so didn't mind when children ran up to me. But as a kid, with Narayana, I always had someone rowing with me, convincing the world it was ok. Now, I was just some random skinny chick coming out of the bay like the Creature from the Black Lagoon. As I adjusted my street clothes in the double plastic bag I kept them dry in, I wondered, probably for

47

the first time, where I was headed. The ability to thoroughly kick ass combined with an addict's drive to train doesn't lend itself to many healthy life options. The Little Kid was halfway through college, DJing, and growing the fuck up. I sat on an old junk more days than not wrestling with the ghost of a mystery man. The fitful fire that grew in me could only be quelled by swimming that final distance to Sausalito. But in that time I found a small doable change I could accomplish. I could talk to my Mom.

I showered as soon as I got home. Rather than my usual sweats, I wore the red blouse and the jeans. I even brushed out my now shoulder-length nappy black hair instead of just braiding it tight. I practiced my smile.

At her door I heard laughing. Not her drunk back in the day laugh, but sincere sweet laughter. I had to knock. When she came to the door, she almost looked happy to see me.

"Well, this is a surprise," she said, though she still blocked her entrance.

I wanted to know if I could take you out to dinner, I said.

"Praise Jesus, Brother A.C.," she shouted back into her house. "It's a miracle!"

"Testify!" a familiar voice shouted back.

"My prodigal daughter has returned offering gifts, praise his name!"

I can leave if it's a bad time. I wasn't used to the religious blabber or someone else's voice coming from my old home.

"Meet her well with this feast we got here," the voice inside offered.

The house smelled of spicy crab and baked apples. A guy, Latino looking and younger than I expected, descended the stairs looking like a reject from a '90s rap/rock group. He wore a black bandanna around his head, baggy black cargo pants, and a shiny skin-tight black T-shirt.

"They call me A.C.," he said, offering his hand.

Have we met? I said, holding his hand and feeling like I was pantomiming.

"Doubt that!" Mom said coming up behind me. "Brother A.C. doesn't do much but work, praise the Lord, and cook up a storm. I met him at church."

I nodded, freaked by the familiarity A.C. had with my mother and my sense of recognition. They seemed like old drinking buddies, but I had met every one of them and he wasn't familiar from that scene. I sat nice and polite taking bits of crab and shrimp they had baked for a Sunday feast as the conversation shifted between gospels and Skip James.

Every now and then A.C. would give me a knowing glance, like we shared some secret. When I looked over the balcony and saw his trench coat with an anarchy symbol painted on it, I could almost grasp what we had in common, but then it slipped away.

"Chabi, you listening?" Mom's words shocked me back to the conversation.

Not in the slightest, I said, disappointed in myself.

"I said despite being too skinny, you look very pretty." And she kissed my forehead and patted my hands. If a stranger wasn't sitting across the way, I would've grabbed her and held tight. Instead I let her excuse herself to the bathroom.

"Want to see something cool?" A.C. asked with that same in-joke expression on his face.

Sure, I said.

"Just need one promise," he said, standing up from the table and walking back into the kitchen proper.

And what's that?

"No matter what you see, you won't try to hit me."

I thought about it hard for a few seconds. You try and hurt me or my mom, I'll swap your throat out for your balls.

"Trust me when I say this trick puts me in more danger than you."

49

I don't know you, how the hell am I supposed to trust you?

"I'm trusting you to keep your word."

Go on then.

A wind crossed my face despite the windows being closed. And just like that, a fluttering of my eyes, and I knew who he was. The guy who had been on the *Mansai*. The thief, the one I had forgotten.

Chapter Five
A.C.'s Entropy War

"No more drunk fights," Narayana told me the third weekend of my senior year. We were on top of Mount Tam, using the abundant turkey vultures as target practice with bows and arrows. I was only allowed to bump their left wings. The craggy cliff bases and arid afternoon air seemed to keep all other hikers and nature nuts out of our eyeshot. Anyone who caught sight of our activities from distant hill peaks didn't seem to mind much.

It's getting too easy, anyway, I said without a hint of ego. Raj grunted in agreement either with my statement or my shot that took exactly two feathers off a vulture circling fifteen feet in the air.

"What you aim at?" he asked with genuine curiosity.

The buzzards in the air.

"What part of buzzards?"

The left wings? I asked. He had told me to aim at their left wings not twenty minutes earlier.

"What part of the left wing?"

I paused, barely understanding the didactic teaching technique.

The entropy of the left wing is what I should be aiming for, I told him finally, stopping my bow draw and looking at him. What passed for an educational smile crossed his face.

"And you strike with?" Raj asked, pressing the point.

The generativity of the bow. The part of it that creates.

"No!" he snapped.

Of myself! I meant myself!

"Why?"

Because weapons have no generativity, no entropy of their own . . .

"What?" He heard the question I was thinking.

Well, what would that be like? Weapons with their own entropy. I'm just saying that's how most people think. You know, people aren't the problem. Guns are.

He swore in his native tongue then stomped over to a boulder about a hundred times his weight and height. It was as wide as two redwood trunks. Maybe he closed his eyes to prepare but maybe he just exhaled completely. What I know for sure is that not a second later, with one blow, he shattered that boulder. Roughly even-sized diamond shards of shale and rough granite splintered from it, making hard rain sounds as all assembled critters, turkey vultures included, dispersed. All I could think was, Beautiful.

"People are stupid. You don't want entropy weapon. Too much weight," he said, dusting himself off.

No more drunken fights didn't put an end to my fighting. Narayana started me in the highly profitable world of underground bare-knuckle fighting. That was probably where Dale's friend saw me. But by this point it seemed like an insult. I'd adopted Narayana's understanding of the fist as the last tool of the precision fighter. It was the same with death. An idiot child with a gun could kill. But to maim, to inhibit with purpose—while remaining untouched—that was the true challenge. That I'd be facing off against people who'd prepared for me was good. But their aspiring mixed martial arts mindsets made the fights seem more of a hoop to jump through than a legitimate challenge.

"Everyone has a plan till they get punched in the face," Narayana had told me a thousand times if he'd told me once. The first time was when we first started training, just after my near-rape. He sat me on the deck on the *Mansai* and blurted out truths in between beer burps.

"So I either punch you in the face all time or you learn how to fight with no plan. Which you like better?"

Guess.

"Both good plans." Narayana laughed. "But ok, I no punch face. Fist? Loser weapon anyway. In ring, ok, because rules are there. But real fight, fist is . . ." He began to ramble in his own language—a mix of Burmese, English, Spanglish, and god knows what else.

Big? I offered.

"Big and stupid. Like ox," he said. "Big and smart good, like elephant. Elephant fight ox. Ox wife widow. Hand can be elephant, but better finger snakes, yeah?"

Like poisoned?

That stopped him. He looked at me for a long time before saying anything.

"You no use poison. Poison for cowards. I no train cowards." He knew he had no reason to be mad, and I wasn't sure what I said, still even with his controlled breathing I could hear his anger. I thought I reminded him of the snakes on the dock but it was something older, deeper. What had he said to the snake? That he was free?

Ok, I'm just trying to understand. Fingers like snakes, I don't know what that means. What? Flexible? Deadly?

"Yes. Strong, flexible, quick, unpredictable, deadly. But no poison."

And no fist, I said, letting him know I understood.

"Fist is better than nothing, but the way you train, you think, later, fist is last option. Yeah?" he said, back-flipping and walking on his hands to his cooler.

Yeah.

My first bare-knuckle fight was an open brawl in the basement of an El Salvadoran bar in East Oakland. The size of half the block, you could find all manner of drugs, prostitution, and guns in the crowds.

Blood splatter wasn't of concern enough to clean off the mat, and I'm pretty sure there was cock-fighting going on somewhere else in the basement. Easily two hundred people stood around the square ring and all of them were screaming.

Fifty dollars bought you in. Anyone could fight. No rounds. No breaks. Tap out, unconsciousness, or death were the only ways to get out. Two in the ring at a time and no weapons were the only rules. My first fight was against some Guatemalan ex-military with no fear and way too much energy. The holes in his shoes meant he couldn't afford coke, so he was probably a meth head. Narayana had warned me about the possibility. The yellow-skinned fighter was mad that he had to fight some skinny pie-faced girl. In Spanish he said my whore black bitch of a mother must have wanted extra soy sauce for her fried rice and didn't have any extra change for his crew. That was the last thing he said that night. The moron walked up to me with no guard. Salamander's Tail—angled low back leg kick—twisted to Gryphon's Repose—three fingered eye-nose rake upon exhalation—and the Rooster's Defiance—all hip-driven knee strike to his solar plexus—ended the man. I'd practiced my techniques so many times against invisible enemies much larger, stronger, and better prepared than the dope fiend in front of me that my bones and muscles, made uncommonly strong and flexible by Raj's training, barely recognized that I'd actually made significant contact. For a second, I was actually disappointed. Then something unexpected happened. The crowd went wild. They loved me. I scanned the tan-faced crowd and saw my favorite dark spot collecting his winnings and betting the next fight.

The adoration was intoxicating. I think it always is.

The next one was a wrestler, mixed martial arts style. He was white and just as poor as the Guatemalan who would now have breathing problems for the rest of his life. For some reason the white guy's ponytail offended me—who goes into a no-holds-barred fight with an easy grab?—so I wanted to beat him with it. When he tried his college wrestling takedown on me, I let him get close enough to wrap his arms around my waist, but then pushed his neck to the mat and landed three Coal's Nails—two-fingered prolonged pressure strikes—on his neck before he could push back. Just as I was about to grab the ponytail off his defunct body, I heard the slow slide of metal against the mat. He'd hidden five minuscule shaving razors in his hair. I respected the ninja move but couldn't abide breaking one of the only two rules so I plucked the razors out and sent them flying at the peanut gallery in his corner. The crowd loved the theatrics. Even Narayana offered a silent nod of consent.

My third opponent landed one kick. In my defense, he tipped the scales at 280 and had obviously graduated from gladiator academy young to earn his penal Ph.D. in ass kicking. If the braids and the barely visible tats on his coal ebony skin hadn't informed me of his pedigree, the hosts of uniquely jail-inspired rape epitaphs he hurled at me as he came marching would have.

They also got me mad. Which made me lose my breathing and focus. So when jail muscle man pulled off an elegant leg sweep, I fell for it. And fell. I landed fast enough, well prepared for my opponent to try to make good on his threats of sodomy and mutilation, but the blow of the crowd's gasp was harder to recover from. I even risked a glance at Narayana and saw his disappointed face. I stymied the jail man's attempt to kick my head off but didn't bother getting off my back. When I landed a shin kick that buckled the bruiser, half the crowd loved me again. Jail man got so frustrated he jumped in the air like a TV wrestler, trying to land an elbow. I bicycle kicked from the ground into his jaw and groin with precision even I was impressed by. It took half an hour to revive him even with the crowd going wild for me.

By the end of the night Narayana gave me five grand, half the winnings. By the end of the month, the owners were simultaneously barring us and begging to represent me as a headliner at other spots.

Raj would hear none of it. Staying out of the spotlight was an absolute necessity according to him. So we went through the ethnicities, Latinos, Asians, Blacks, and Whites—all the underground fighting communities. And by the time finals rolled around, I'd taken them all on. I never gave my name but me and Raj were a hard duo to miss. By the end challengers would drop out as soon as we walked into whatever dive the hardest of the hard were supposed to populate. I felt invincible.

Promises be damned. I jumped across the table and threw all my silverware at him at the same time. Another fluttering of wind and just like on Narayana's boat, A.C. was gone. Only not far.

"Come on now, you promised," he said calmly from the ground floor. He was putting on his jacket.

Stay in the bathroom, Mom! I shouted as I jumped over the banister to be eye level with the man.

"We're in flux right now, Chabi . . ."

We're in Sausalito, dipshit. What the fuck are you doing with my mom and what the fuck were you doing on my boat? He smirked. And how do you keep doing that disappearing, forgetting thing?

"How do you talk without moving your lips?" It took all I had to not punch him for that comment. No doubt he saw the effort it took. "Ok, ok look we're in flux right now . . ." he said slowly, making his way to the living room porthole. Lifting the blinds, he invited me to look outside. The entire world was on a forty-five-second loop. The same waves came in, came out, the same kid dropped her ice cream at the general store, the same gull made the same screeching sound on repeat, every forty-five seconds. I looked back at A.C.

You did this?

"No, this always happens. Little fluxes, big fluxes, hiccups in time and space. Come on, you put your keys on your dresser one second, the next they're gone, the one after they're back again. If you hadn't been paying attention for that one second, you would've never noticed. Time is relative and illusory."

Who are you?

"They call me A.C. I live mostly in the unnoticed seconds. I'm like a . . ."

Rectal irritant is what you are. What the hell are you doing anywhere near my mom?

"She was the safest way to get to you. To prove I'm not a threat."

Prove how?

"I've been in this house for hours. Your hours, not my hours. I could've done anything I wanted to her and you can testify that she wouldn't have remembered it. Shit, I didn't even have to let you see me truly. Your mom is safe. She thinks I'm a member of her church."

You're not?

"Fuck, no! I'm not even here."

To prove his point he moved his hand through mom's bookshelf unhindered.

I shook your hand.

"Yeah and you speak. Fuck, do you even know what you are?"

I sat down on the beige pleather couch of my youth and squeezed the bridge of my nose, hoping to stave off the inevitable headache. So what am I?

"Liminal."

What the hell does that mean?

"It means there's normal people, like your mom. There's people like me who train, study, barter, and bargain their way into certain skills and powers. And then there are liminal people. You and yours are born with some of the weirdest collections of gifts and curses ever assembled on this planet."

I'm liminal. What are you saying?

"What, you thought you were normal?" he said, relaxing as he sat on the couch, or rather I perceived him to sit on the couch. I noticed the pleather didn't give way to his weight. "I mean come on, you run and swim like you're training for an ultramarathon but you never break a sweat. You've shredded some of the most cutthroat degenerates with an afterthought. What, you imagined you'd marry the high school football star, get fat with babies and move to the suburbs all while not moving your lips when you spoke? You are a liminal girl. In between . . ."

In between what? I shouted.

"That's the problem with you and yours." He smirked. "Never can tell what your kind is betwixt and between."

Everybody is always between something, asshole.

"True that. But you liminals, your decisions matter. Where you go, so does the world."

Hey, shit bird, you are giving me a headache. Start making sense.

"I'm afraid I can't. Well, to be more honest, it doesn't matter if I can. See, I'm not really here."

What. Does. That. Mean?

"I'm riding the consciousness slipstream. Some call it the syn-chronistic highway."

Where are you riding your slipstream to?

"To you." Again that fucking smile. The sad thing was it was beginning to work. "There's a time when I can be a choice for you."

You're not my type.

"Liar," A.C. said, standing. He walked into the sunlight that was only partially blocked by the blinds. The shadows of the blinds hit the rest of the room unbroken, but not where he was standing. "Sadly, that's not what I meant. Me and mine, well, we're at war. And we're losing. You could help us turn the tide. But it has to be your choice."

So make your pitch.

"Can't. You'd forget it. Byproduct of my talents, I'm afraid. Memory can't abide me."

I wanted to yell bullshit, but then I remembered forgetting him twice.

Jesus. I laughed. You can't really touch anything and you're infinitely forgettable. No wonder your side is losing.

"I know, right?" He smiled again. "There are ways I could be more substantial in the here and now, but that could be just as much a weakness as a strength depending on . . ."

On what I decide. His smiles hadn't worked that well. A lifetime of being suspicious left me sensitive enough to know A.C. was cautious as well. This all has something to do with Narayana, doesn't it?

That shocked him. Then a slow grin came to his face. "He told you his real name?"

I debated for a second, then asked him the question I wasn't sure I wanted an answer to. What is he?

"That answer is about ten times more complex than the question."

I'm going on record as hating your ass. What the fuck are you even here for?

"Sometimes, if I'm subtle enough, light enough, just a piece of me, a scent, a phrase, something can stay behind after I'm gone and have an effect." He seemed less substantial and more human then. Like it had all been a joke up to that point. But I saw the strain on his face as it was literally fading from sight.

What do you want to say? I stood up, quickly moving towards him, already feeling the mist of him evaporating. His voice changed from confident and jovial to the sound of miscomprehension and wind mistaken for word, but I heard it. Just before I forgot him. "Stay close to your mother."

It's not that I woke up. More I became aware that I had been doing something else, engaging in a way with something that gained less importance with each passing second. When Mom came out of the bathroom, she recognized the diminishing knowledge in both our eyes, but not the source of it.

59

"Thanks for coming over, baby. It's been nice spending time. You want some baked apples to take over with you?"

I wandered back to the *Mansai*, thankful to Mom for cleaning up the crab mess I'd left. The *Mansai*'s deck made me minimally shaky. I didn't eat enough. I barely acknowledged the lack of crab taste in my mouth when I saw Dale's truck parked in my parking lot. Shotgun came out from behind the ride, hands open and at his side, walking slowly. By the time he got close enough to speak, I was annoyed at his caution.

"I want to reach in my jacket pocket," he let me know.

If I wanted, I could've ripped any weapons you had off of you two minutes ago.

His lightweight anger faded before it flew. Matt passed over an envelope fat with hundreds before he said, "I know. That's why I'm here."

I allowed him on board. Even gave him a chair and offered him orange juice, the sole contents of my fridge. Then I sat back and waited for him to speak. I don't think he could help sounding like he was bragging all the time.

"Roderick found some high-class buyers. International jet-setters into overseas distribution."

Congrats.

"There are rumors." They must have been major rumors because Shotgun had never been the cautious one before. "Everything from cannibalism to a demonic cult. So we're limiting our exposure to them. I'm the face. Roderick was wondering if you'll be the muscle."

I stare at him.

"His word was backup."

I smiled.

"He did make one request." It was his turn to smile. "He wants you to dress up."

Chapter Six
Naga Suites

I found my music by accident. The Little Kid had latched on to me. His signature on his email was his website. He was the first person I knew who only used numbers for his website address. Something about hacking. On his Hobbies and Interests page, next to the geekiest Botany and Biology fan page, I found his "Jungle" tab. It was music . . . of a sort. Obviously derived from the same musical tree as hip-hop, the vocals were more dancehall influenced, the beats faster, more repetitive. Two of the mp3s I downloaded from him had chaotic breaks filled with sirens and horns that would make Public Enemy jealous. The controlled chaos of it put me in mind of a car wreck, though I had no idea why. I put it through my speakers one night and felt the difference between headphones and speakers for the first time in my life. Some music needed to be played out loud.

"It's not my music," Mom said, standing in my doorway listening, "but I could see how you'd like it." I think she was just happy I was doing something that resembled a typical teenager. When I played a Congo Natty track for Narayana that night, he smiled.

"I like Wu-Tang better."

That's Method Man on the mic, Raj, I said, pointing to his paltry speakers. It's a remix or something. You said find my sound. I think this is it.

"Dance," he commanded.

With you?

"No. Alone. Your sound knows your body. Show me."

Back then, aside from salsa, which I treated like combat training, I did not dance. In that one order I remembered Narayana's genius. In dance, there was no combat, no attraction, just creative union. I couldn't begin to fathom how dancing could be turned into bone-shattering blows, but Narayana could.

I let my knees bob to the beat, felt my hips slide to the synths, switched my head to the bass, skanked my legs to the snares, and flexed my arms whenever they felt the need, all to Tenor Fly's "Born in the Ghetto." Anyone watching it from the other decks probably saw the most subdued dance a body could perform. But I felt freer that night rocking out than I ever had before.

"Attack," Narayana said softly. I hadn't realized I'd closed my eyes. When I opened them, a skeleton was directly in front of me. My peace and joy was shattered. In as few seconds as possible, the bones of the skeleton from pelvis upward were shattered as well.

"Good start." Raj smiled, examining my handiwork. "But you strike with fear, not intention. Big difference."

I don't know how I did that, I said, trying desperately to control my breathing.

"That's why it's only a start. Learn your music. Watch how others move to it. Find joy and peace in the breaking of bone. Then you're ready for the next level."

It took the rest of the year. I became a Junglist, eating, sleeping, scrapping, and studying with a constant diet of Shy FX, Congo Natty, General Degree, and the like. Saturdays I woke up, rode the damn fixed-gear fifty miles, did my homework, cleaned my house and the *Mansai* and practiced the eighty-nine katas all while listening to Jungle and dubstep tunes. At night I'd find my way into 330 Ritch, the Mezzanine, or any other club in San Francisco that spun the tunes I liked. I'd usually watch for an hour then throw myself on the dance floor in part-emulation, part-innovation mode. Breakdowns of the low bass parts were my pornography. Everything else was lost, my voice, my mom, my training, my ever-worsening grades; everything went away on the dance floor. Any guy who tried to dance with me risked his life, a fact most came to recognize rather quickly. It was usually the gay boys, who just wanted to dance because they appreciated my moves and not my breasts, who survived the interaction.

I keep thinking of people as meat skeletons, I told Narayana one night after he prepared a stewed chicken dinner for both of us. We sat in his cabin listening to GZA's *Liquid Swords* album. He sighed and scratched his head.

"Human body is perfection and fragile. Yin and yang. They have to work together. This is youth; think anything is all one way or other. It is meat skeleton, but skeleton is also meat transportation. What, I train you to find skeletons to break? It's only where it starts."

The next morning I woke up at five, put my headphones on and stared at that first skeleton all day. I studied every fracture and splintered bone as I listened to every jungle tune I could find online for free.

By eight p.m. I was ready. I went over to the *Mansai* and silently presented myself. Only when he brought up another skeleton did I take my headphones off. I still heard the clicks and synths of the beat. For the first time that day, I let myself dance. This time with no restraint. I wasn't even thinking about the skeleton; the ethereal jungle beat in my head held me in its trance. It was only when I found myself eye to eye socket with the skeleton did I remember the fractured bones I'd been studying all day. Rather than strike, I breathed in slowly. With my exhale I reached out with my fingers and found places where that universal beat and my pulse couldn't find a counter pulse. In these places I struck in time with my pulse, the pulse of the world. And bones splintered. With each one more vulnerabilities of the skeleton became clear. It was like massaging in reverse. I wasn't as fast as Raj, but by the time it was done, the final massacre looked the same.

It took me a while to find something to wear to meet the cannibals. Shotgun gave me a week to get it together. I tagged the Little Kid for fashion advice. College and age had done well for his fashion sense when he wasn't playing at being the poor man's Diplo. Plus he couldn't even imagine how to lie to me, so flattery wouldn't be an issue.

I settled on a charcoal-colored two-button single-breasted business suit and, at the Little kid's insistence, had it tailored, sucking in the shoulders and tapering the waist. In the end it seemed more like a uniform for a bannerless army than anything. For kicks, I preserved combat readiness and bought a pair of oxblood Doc Martens and told the Little Kid's protest to fuck off. Dressing the part was one thing. It was still a job.

I had to dead-stare the Little Kid for a full ten seconds before he'd accept the grand I gave for his fashion eye. He tried to ask me what it was for as I left him standing in the mall in downtown San Francisco. Four hours later, back at the dock when I walked within striking distance of Shotgun and he didn't notice it was me, I knew it was money well spent. I'm sure brushing and combing my hair out also helped. I tapped the window of Shotgun's truck as he sat parked by the dock.

"You look . . . human," he said, meaning "hot," when I stepped into his truck.

Don't let the look fool you. Where's the product?

"This is negotiation, not delivery. You ready?"

Whether it was driving into the city or just being nervous I couldn't tell; all I knew was that it would have been easier for him to go through Oakland to get to our destination than going over the

Golden Gate Bridge. But I let it go. I didn't bother speaking until we were at the hotel. Sorry, not hotel. Naga Luxury Suites. Right on the border of Hayes Valley and downtown San Francisco, the building distinguished itself from the posh restaurants and fashion boutiques around it by having a circular driveway with a shed-sized fountain as its centerpiece. The fountain was shaped to resemble a giant cobra spitting water from its fangs as it encircled the world. Someplace nearby that dark dubstep sound I loved and feared was playing.

"What the fuck?" Shotgun stammered. He stomped the clutch, afraid to even enter the driveway. I couldn't fault his reaction. There was something alive, almost in motion, about the sculpture. It could have been the water bouncing off the snake's body, or maybe some slow rotation motor built into the globe, but whatever it was, the concept of the image itself was threatening. The real threat that I felt was the irresistibility of the image. Much as it screamed danger, neither Shotgun nor I could take our eyes off of it easily. The building itself had a similar effect; white silver, beyond modern sheer glass and polymers coated its outside and made it seem more like a monument to impossible heights than a place you'd actually enter. From jump, the Suites were intimidating.

You going to pull out now? I asked genuinely. He could've gone either way.

"Last time I felt this tweaked," Shotgun started, regaining his composure and pushing the truck into first, "four dudes that did better in the Hole than in Gen Pop were all moved to the cell next to me."

Don't worry. I'll protect you. For the first time ever, that sounded false.

Shotgun got more nervous when he turned his keys over to the valet. I acclimated to the Naga effect quickly but Shotgun's breathing just got more erratic; his movements were jerkier. Luckily, he pulled himself together enough to speak at the front counter.

"Welcome to the Naga Suites. How can I be of service?" the small Asian receptionist asked with subservience too genuine to seem born of a paycheck.

"We're here to see Rice Montague." The perfectly manicured woman gulped slightly at the name then stared incredulously at Shotgun.

"And you are?" Even I could tell that Matt should have spent more time on his wardrobe. A pair of Dickies and a long-sleeved chambray shirt covered by a full-length double-breasted leather duster can only take you so far in this world. After being assured that we had an appointment, she pointed to the back elevators and with a humble glare said, "He's in the club."

The elevator buttons didn't have numbers, just icons. Above the door, correlates to numbers as well as locations of shopping floors, massage floors, and "The Club" were posted. Of course, we were heading to the basement. That supple dubstep tempo that teased my ears upstairs threatened to destroy them as we descended. Shotgun became even more nervous. But the music was so . . . good; I almost forgot I was on the job.

"Chabi . . ." Shotgun murmured as we exited the elevator. It wasn't the bass, the flickering purple, red, and yellow lights, or the mass of over four hundred people—pure body funk mixed with every trendy perfume release in the past last three months. It was the bouncers. Two thick-necked Samoans, one checking ID, the other doing complete and thorough pat-downs. Not that he needed to do that much to catch the sixteen-inch shotgun strapped like an extra limb to Matt's back under his broad-shouldered jacket. I'd been hearing the thing shake loosely since he got out of the truck.

Me first, I told him, squeezing in front. Before I could speak, the Samoan waved me and Shotgun past the line of sequin-and-black-dressed waifs and costumed club kids. The Samoan's only interruption, a small stamp on our hands, a silver snake that glowed in blacklight.

Don't ask how I found them. You'd only get confusion. What can I say? I smelled them before I saw them? They called me? You ever long for something you've never seen but once you find it, you're repulsed by it? That was me the first time I saw them. At the dead center of the dance floor, defended by four pillars shaped like red and silver pythons intertwined, five of the most beautiful people I'd ever seen in my life reclined on a slightly elevated black sectional couch. There were no guards but no one even approached the mini stage, or those that reclined on it. They looked bored and fashionable—at least three of them did. One, the palest smallest woman, wore silk pajamas and seemed unaffected by the heat and music of the crowd. But the youngest, an olive complexion guy with an almost crew cut and eyes so black I noticed them through the darkness of the club, couldn't stop staring at me. As we approached I saw his v-neck, tan shirt show a chest with no hair and a mouth that had the perpetual beginnings of a smile.

"You Rice?" Shotgun asked the black-eyed man as we approached the bed/throne/couch.

"You don't look like you're carrying eighty-five pounds of marijuana," Rice said, standing but still staring at me. "Are you carrying it?"

I'm just the eye candy, I said and felt the echo of my Voice in his head. That almost smile grew to adulthood. But the pajama woman, whose face up close looked like that of a pleased rat, turned as I spoke and stared at me. All the beautiful people did. Shotgun barely noticed.

"I'm not about to bring all my product to a meet-and-greet. We haven't even agreed on a price." Still not taking his eyes off of me, Rice reached into his back pocket and pulled out a black credit card.

"Six hundred thousand dollars on that."

"I don't take credit cards."

"I don't give them. That's a black card. Any ATM, every bank accepts them. No proof of ID necessary. Think bearer bonds for the twenty-first century."

"I guess that works," Shotgun murmured and reached for the card. I knew this was just the sort of thing his uncles sent me to protect against, but I was surprised how easily the kid was falling for it. I slapped his hand back and noticed a weird narcotic haze jump off him.

"Eye candy has teeth," the rat-face woman said. Not just her face, but if I looked at her mouth long enough, just a second longer than normal, I saw a thousand pairs of tiny rodent teeth in her mouth. But that didn't matter. Another part of me still saw her as gorgeous.

ATMs have cameras. So do banks. Computers leave trails. Cash is king. With each of my words, the small-toothed one and Rice exchanged furious, confused looks.

"Let's all have drinks, discuss this," Rice offered. Like nothing I've ever wanted before, I wanted to please him. More than I ever wanted to please my mother. The feeling sickened me, reminding me of my Narayana. But I couldn't think of a reason to refuse, so we sat.

"At four eighty an ounce, we're looking at six hundred fifty thousand dollars," Shotgun said after the woman made some invisible signal and got a waiter to come over and pour champagne for us all. The other three beautiful people, all men in four-thousand-dollar suits, were older and out of place. They seemed bemused and slightly annoyed by us. Me in particular.

"That's a lot per ounce. Where's the bulk discount?" Rice asked playfully.

You hurting for cash? I asked looking around. Besides, we all know you're going to slap another forty percent on top of the sticker price when you sell it overseas.

I couldn't tell if it was what I said or how I said it that got the other three beautiful men to take notice of me. But I'd almost wished they hadn't.

What's your name? the small-toothed woman asked, her high-pitched voice suddenly echoing through my head.

Chabi, I answered, and then wondered why. What's yours?

"They call me Poppy. Now what makes you think my cousin is at all interested in resale?" Something in her voice was also telling me to go fuck myself, but I couldn't find it in her tone or vocabulary.

Eighty-five pounds of weed? I fake laughed. You could give everyone in this room a joint for that and still not even make a dent in your pot pile. You could be trying to go the legal route, sell to the clubs, but high rollers like you, able to hand out black cards like Halloween candy, you couldn't see enough profit from a cannabis club unless you owned it. But you take this Cali bud to Europe where they're sick of all that high-THC hash, you can name your price.

With each word, the silent pretty ones became more irritated. Poppy ground her thousand teeth together but still managed to act like she was smiling. Only Rice emanated curiosity over anger. When one of the silent ones finally did speak, it was to Poppy.

"Teach this girl her place and let's move on with this."

You're welcome to come over here and try, big man. No need to hide behind little miss skinny.

You understand me? He looked absolutely shocked.

"You heard him," Rice stated more than he asked.

I said yes quickly then realized something unsettling. The big man's mouth hadn't moved.

"Listen, I have no desire to get into the international pot business. The truth of it is we throw eight parties a month like this. S.F., New York, London, Barcelona, Kotte, all over the world. Let the masses drink, smoke, pop what they like. It's of utmost importance that the VIPs only have consistent high-grade party favors. We don't have to quibble over dimes and nickels." He looked to Shotgun, glassy eyed and slack tongued. "Six hundred thousand is too low? Fine. Seven hundred thousand. Cash. Delivered tomorrow morning."

"Ok," Shotgun managed to get out.

"You are overly eager." The last of the formerly silent finally spoke. Again his lips didn't move. None of the pretty people's lips were moving. "Demand what you will from these weak wills and see it done."

An ancient pain began to light on the skin of my back. I tried to ignore it but it came with an equally ancient anger.

A lot of reckless tongue wagging is coming from that corner over there. Don't see a lot of action, I barked using my Voice.

That got the pretty man's attention. He stood, a clear foot and a half taller than me, in a soft steel gray suit obviously custom-made by a tailor far better than mine. It fit his vulture-like chest span perfectly.

"What are you?" Had he been using his mouth, no doubt spit would have been flying from it as he spoke.

The one that will end you if you don't sit . . .

He hit me. A right-handed slap across the face, starting from his left shoulder. It was old school and theatrical, the way an actor would strike a stage harlot. I saw it coming but I couldn't stop it, couldn't delay the blow. No. I could have. I knew the defense and how to implement it. I just didn't. I knew the counter, right foot Dragon stumble to left side to change levels followed by Phoenix Ruffle—vertical elbow blows to the body with right leg bent slightly more than the left to confuse defensive blows. But I couldn't think of it fast enough. No. My body wouldn't react fast enough. I was on the ground, slapped, one tooth loose as a result.

The warmth on my back grew white-hot. Every suppressed grunt, shout, and vitriol I'd ever managed to contain lobbied its jailor and demanded freedom. While Shotgun sat stupefied, Rice shielded his head with pity, and the other pretty people laughed, I stood up. The slapper saw me but didn't care. His mistake.

I full-body struck him, using the dubstep track to find the entropy of the man's bones. The agony in my back lessened after I'd struck the slapper eighty-five times in fourteen seconds. Each blow was like jamming a finger into a concrete block. But Narayana had me do that when I was fifteen. The sight of the confident slapper falling back in horror and pain was worth it. I'd never found the entropy of a living person's bones before. Somehow it felt less world-shattering than I thought it would have.

Then I passed out.

Chapter Seven

Alter

It was all coming together for me as the year went along. Narayana left me to maintain my training, throwing the occasional challenge at me just to remind me he was always watching. He had me swim from San Francisco to Oakland at four in the morning, for example. He'd only told me about it forty-five minutes before. The whole way over Raj rowed his little dinghy nearby demanding I swim like a fish or at least a sea lion. My reward, of course, was worth it. "Good girl," he told me when we reached Jack London Square.

Grow up without a father or anything other than a moderately depressed alcoholic mother trapped in a dead-end job and you'll never understand why the captain's "good girl" meant so much to me. No one else saw the work I did with him. We both took my training with such seriousness that other eyes on that relationship felt like an invasion. His rewards, while few and far between, had the comfort of being well earned.

One time the prize also included breakfast at a vegan soul food joint. The restaurant had diminutive triangle tables off on its side street so we could people-watch as the Captain ate soy sausages and hash browns like they were made of crack. My only concern was warming myself with the thick wool sweater and down blanket the old man provided. It was 10:30 in the a.m and I was thankful for the sun.

"Soon you find entropy without music," he told me in between impossibly large bites.

Because entropy is everywhere. I tried to not shiver and speak as though I knew why it was important. It's hard to find specific entropy.

"You have sex yet?" he asked as cars began to risk themselves against lights and peers.

With what free time? I asked instantly flushed.

"Still woman. No matter what, still woman. Women must have sex. Know where life begins, know how to end it. All healers are poisoners. Remember that."

I was about to stutter some protest when a nearby Camaro, driven by a hyphy boy with shoulder-length dreads, lost its front axle as it crossed the street. The car dipped fully to the right side, scraping concrete against metal, making an awful sound. The rear of the car fishtailed into the side of an absolutely beautiful, slightly graying middle-aged white guy. Even as the car crumpled around the man like he was made of metal and not flesh, I couldn't stop staring at the man's chest. I felt remorse for his ash gray silk suit as oil and hyphy child blood stained it. Even the thoroughly unnatural sound of metal meeting whatever substance that man was made of couldn't detract me from the glory of his two-day stubble. I reached out for Narayana's hand, fearful of the trance I was falling into. His absence shocked me back to reality. I looked around and saw nothing, but as I was about to call out for him, I felt three of his fingers on my back directly behind me.

"Be still. Be quiet." And I felt fear. Not just from his words but also from the attention the beautiful man almost gave to us. He was in the middle of yanking the hyphy boy out of his car when Raj spoke in a voice that mirrored my own true Voice. And though the supposed victim of the crash continued to move efficiently, smashing what remained of the windshield with one hand and tossing the boy across the street like a bowling ball, the cock of his head proved his attention was truly toward us.

Raj drew characters on my back that I instantly knew how to speak, though their home language was obscured. The beautiful one looked annoyed then, like the sun was in his eyes. As always, I did what Narayana told me to do and was quiet. One second more and the beautiful man was gone down Broadway to the train tracks that ran parallel to the Bay. I saw him survey one more time, then he was gone, hidden by an Amtrak I didn't see coming. When he left, so did the words written on my back.

What the fuck was that? I turned hard to face Narayana.

"Doesn't matter," he said in an accent so foreign I thought he might be stroking out or something. "You will forget soon enough."

Like hell!

"Remember only his grace," the Captain said as though he hadn't heard me. "The elegance of his movement, the tempo of his strike. That one is true with his form. Strive to be like him in that way alone."

"Oh my god, what happened?" Our waitress came running out of the restaurant as if she'd just heard the crash.

"Some dumbass kid done crashed his car. Sent himself through the windshield, Lord have mercy," an old black homeless man on the street informed her. Just as I was about to correct him, Narayana spoke.

"Back to the boat." I obeyed but listened for trace elements of what I thought I'd heard in his voice. Fear. It was an impossibility I needed verified. I listened for it as we went back to the dock, on his boat, and back to Sausalito. But the farther we went from Oakland, the harder it was to remember what I was looking for and why. In the end, all I had to hold on to was the memory of the efficiency of human motion in action.

I usually woke up in a second. I'd be asleep then I was awake and could tell you how long I've been out, what time it was, and who was in the room with me. I was like that before Narayana and he only made that sense more acute. So understand the mid-level panic I felt when I woke up slow.

It took me a good minute to figure out where I was. It was an extreme source of shame to have to use my eyes to scan for clues, but when they fell on the black business card with the silver snake coiled around the globe, the previous night came flooding back to me. I was in the Naga Luxury Suites.

Without hearing a sound I knew the pretty boy Rice was on the thirteenth floor. He wanted to see me, I knew that as well. I didn't *know*. That's too strong a word. I felt it. And I didn't like feeling without knowing.

I'd been laid out on an obelisk of a bed with black sheets. I was still dressed. A quick thought of rape ran through my head, but my privates seemed unmolested. My boots were placed together at the foot of the bed, but other than that there was no evidence that anyone had been in the room since it was furnished. No note from whoever deposited me. No signs of life. It creeped me out. In the hallway I almost banged on a random door just to get a sense of another person being alive. Everything was too perfect, not a hint of dust anywhere, small tables with courtesy phones and candies were laid out as though no one had ever touched them. Not a thread was out of place on the double-knit silk red-and-silver Turkish rugs or the practical rugs underneath. Everything was so quiet. I couldn't hear TVs from other rooms, the traffic from outside. I put myself in combat mode. When the elevator chimed, as they do when you call for them, I nearly roundhoused it. Instead I stepped inside. My body went to press the sigil for the lobby. But the curious side of me stopped my arm at the sigil for the thirteenth floor.

The floor I'd been on had fifteen different rooms. And while the elevator had glyphs, the rooms had numbers. Except on the thirteenth floor. And it only had five doors. I walked by the door with what looked like seven smaller circles all connected by a single squiggly line to a larger one with black small pointed triangles, almost like teeth, in the middle of it. I heard a familiar voice using an unfamiliar tone. It was Shotgun and he was apologizing. Not like a kid caught doing something wrong, but like an accused man who didn't know what he'd done was a crime.

Just as I was about to launch myself at the door, it opened.

"Relax, he's fine." It was Poppy in a white bathrobe, which she let reveal her red bra and panties. Anyone else would have caught a Rising Rooster to the jaw, but that would let her know she spooked me and I couldn't have that.

You got him tied to a bedpost or something or can he come out to play? I asked as casually as I could.

"Matthew, darling. Your eye candy wants you." Ever seen someone who just had his heart broken? Like that second? There's a desperation mixed with a terror that takes over the eyes. The mouth can't decide between screaming, laughing, or crying. I once saw Little Kid right after he asked some pink-and-gold-clad Latina to a dance. I didn't catch the words but I could tell he'd need some super strong glue to put his heart back together. When Shotgun materialized, he had that same look on his face. Only his voice tried to convince me otherwise.

"Oh, Chabi. I'm so glad you're ok." He hugged me. Like a sincere hug. He was flush.

Fuck is wrong with you? I asked forcefully, pushing him off me.

"Nothing. I was . . . Me and Poppy were talking. Just so you know, she said a lot of things that make sense."

I let my eyes flash over to Poppy for a quarter of a second and somehow she managed to display her million-teethed mouth in the form of a smile. She was the skinny white bitch that all normal looking women despised. Her wiry jaw and atrophied arm and leg muscles screamed weak just as her attitude displayed insane confidence. Her hip bone sticking out above her panty line infuriated me for some reason.

"And look!" Shotgun yelped as he reached around the corner and pulled out a briefcase. "Seven hundred thousand dollars. All of it." He was gleeful. Then a second later, repentant. "Oh, Poppy, are you sure? I . . . I don't want money to fuck with you and me."

"Baby, it's like I keep telling you." Poppy moved her pelvis on to his thigh then her hand to his ass before I could gag. "It's only money. And you have so much more to offer." Something about the way she kissed him, her jaw undulating like that or the fierce grip she had on the back of his head made it look like she was devouring him.

I wanted to do something or say something at least. But what? "Hey, stop kissing the super hot half-naked chick because every now and then she's got a million baby rat teeth in her mouth?" Right before I was going to make up a more suitable excuse, Poppy stopped sucking him dry. Shotgun barely moved from her.

"Rice is over there. He's dying to speak with you." I followed her bony finger to the door diagonal from hers. When I turned back, Poppy's door was closed.

I knocked on Rice's door determined not to kiss him. The door opened on its own and let a serious amount of noise out. Rice sat on a steel gray couch in front of a seventy-five-inch screen with a video controller in his hand. The game on the screen seemed to toggle between first person shooter and mêlée martial arts at will. Rice was engrossed.

"Just give me two minutes, Chabi. I'm about to rape this game," Rice begged me. I watched as he conquered the challenge on screen. In the animated victory short of the game, a silver glove that the main character wears transforms into a giant silver snake and wraps itself around the main character's body, a customizable character obviously, because it looked a lot like Rice. Close-ups showed the bulging feet, hands, and mouth of the character. Then an explosive flash of light and the main character is transformed. He wears a suit of armor that looks like skin. The words "You are the Silver snake!" appeared over the character's head in a cheesy font.

"Cool, huh?" Rice finally asked. Somehow that gave me permission to look around the rest of the suite. It was easily five times the size of the room I woke up in. The ceilings were twice as high. No wall separated the front living room we were standing in from the gourmet level double-sink kitchen. There was a second floor above us with two doors and seemingly connected bedrooms. The opposite wall from the entrance door was one great window. Outside, a glass patio jutted out like a splinter from a tinted highly soundproof sliding door. This was no hotel room or even luxury suite. This was a throne room.

Why not the penthouse? I asked out of nowhere. Nothing was comfortable. Not standing, sitting, speaking, leaning. I felt fundamentally discombobulated in my body. Which never happens.

"Fucking passé wannabe elite bullshit," Rice announced with a smile as he flipped back over his couch and made his way to the kitchen. "You want to control something, you dominate the middle of it, not the top."

You control this hotel? I asked, watching my feet follow him. Rice pulled out two Japanese beers from the fridge and tossed me one. I caught it more on instinct than thought.

"I better. My dad owns it. Twelve others as well. All over the world." He raised his coal black eye at me, searching for an impression he failed to make. What did I know about hotel owners and suites all over the world? He could've said he was a world-famous physicist and it would have meant just as much to me. He read my indifference as a challenge, and for a second I tensed. But then he opened his beer and started talking again.

"Fuck me, though. Check you out. Pulverizing the bones of one of the old-timers before he even had a chance to react. I love the way you took the first hit to justify your reaction. Fucking clean!"

Just before I took a sip of beer, the ass-kicking came back into perfect view. It staggered me, but also brought me back to my senses. I put the beer down and assumed the Ember Stance—right leg before left. Left foot pointing out for maximum balance, knees bent, shoulders loose, chin down, hands open, ready.

I don't drink, I said, scanning all the doors, waiting for cops or security to rush in.

"Oh, relax, why don't you?" Rice said taking a drink. "You're under my protection . . . Ok, my father's, but still. Even if Samovar, that's who you broke by the way, Samovar Khan. Even if he could stand, he wouldn't dare do it here, now. He'll come for you to be sure. But not here and not now."

Why not? I asked, surprised the man was even still alive.

"It would reek of desperation, of need. Let me tell you something about Salmy, as his name doesn't appear to mean anything to you. Mr. Khan is a corporate raider on a global scale. He dismantles companies for parts, puts small towns on the map and dissolves LLCs before they even know they've joined. He's a major player. But before he does any major deal Salmy goes to this resort in the hills of Ecuador. A thousand dollars to have volcanic ash shot up your ass type stuff. So Salmy is wrapped in ancient seaweed, which is keeping some special mud tight to his pores or something. Important thing is he's bound; super tight, no wiggle room. Get the picture?"

I nod, fascinated by the glee with which he's telling the tale.

"Ok, so on the other side of a town a guy who doesn't want whatever deal to go through hires five gun thugs from Guayaquil to make sure the deal doesn't happen. And these guys are not street level. We're talking hitters, salt and peppered in the game. Smart enough to know to wait until Samovar is wrapped in the seaweed and having his alone time. Ok, so naturally no one knows what actually happened in the room, but Poppy got a copy of the medical reports for each of them. One's floating rib punctured his lung. Another's fifth vertebrae went missing. Not shattered, not broken, just gone. No surgical scars either. One just couldn't stop screaming. No injuries, he just couldn't stop screaming his head off. Another's testicles ended up in his mouth. And let's be clear, not his scrotum, just his testicles ended up on his tongue. And the last guy. His sole injury was a permanently prolapsed anus. And that's not the best part."

He was in genuine hysterics at this point so I didn't bother speaking. But in my mind I was glad I'd broken the man's bones. The wounds he produced were sadistic. Not meant to defend but humiliate.

"The best part," Rice continued, "is that when those poor Ecuadorian women came back in the room, Samovar was still wrapped in the seaweed."

And that's the man I . . . incapacitated last night?

"Yeah, how about that?" Rice stepped from behind the counter in the kitchen and took a seat on the stool closest to me. "Those were some nice moves you had there. Where'd you pick them up?"

Here and there. No lie had ever come so easily to me. For all of Rice's considerable charm, I could tell we were finally getting to the thing he wanted to know.

"Wow, that's weird 'cause I've been here and I've been there and I've never seen anybody like you." He tried to meet my dead eye. I was surprised by the seriousness of his face, but it still didn't match mine. I felt my back get hot again and saw an instant response in Rice. "Don't mistake me for an enemy, darling. I am no combat man. I'm a lover, not a fighter. All I'm saying is I could use some more fighters around. You interested?"

Last night was a mistake. That's not what I do. If that's what you're looking for . . .

"Satisfying as it was to watch one of my dad's generation overplay his cards and get schooled for it, that's not a business I'd invest in and expect consistent returns. No, look, we're just starting this whole monthly big bash thing in San Francisco. That's new dealers, new drugs, new crowds, new everything. I don't know who to trust and who to let loose. I'll figure it out soon enough, but in the meantime, if I let the wrong folks get too close, I might need you to escort them out the front door."

Cover your mistakes is what you're saying.

"If you want to put that taint on it, sure. Come on, look, I'll smooth things over with Mr. Khan for you, keep buying from your boys and throw in ten thousand dollars for every party you come to. If I need you in between parties, I'll kick you another five grand just to see you. Plus you can stay in the suites whenever you want."

You just want me close by, I meant to say to myself.

"You're right about that." Rice smirked, looking me up and down. It felt gross . . . and good to be desirable. "But I swear this is all business. Say yes. Please?"

I'll think about it. The early morning light was beginning to reflect off of his clear patio causing a flare to lance across my eyes.

"I know you, you'll say yes. I can tell." Rice moved his hand in some odd motion and the blinds went down. He fished in his fridge for another beer and an apple as well. "Besides, you have too many questions you want answered to not hang out."

Careful what you think you know, I tried to quip back without sounding harsh. I'm going to go scoop up my friend from your girl's spot now.

"He's not yours, is he?" Rice asked.

What? Like boyfriend? Nah.

"Boyfriend, right. Yeah I think he belongs to Poppy now. Might be a while before he's ready to leave her side. Just chill out. Finish your beer."

I told you I don't drink. But when I looked down I'd drunk half of it. Rice did that half smile from last night and I knew the correlated emotion for its true name: Mastery.

I left the room quickly and banged on Poppy's door until she let me in. I half dragged Shotgun out of the room with the cash. When Poppy tried to get in the way, I put both the cash and Shotgun down and squared off for her. She got the message and promptly moved. After Matt recovered from the shock of being away from his woman, he had one insistent request, "Please don't tell my uncles."

I wasn't sure what not to tell them, but silence was my preferred mode anyway. After dropping me off at my harbor, Shotgun pulled out a prepaid cell phone from the glove compartment and gave it to me. I was already out of the car.

"I was supposed to give this to you last night. But you know, so we can call you instead of just showing up." I nodded and walked away.

Back on the boat I threw up four times before I could lie down. I felt a deep sickness beyond anything half a beer would've done. Dizziness was where it started, but with each memory of the night, nausea crept up. The beautiful ones, I'd seen them before. Not them, but someone or something that looked like them. And it was cruel. People so attractive should not be allowed to be so hard, I thought. But when I searched for evidence of hardness, I saw only my own. They negotiated in a way that was fair, that benefited Shotgun's family in the end.

But then there was the slap. It had been a while since anyone got the drop on me, sure. But even when they did, it was never a full-on slap like that. I rubbed my cheek and felt it still slightly swollen. There was no way a normal man in his late sixties should have that type of power and speed. But if Rice's story was to be believed, Mr. Khan was no normal man. So what kind of man was he?

And there was something else about all of them. Something to do with their mouths and the way they spoke. Maybe it was that accent that I couldn't place. Maybe it was they sounded a bit like me when I spoke. But I didn't use my mouth when I spoke, and they did. Didn't they? Even the stamp on my hand to gain entrance had faded. I wondered if this is what it felt like being drunk, being sure something had happened but not knowing what.

I twisted and turned in my bed for hours trying to get the smells and images of the previous night out of my head. I'd found the entropy in a man's bones and he lived to tell about it. That just shouldn't be the case. The most infuriating part of it was my strong desire to go back. All at once, I felt the inadequacies of my life, living hand-to-mouth on a boat. At that moment, I could be staying in a luxury suite. I could be eating fine food and drinking the best drinks.

I sat up from my bed, Narayana's bed, furious, my back slightly hot. What the fuck am I thinking? I don't eat or drink like that. These are not the fucking things I want.

I jumped in the shower enraged but with no direction for it. Finally I settled into my katas. It was two in the morning so I didn't see any reason to dress. It was only then, in that cold night air, that I was able to lose what had been done and what I did in the previous night.

Chapter Eight
Riot

By the tail end of senior year Mom pretty much stopped talking to me.
I took that. She also stopped worrying. When I came in with lightweight wounds my opponents could land—a sprained finger one
night, a scorched shoulder the next—Mom didn't even ask. I took
her disregard as a form of respect, like she knew I could handle
myself, though I knew that wasn't her intent. Mom acted like I did
drugs or like I was sleeping with Narayana. I wanted to scream,
"He's turning me into a bona fide badass, Mom!" But I was afraid
of my own voice.

The Little Kid invited me to his after-prom party. His mom
owned an open-faced sandwich shop in downtown Oakland and
she'd be gone that weekend. He told me he'd pay me a hundred
dollars.

What are you asking me now? I asked. He thought he'd offended.
Really, I just hadn't been paying attention until he mentioned money.

"No! Not for sex." A little too loud. The catty bitches on the
school's lawn giggled. I stared until I vanished their Forever 21 asses.

"Security. I think that's when I'm going to make my debut."

You gay?

"No. My debut as . . ."

A woman?

"I already said I'm not gay . . ."

Yeah, but you could be like a woman trapped in a little kid's body. That's not the same as being gay . . ." I kept a straight face until he looked like he was about to cry. Your debut as what?

"A DJ," he chirped like a small bird as he searched his backpack and pulled out cards and posters in bright red and yellow. I'd seen them already posted around school, though there was no way I could have known they were his. Under DJ it said "Special Guest."

What makes you so special? I asked as we headed to our homeroom.

"Nothing. But if I suck, I don't want it ruining my chances to spin someplace else." He was off like a squirrel after nuts in his bag, looking for essentials for the next class. I'd given up learning anything at school almost a full year earlier. Even the pretty black teacher stopped trying with me by this point.

Fair point. But why are you trying to molest me on the loot? I demanded, pointing to the five dollar cover. Half the door and I'm in.

"No," he said, so forcefully I wondered if he was reacting to something else. His posture didn't change, he didn't stop rooting through his bag, just his voice got definitive. I waited until we got to class and he was sitting to speak again.

Come on, Little Kid. Even if just half your science geeks come that'll be . . .

"Look, I budgeted properly," he fumed. At me. The Little Kid fumed at me. "My mother's business hasn't been going well. If can do this right, I can pay rent for a month. I need that money. I wouldn't even be asking you for this but . . ."

But what?

"Well, I kind of went crazy and announced it on my website so I don't know how many people are coming."

On the *Mansai*, Raj told me I'd done the right thing by taking the job. We discussed it as we went through the seventy-seven forms of motion he'd first taught me. I'd never forgotten one of them, but senior year was when Narayana taught me their names.

"He see you fight?" Raj asked, retracing his arm from Excise Griffin; a hard wrist, soft finger strike designed to paralyze from the diaphragm down to the distal phalanges, and arching his back for Medusa's Rise, a single-leg overhead strike.

Nah. Just the trouble I gave a wannabe gangster at school. But you know, rep, I said after landing from the rise and extending my right arm to the side for the Phoenix Bow—from extended right arm, hip twist into right elbow, move left hand back to the cheek like you're stringing an arrow in a bow, then forward approach driving left fist into the target.

"He not hire you." Narayana laughed, his bulletproof belly not betraying a single shudder as he did. "He hire your rep. Know what that means?"

Testing the rep, I said, twisting and crunching into Flame's Descent—front leg kicks out back leg of opponent while back finger rakes the eyes of falling opponent, while I squat low to prevent an attack on my legs.

Only ones who come are the ones who need the rep the most. It would be the gang banger. He was not happy that a girl had punked him. But he had it coming for going after the Little Kid for no reason one lunch period. If he was dumb, he'd come alone. Either way he'd be strapped. As my calves ached from the Demon's Tears pose—legs parallel and bent, weight on the left, right ankle loose for a snap kick to groin or face, right arm protecting vital trunk organs, other arm chambered and relaxed, ready for whatever came, Narayana smirked.

"Good girl."

But I didn't do anything, I said, my concentration broken.

"Sometimes you good girl without knowing," was all he would say as he descended into the main cabin. Just as I was about to give up Demon's Tears, Raj came stomping back up the stairs.

"How come he only ask you for after prom?"

Huh?

"He should take you to prom." I almost choked laughing. "You not ugly," Narayana barked, like my laugh had insulted him. "Where I'm from, many man pay good money for night with you. Bring flowers, food for your whole family, and money."

Thanks? I smirked, really trying to take it as a compliment. Here, though, these dudes want white chicks, or light-skinned black girls at least. They've got to be able to do whatever they want to them, like control them, you know? Girl stands up for herself, doesn't dress like a slut blow-up doll, it just doesn't work, you know?

I was speaking purely speculatively, I realized, as the dark small man crossed his deck to me with an inspective eye. Slower than I'd ever seen him move, Narayana reached his manicured hand to my face, bracing my Mongolian father's cheeks in between his hand. Fish sauced wafted off his breath as he gently pulled me toward him.

"I am Narayana Raj. You are my one and only pupil. Between me and you, no lie. I tell you this and you listen like when I teach Ashes Ascent or Salamander Strike." He waited until I nodded before speaking again. "You are beautiful."

Not sure why that hit both of us so hard, but we held each other for a while after that. Me holding back tears, him singing gently in whatever his home language is.

I'd prepared the way Narayana had told me to; I'd gone to the indoor shooting range with a bow and arrows he'd forced me to make two weeks earlier, and practiced my aim as small-caliber fire went off all around me. I perfected the light-touch pulse interruption Narayana called Ember's Kiss, and made my blade dance in my hand like a crackhead trying to earn enough for her nightly fix. For the final touch I waited until the last minute. I needed Mom.

I got this thing, I mind muttered, interrupting her Carolina Chocolate Drops listening. Mom was reading sitting on the couch in the living room downstairs. She'd stopped with the hard liquor but still sipped on large goblets of wine. She turned in her chair slightly to me. I need to get dressed up for this thing tonight.

"What kind of thing?"

It's a dance. I'm . . . It was like we hadn't been distant and cold for a year plus. I'd never seen her so animated. My closets were filled with decomposing skeletons and weird weapons. Mom's were filled with pseudo silks, rainbows of short, mini- and long dresses. The variety of sizes told me she'd never thrown a dress away. She had dresses in there I vaguely remembered from my childhood, back when she was still an elegant drunk. When she pulled out a deep blue skintight pencil dress, I almost ruined the moment.

I've got to be able to move, you know? The flash of despair in her face made me want to pull my words back into my mouth. But Mom took a gulp of wine and kept her eye on the prize.

"Good point. You don't know what these boys out here will try. Besides, you can't go from jeans, T-shirt, and hoodies to a piece like this. Might cause some heart attacks." We laughed. Together. In the end she fitted me with a gray blouse that left my back exposed and a blood red skirt that showed more ankle on one leg than the other. I let her do my makeup but disappeared before she could say anything about my toe socks. I lived near barefoot and a hundred bucks wasn't enough to get me to try heels.

From his deck Raj looked over the pier to see me and nodded a noncommittal affirmation. His attention was split by the small TV he had playing UFC fights or, as he called them, comedy fights. "Remember Peacock's Forever Glory requires clear mind as well as contracted diaphragm."

I look all right, Raj? I twirled in front of him on the pier to show the trickery that Mom had worked. He threw me the keys to his rusty Cutlass Royale.

"Clothes, paint on face don't make you good. Has to come . . ."

For the love of Christ, Raj . . .

"Yes, ok? You pretty. Make good money if you sell it. Now go protect Little Kid." With no one else around I felt ok to grin.

While everybody else was at prom, the real prom, Little Kid and I were transforming his mom's sandwich shop into a den of music, dancing, and underage drinking. When he first saw me, Little Kid looked like he wanted to say something, but then couldn't find the words so resorted to trying not to look at me directly.

Little Kid was smart; once we moved the trash cans out of the small enclosed back area, it made a great keg garden and smoker's refuge. I didn't bother asking where he got the three kegs. A storage balcony that usually served as an office for his mom was the perfect DJ booth. We moved the meat coolers to the back—luckily they were on wheels—and rearranged the lunch tables so that they made the borders of what would be the dance floor. He'd already taken the chips and sodas out of visual range by the time I got there. I only had time to demand Little Kid play jungle once before the chess club came a-knocking. Half of them were already drunk.

Little Kid was spinning his slightly alternative top forty tunes for an hour before anyone I didn't recognize from school began showing up. Eye checks and the occasional Ember's Kiss kept the five-dollar tolls coming easy enough.

Around one in the morning I noticed the lack of my favorite Latino gangster wannabe. The loss of that ass-kicking wasn't that severe, but it alerted me to the lack of new bodies coming in. I stepped outside for the first time in an hour plus and saw Oakland on fire. Turned out it wasn't the gangster I had to worry about. Just the overtaxed, underprepared, and trigger-happy Oakland Police Department.

A moron of an undertrained Oakland police officer had fired a gun at point-blank range at a twenty-two-year-old Oakland kid who was unarmed. And handcuffed. Facedown. The cop was white and lived in the rich suburb of Antioch. The kid was black and lived in a part of Oakland known as The Bottoms.

The cop's excuse was that he thought he was pulling his Taser. Oakland wasn't buying it, but the jury did. They gave the cop the lightest sentence possible. Oakland answered by lighting its streets on fire. That's what the news reports said, at least. In truth, it wasn't the mourners of the dead Bottoms kid or the righteous anger of the Oakland protestors that started lighting garbage cans on fire. It was bandanna-faced trustafarians who got off calling themselves anarchists alongside the usual opportunistic infection–type people that avail themselves of whatever tragedy they can find to grab whatever they can. They were the ones who maintained the chaos in the streets.

In response, the Oakland Police Department strapped on their riot gear and swung for the fences, trying desperately to maintain what crumbs of order they could find. Of course I knew none of this at the time. I just walked out of my first and only high school party and found a full-scale riot jumping off.

Party's over! If anyone wondered how they could hear me over the music, they didn't bother asking. I had to use my Voice. They were all following instructions, packing up and figuring out how to get out of the sandwich shop, except the Little Kid.

"What the hell?" he yipped at me as I went up to his balcony.

Riot. Big time. All downtown, by the smell of the fire. He understood quickly enough and killed the music just as the sound of breaking wood from the beer garden made him jump. Me too, only I leapt from the small back window on the second floor balcony to the beer garden. A skinny dread anarchist had already made his way over by the time I landed. His friend was trying to make it over the fence as well. I let his ass meet my knee.

You're not welcome here, I whispered as I threw him back over the fence.

"Fucking pigs are everywhere," the remaining white dread moaned as I stepped off the keg, resting on the balls of my feet softly.

Your problem. Not mine. The smell of his fear came in waves almost masking the smell of burning tires from Franklin Street. You get one chance to leave here on your own.

He did not choose wisely.

Back inside, nine mathletes and debaters formed a circle around the Little Kid. He'd been smart enough to lock the front door and turn off all the lights. The front gate to the plate-glass shop window had already been locked down. Across the street we saw a troop of helmeted baton-wielding police officers making their way from their headquarters on the border of Jack London Square to the main riot center in front of City Hall.

Did I stutter the first time? Go home.

"They, we were all going to stay here." Little Kid stepped up as the others retreated from me.

Um, riot equals change in plans, no?

"Where are we going to go?" a mousy girl who made me ashamed to be a female cried. "Bryce called. He said some of the others had been attacked. BART is closed."

"They all told their parents they were going to be out all night. At each other's houses. But we were going to spend the night here. Kind of like a sleepover. We've got sleeping bags . . ."

For the love of all things non-nerd I beg you to stop talking. I looked at them in earnest for the first time. They were the last of the two hundred who had come, and the first. The intelligent outcast. They were as new to fashion as I was. It was a costume for them. For many, maybe all, it was their first night out. Around 190 bolted, some paid the price. But these ten, plus Little Kid, had stayed loyal through fidelity and fear. What little sentimentality I had asserted itself. I would get them home.

New plan, Little Kid. Your mom is on vacation?

"Yes?"

Then that's where everyone is going. Your house. You all got here. You can all get gone if I get you to your cars, right? They mumbled and nodded.

"Some of us have been drinking," the mousy girl whined. My dead eye was the only response I could muster.

"We can make it. We can make it," Little Kid chimed in.

Good, I said, snatching the mp3 player from his pocket. Better have some Benga on here.

We were on Clay Street; the riots were primarily on the other side of Franklin, though the smart anarchists and other rioters thought they could use Clay as a back door the same way the cops did to get to the main mêlée. But the Little Kid got his smarts from his mom. Her sandwich shop was three blocks away from downtown Oakland's federal building and two blocks away from the police station. I led a crew of eleven past battalions of police to their cars on San Pablo Avenue. Luckily, the freeway was only a half a block away.

"I'll never forget this," Little Kid said, sitting in the back of his friend's father's luxury SUV.

Hardest hundred dollars I ever made, I said, messing his hair before I slammed the door. Then I was alone.

I felt like I should have a cigarette or a toothpick in my mouth as I strolled the half-naked streets of Oakland toward the ruckus to pick up the Cutlass. I'd parked it just off of Broadway. I could hear the old man in my mind yelling about how I destroyed his car the first time he'd lent it to me. Then I realized I did hear him yelling. In my mind, but in my ears as well.

"Chabi!" his small voice made big by panic. I was running before I knew it. Into the madness of downtown. A thug lost his ability to balance forever for getting in my way. It was an afterthought. I barely registered the .45 I pilfered off a cop who tried to stop me from entering the chaos of downtown proper. Only the echoes of his broken hip and jawbones registered. Narayana was in a frenzy and, like a lightning bolt, I went to him. "Chabi!"

He was at once poetic and barbaric when I finally caught sight of Raj. The tale of his journey was clear. His EMT overall tops were tied around his waist. He'd come into the riot in uniform hoping it would make it easier to find me. I knew he wasn't scheduled to work. Seven cops tried surrounding the wiry old Indian who trained me to have 360-degree situational awareness constantly. I felt bad for the cops but worse for the assortment of rioters littered in Raj's circumference that held broken bones and struggled to stop bleeds. My mentor didn't stop moving but his bloodied knuckles and fingertips told me he'd been holding his ground for a while; all the time calling out for me.

Narayana's low leg kicks hobbled two cops before he noticed me. There was no restraint in him. It took about a second.

"The dinghy is at the dock," he said almost to me alone as he used the cops' numbers against them, moving in close to one so the others wouldn't fire, incapacitating the close officer then quickly jaunting into the shade of a half-finished alley or some corner. I struck at the periphery, taking advantage of the intentional blindness the cops had toward me. I was not on their mental threat list.

Not without you, was all I said. Three SWAT members with automatic weapons turned to me at that point. Safeties off, fingers on triggers, all with body armor. I pictured pulling the pilfered .45 and nailing each of them on the faceplate with it. But just before I drew, Narayana left his shadow, striking one officer so hard he flew into his colleagues that had drawn a bead on me.

"Don't you touch her!" he shouted with a rage I'd never felt from him. I sidestepped the final standing officer and put him to sleep with the Dragon's Tooth strike, an open palm strike to the carotid while soft-striking the trachea in two spots with my fingers. Sure, more cops were roaming the streets but none that had faced us.

"You ok?" Narayana said, touching my face gently.

I'm fine. I swear.

"Still a woman." He clucked his tooth. "I tell you go, you go."

I don't go anywhere without you, Captain.

We walked quietly, patiently, our hands out of our pockets for all the cops to see. I told him where the car was but the old man didn't change his stride. We went to the docks in Jack London. Narayana had barely tied his dinghy off properly. On the way home he demanded I share his sake.

Two days later I ran from Sausalito to the Marin headlands, home of every impressive picture of the Golden Gate Bridge. But I still couldn't get Rice out of my head. More specifically, the beer incident was still echoing for me. He'd offered the beer. I caught it but didn't drink it. I remembered. I could track every word he said in that conversation, every move. I was locked in. So why didn't I notice myself doing the very foreign thing of taking down beer? The last time I drank was after the riot with Narayana. Mom's previous problems, and the lack of focus it offered, always made alcohol seem like an intentional poisoning. But underneath it all was this awareness that Rice wanted me to drink. And what Rice wanted, I was getting the sense, he got. As I stood breathing loosely at cloud level looking down at the Golden Gate Bridge, I wished I could find Rice and force all his secrets out of him.

I could almost hear his voice in my head saying, "Come find me." What was definite was a pull toward San Francisco even though it was in the opposite direction of home. But I didn't have anything else going on that day so I followed the impulse. I went quickly, easily tearing down the mountains that buttress the Bay and on to the famous suicide bridge. I tore past tourists and seasoned runners with the same ease. Once past the metal and the cars on the other side of the bridge, I quickly cut through the Presidio's woods. It was early afternoon on a Saturday so I had to contend with all manner of picnicking, homeless panhandling, and cops on authoritarian power trips. I dealt with them all in the same way—speed. I was a blip in their day, nothing more.

Out of the Presidio I cut over to Marina Boulevard and followed the Bay over to Fort Mason, an old retired military base that's rented out for corporate and non-profit events. Ask me why and I wouldn't have been able to tell you. That is until I saw Rice. He was surrounded by five short stubbly guys, obvious computer programmers, and two girls that were either "fans" of his or very convincing high-end escorts.

"Chabi, you made it!" he said with genuine affection, as he left all his other guests to come to my side.

Didn't know you were going to be here, I managed to gasp out. I was sweating, gasping for air. It wasn't the run. I'd run twice that distance in less time and not felt any worse for the wear.

"If that's what you need to believe, so be it. Just don't hit me, ok?" He giggled, then called his entourage over. He introduced me as a member of his personal security team. I instantly forgot the others' names. If I had to think about why, it was simple: they weren't as beautiful as Rice. I knew them instinctively to be normal and for some reason that wasn't good enough.

Why am I here? I asked after taking a long drink of water from a fountain and changing into my non-running clothes in the bathroom. Rice sat schmoozing with computer types and business folks in a large makeshift auditorium. Obviously it used to be an airplane hangar, but the building was cut in two by a large partition.

"I figured you'd get a kick out of this. I know you're all into martial arts and the like. Well, this game I'm about to release is going to be the best martial arts RPG ever."

So now you design video games as well? I asked, remembering the game he was playing when I walked into his suite.

"Design? Just the storyline, some of the key characters. Not the heavy design lifting. I hire people for that. But it's my production company. Check it, cross platform, from an app to your game console, *The Saga of the Silver Snake* will be available for everyone. You buy the app, you get one level of game play, buy it for a console, it's a whole other experience. All of it involves the kicking of ass."

That seems . . . cool. I kept getting confused. He kept not speaking with his mouth, kept using that mastery smile. But he wasn't doing anything nefarious. He was just a rich brat showing off his toys. I couldn't even remember why I was so resistant to coming in the first place.

"I know you don't drink but I promised Poppy I'd bring her two glasses of champagne. Could you do me a favor and deliver them for me?" He spoke as if he had two glasses in his hands. I said nothing and went to search out the champagne before I asked myself what I was doing. It was getting too much. I was about to leave when I saw Poppy lounging, again in pajamas, though these were black silk. Infuriating as she was, finding Shotgun with her, sitting at the foot of her couch, sent me over the edge.

What it do, Matt? I asked, interrogating him with my eyes.

"Oh, Chabi. Do you have my champagne?" Poppy asked, not even looking at me.

No, I told her. You good, Matt?

"Why not?" Poppy almost shouted.

"Don't worry, honey." Matt scrambled off his ass to get up. "I'll get you some champagne."

"No you won't," Poppy continued, standing herself. "Rice told his little friend to bring both of us champagne and that's what she's going to do."

Twat, sit down before I end you. The heat up my back sent spasms through my arms and legs begging for release. Poppy's rancor had caused a scene. Now she didn't know how to back down without losing face. But she also knew if she kept standing I would do more than knock her down.

"Chabi, enough!" Matt snipped, pulling on my arm. I saw Poppy think about trying to take advantage of the distraction to slap me, but then she remembered what happened to her pretty elder. I let Matt pull me to the open bar.

What the fuck are you doing here, man? I snapped at Shotgun.

"You can't talk to Poppy like that, Chabi. It's not right." He was shaking with fear.

What's not right is you right now. You see yourself, Angola boy? San Quentin man, what's this chick got on you?

"I love her, Chabi." I was stunned. I had no response. "We've been talking every day we haven't seen each other. Chabi, she gets me. She understands me like no one else does. Not my uncles, not even my mom got me the way she does."

You've known her for under a week, I said, more shocked than I'd ever been by anything since Narayana. There were no words for this. Shotgun was gone. His usual tense jaw, the frustrated focus in his eyes, his manic energy, all of that was spent. In its place, fawning over a woman obviously gorgeous, but equally obviously fickle.

"Don't take this away from me, Chabi." It was as close to a warning as he could muster against me. "Aside from that one time in the woods, I've never gone against you, I've never asked you for anything I wasn't willing to pay for. We don't have debts between us and we've done good business so hopefully I've got a little clout with you. I know you like being . . . the way you are, hard and dissatisfied with the world. That's fine. I'm not here to judge you. But I want some joy. And she makes me happier than I have a right to be. Please play nice, Chabi. And if you can't, can you just stay away?"

He took two glasses of champagne and went back to Poppy. She looked over, only to smile her rat-toothed smile. My hand was around the exit door when the lights went low and Rice's video game documentary began to play. Tech geeks, some of whom were in the room, some who couldn't speak a lick of English, all gushed about the amount of pride and honor it bestowed on them to be selected for such a project. Interspliced with them and famous voice actors' scripted cameo interviews was game play of the main character: a feudal lord who has to battle other lords and armies for the world's ultimate weapon, the silver serpent. I found the whole thing boring until the lights came up.

"Now for those of you that don't know, we used some very precise and, well, let's be honest, expensive, motion capturing software to help make Double S possible. I'd like to introduce you to the men and women whose moves we've now made possible for you to control."

Thirty men and women took the stage to the roar of applause. They all walked confident, strong: fighters. Mostly stage trained though some real combat talent was hidden in a few of them. Some were supple and deferential in the applause while others were ego-driven and raucous. By their stances alone I could tell their vulnerabilities, which ones had broken bones early in their careers that had never healed properly, others who relied too much on one aspect of their skill set and neglected others. All of them were skilled in one-on-one combat, half could maybe take three at a time, but none of them had fought bare-knuckled up and down the California coast. Out of the corner of my eye I saw Rice. As others were asking the martial artists questions, he was looking at me. After things went back to schmoozing mode, Rice called me over again.

"Chabi, I want you to meet someone." He was big-shouldered, a foot taller than me, with eggshell white skin. Younger than Rice, older than me by maybe a year. He was beautiful. And even though I kept forgetting it, I could see that he was not speaking with his mouth. I took his hand to shake it and was caught instantly. "This is Peren. Don't tell anybody but he did most of the modeling for the actual Silver Snake."

Your mother must be proud of you, I said, hoping he'd let loose his grip a little. Not only was it tight, it was manufactured. With some hold I'd never seen before, he was slowing my pulse rate down.

"Wouldn't know. Haven't met her," he said with a far more menacing smile than even Poppy had thrown my way. "I heard you put down Mr. Khan."

Well, like most men, he didn't know how to quit when he was ahead. I controlled my panic and went back to my breath. The grip game was his. He'd won because I'd stepped into a trap without knowing it. I had other options.

"You misunderstand me," Peren said, increasing the angle and the weight on his grip. "I . . . train with Mr. Khan often. I find it hard to believe that a young woman as unskilled as yourself could . . ." I gave into his grip quickly, dropping to one knee. Some people would have loosened their grip, but he made his tighter. More's the pity; I stepped in under him then pivoted all my weight into my other shoulder and sent my elbow spinning into Peren's face like a whip. His grip instantly loosened but didn't break. That was fine, I used the Flame's Retreat—two-fingered nerve strike to paralyze his gripping hand. The whole incident was over in four seconds.

Just because you find something hard to believe don't mean it's false, right? I asked as he retired to the bathroom. I got as far as outside Fort Mason before Rice caught up with me. He made sure to not impede my progress with touch.

"Wait, why are you leaving now?"

I know, right? I'm just fickle that way. I hate being set up and all.

"Hold on. I set him up. Not you."

Explain yourself. I was getting sick of being surprised.

"Look, guys like Peren and Samovar are all kinds of deranged about their abilities as fighters, ok? Plus they've got that macho man crap about honor and debts and all of that. I knew that once Peren heard what you did to his master or sensei or whatever, he'd come for you. So I told him who you were about a second before he met you.

I knew he'd have to make a move and anything other than a full-on assault I knew you'd be able to handle."

The fuck you knew, I spit out. You were testing me much as much as he was. You wanted to know how I'd react.

"Yes. Ok, I admit it. I want to know how my chief of security handles surprise situations."

I'm the chief of whipping your ass if you don't back off me. Rice took five deliberate steps back.

"A hundred thousand dollars a year. Base. Just for San Francisco. If you come with me to the other suites I can triple that. You only work when I'm in town."

I don't want your money, I said, literally running away.

"Then what do you want?" he yelled in the back of my mind.

Chapter Nine
Rice

I did a month of heavy training. Taking no days off, I ran fifty miles, swam fifteen, did katas for two hours, and worked a heavy bag filled with sand, then pebbles, then finally granite, for an hour and a half every day. I made sure to be clear of Roderick and Dale's farm, unsure of what I'd say if they questioned me about Shotgun. I didn't go dancing and stayed the hell away from the Naga Suites. For all of Rice's flirtatious flattery, it was his final question that got me. What did I want? Rice was kind; he obviously thought I was attractive. He wanted me around. All I had to do was what I'd trained for since I was twelve.

But the low-level disgust was still there. The repulsive nature of something, the money, the lifestyle, maybe Poppy just made the offer hard to stomach. It was the way Peren looked at me when he thought he had me, like all was right with the world because I was under his thumb. It was the way Poppy simultaneously ignored and encouraged Shotgun as though he were her pet. It was the way I felt Rice constantly tugging on me for my attention.

I could feel when he was closer to me. I could almost smell his breath sometimes, and I wanted it. I wanted him, sexually, mentally. I wanted to beat him up then I wanted to molest him. I wanted him to admit that he liked it and somewhere, hidden under years of confusion and shame, I wanted him to do the same to me.

I went to Mom. She was the only person I knew that had a full-time legit job. In fact, she'd moved up in the world from night receptionist to full-time manager at the hotel she worked at. She wanted nothing but my happiness. But when I tried to explain my misgivings, I sounded foolish.

"So wait. He wants to give you one hundred thousand dollars a year just to be his personal security?" She was sunning herself as we sat on the dock drinking iced tea. "Hmm, well, either security means something different than what I thought it did, or he has some serious enemies."

Maybe it's a little of both? I asked.

"I'm not used to you sounding this unsure of yourself," she said. I couldn't see her eyes because of her face-sized sunglasses. "I thought I'd like a little humility in your voice."

It's just that . . . I started. I'm not worried about his enemies. I can take on whomever . . .

"There's my cocky daughter." She smiled in earnest.

It's just that I've got an instinctive thing against this guy. Him and all his pretty friends. But someone else I know, he said that I was happy being miserable. Made it sound like I was messed up for not wanting to party like an idiot with this guy and his crew, you know?

"And you're afraid he might be right." She said it and I knew it was true.

Look, Ma, let's be honest. I'm not the best judge of character. We hadn't talked about Narayana since I emerged from my room those few years ago. It was too painful for me and Mom didn't like to gloat about being right. Maybe that's why I don't like these guys, this job, I confessed. Maybe I see happiness and I get suspicious.

"Little girl Chabi," she called to me like I was a kid again. "Now I don't ask what you do to take care of yourself but let me ask you something, in your various schemes and machinations do you make anywhere near a hundred thousand a year?"

No, but what do I need that kind of money for?

"To take care of your old mother when she can't work anymore." She laughed, sipping on her iced tea. "This is the world of adults, Chabi. And it runs on money. If you've found someone willing to pay you good money for what you love to do, count yourself lucky that you get to call it work and get it done. Believe me, there are a lot of others willing to take your place."

I showed up at the Naga Suites the next day. I actually took BART in, rather than running the thirty miles. A near clone of the first woman who greeted Shotgun and me was at the front desk. Before I even announced myself she gave me a keycard to a room. It was the penthouse. When I walked in, Rice was on a huge projection screen in the main room. Behind him Babylon was in full swing. It looked like someone was shooting bad drug-fueled porn in the background. The music was consistent and horrible.

How do you always know when I'm coming to see you? I'd gotten smart and written down the question before I saw him. Whenever I was in his presence, I couldn't think straight and I had questions.

"Is this a question from my new chief of security?" He sat in a club surrounded by models and those that dress like them.

Yeah. How do you know?

"Hey, I'm the boss. I'll ask the questions!" He smiled with a fake serious tone. "Seriously, though. You like the penthouse? It's yours. I'll keep it reserved for you unless family comes through. Family always comes first, snake heel fucks that they are."

Where are you? I asked, trying to find the speakers to turn the volume down. The techno crap club music was killing me.

"Prague. I'll be back in a week. In the meantime, I need you to check the Suites for anything weird. Head to toe. You've got total autonomy. Leave no stone unturned and all that shit. I don't want

103

you going home. Stay in the penthouse. Everything is comped. Anything weird goes on, you phone me right away, ok?"

What am I looking for? I asked, totally confused.

"Anything suspicious." He shrugged his shoulders. "Oh yeah, saw a guy who kind of fought like you." A lump came up in my throat.

Yeah? Would Narayana be in Prague?

"He told me who he trained with but I forgot. What's the name of your style again?"

I found my legs just before I said, It's not a style, it's the way I breathe, the way I think, it is me. Instead I realized his trickery.

It's called the style of minding your fucking business. I got a black belt in it.

"I swear I'm going to marry you one day." Rice smiled a big grin of defeat then closed the laptop he was on.

It was the first time I'd ever stayed away from the boat for an extended period of time. Even at the Green brothers' I'd get home fairly regularly. I didn't know what to do with myself. I couldn't believe the temperature was so consistent. I realized I didn't eat anything when people were constantly ordering food around me. There were three different restaurants in the Naga Suites. And not buffet "all you can eat" type restaurants, but destination locations with chefs whose names were known throughout the world. Just past the main lobby was a bar that was open twenty-four hours a day. Everything was muddled, handcrafted, and small batch brewed. Narayana would have hated it. Half the people in the Suites at any given moment weren't residents or staff. They came for meals, to have meetings, or sometimes just to be seen. It was a cross between the suit and tie crowd and their hipster younger brothers and sisters who'd just found a cool patch of elite status. A significant cross-section of them were shifty eyed, not used to being in close proximity to other people.

I could tell by the way they moved in the space, avoiding eye contact but taking everything in. Something about them was predatory. I ignored them all.

I focused instead on the staff. More correctly, they focused on me. I woke up after my first night to a timid knocking at my door. A young Filipino woman, no older than twenty-five, smiled but wouldn't look at me. She wore the typical housecleaning uniform.

"The Mr. Montague junior says I take you to shopping floor, when you have the time. I wait here." I tried to get her to come in but she wouldn't hear of it. So I got dressed quickly and took the elevator with her down to the second subbasement. On the way we ran into Poppy. She wore pajama bottoms with a light cream button-up nightshirt.

Don't you ever get dressed? I asked. The Filipino woman giggled then stifled herself hard.

"Fashion tips from you, Chabi?" I was wearing a T-shirt and sweatpants so I didn't have much to say. "Tell you what? Let's bury the hatchet and have some fun. We'll let Rosa-Maria go and you and I can do some shopping together. What do you think?"

"Mr. Montague Junior . . ." the Filipina started to speak.

"It's clothes shopping, my dear, not securing a nuclear weapon. I think we'll be fine. Don't you, Chabi?"

"No!" Rosa-Maria shouted. "Mr. Montague Junior he asked me personally. He said I was to take her. That's what I do. Mr. Montague lets you stay here. You don't own hotel. Please see him if you have problem with my conduct." And in a mix of Spanish and Tagalog Rosa-Maria mumbled as she grabbed my hand and stomped off the elevator, two floors before the final stop.

Want to be my friend, Rosa-Maria? I asked her as soon as the doors closed.

"I no trouble maker. I work good for Mr. Montague Junior. You tell him, yes?"

Rice? Yeah, I'll tell him you're real stand-up, I said catching a whiff of the strangeness.

"You promise? Oh, you tell him, please? Tell him I do good work for him all the time. I get good people work for him as well. My nephew, he work in club downstairs. My son, he park valet. They all love working for Mr. Montague."

Cool. I nodded.

It might not have meant anything to anyone else, but my mom worked in the hotel industry her entire life. I remember people coming over bitching about their jobs, running into co-workers in the street with her as they went over the horrors of rockstar residents and overly demanding crew. But I'd never heard a member of house-cleaning staff not only proclaim how much she loved it, but also how much she wanted her children to be involved with the same hotel. As shitty as my life had gotten, my mother never recommended I get a job with her. Something was up.

I let the ladies in the fashion boutique try their best to get me into something that didn't make me look like a street urchin begging for change. When that didn't work, they gave me richer versions of what I already owned. Instead of sweats they handed me a pair of light harem pants and a thin and velvety soft James Perse tee.

One woman almost got a Rooster's Lament to the side of her head when she brought in training bras for me to try on. I thought my shouting ended the issue until the head boutique operator asked me into her office before I left. The woman was in her late fifties, though her hair, makeup, and frame would have you believe early forties. She looked like she had been attractive once, before age and gravity collected their tolls. Now she perched in her final shop of glamour trying to do for others what she'd done for herself. It was a quiet little room set back from the rest of the shop. The walls were peach-colored and the furniture familiar steel and ebony.

"Just wanting to make sure your experience shopping with us was all you could ask for." The woman smiled, pouring a cup of tea as though I'd asked for one.

It was fine.

"Good. Good. On a scale of one to five, five being the best, how would you say . . ."

Are you serious? I laughed.

"Oh, quite serious, young lady. We understand you to be the new chief of personal security for our Mr. Montague Junior. We want you to not only look good but to also feel comfortable coming to us with any of your fashion needs."

You got it. Next time I need some gear gratis, I'm coming your way.

"Excellent. Excellent. You know, you're quite a lucky young girl to have Mr. Montague Junior . . ."

Anybody ever call him Monty? Or Junior? How about Rice? Anybody ever just call him by his first name? The color drained from the not-forty-year-old woman's face.

"You can rest assured, ma'am, that neither myself nor any of my staff would ever address Mr. Montague Junior in such an informal manner without express consent from him." I let her have her moment, understanding it to be genuine and not some performance for an invisible audience. "I have been in the employ of the Montague clan for over three decades and there have never been any doubts about my loyalty or my commitment."

Long time to work for one family, I noticed. She nodded. Any of your family members work here?

"My daughter and my son's fiancée both served you outside. My aunt is a head sous chef for the roof restaurant. My late husband had the honor of being Mr. Montague Senior's driver for twenty years before he died."

I'm sorry.

"About what, dear?"

I left. Was this what Rice had been talking about? This unnerving loyalty to the point of servitude? It wasn't to all customers, though they did have a high level of customer service. It wasn't even to all pretty folks. Rosa-Maria had no compunction about telling Poppy to fuck off. The loyalty was directed at Rice. No one I talked to in the subsequent day and a half had anything bad to say about him: from the towel boy at the pool to the piano player in the bar at night. The maintenance guys, the operators, the head desk, all reported the Naga Suites as the best place they'd ever worked. More than that, they all had something good to say about Rice. He'd helped them out of a rough place in their lives, he'd lent them money, and by far, the most popular praise of Rice, he'd gotten a member of their family a job. Usually at the Suites.

My third day at the hotel I started getting more proactive. I went to the head of room service and demanded a laptop. A Mac. Big screen. Still in the box. The small Asian man typed for seven minutes straight into his computer then said, "Twenty minutes ma'am. It'll be delivered."

I pulled the phone Shotgun gave me weeks earlier and texted one of the three numbers I knew by heart. Luckily, he was in town. The Little Kid got to my door half an hour after the computer came.

"You want me to do what now?" he asked, after I'd already explained it three times. I couldn't tell if it was because he never imagined seeing me in a penthouse or because of what I was asking. I went to the why of it instead.

Look, something is fishy about this whole set-up and I can't figure it out. I need to know where the fish is. Is it in the hotel or is it in the dude? I want you to check that computer for bugs first and foremost.

"But to leave them in if I find them?"

Exactly. Then do a search for Rice Montague Junior. Do another one for his dad, and then do another one for the Naga Suites International.

"Like just a plain Google search?"

Whatever, man. But then I want you to do a search on your own computer but not here. I don't want you to use the same router or cell tower or anything. I want . . .

"To see if the results are the same," he said, finally getting it. "Ok, first off, this sounds incredibly paranoid of you but whatever. I owe you so this is going to get done. The real issue is that what you're asking for won't get you what you want."

Why not? I asked, curling up on a couch across the room from him.

"If anyone really wanted to give you false information, why would they spend time bugging a new computer with hardware? More likely, he'd identify the IP address and then trace/clone any website you checked out online."

Other options, Little Kid? I said, defeated. I hadn't understood any of the tech talk, but he sounded convincing.

"You know we are the same age, right? Of course there are other options." He smiled and pulled out his own computer. "I'll tether my laptop to my phone and open a VPN to an onion router I have access to. It also has a bare-bones search engine on it so . . ."

And no one here will know it was me? I asked.

"It wasn't you." He smiled again.

Little Kid showed me how to turn off the wireless modem on the computer then gave me a thumb drive with all the info he could grab about the Montagues and the hotel. None of it was illegal though some of it was buried. Like the net worth of the Naga Empire, 7.9 billion dollars. The Suites have been around since the mid 1800s and had never gone out of the family line. Kinda. It seemed that it was a family of foster children. From Rice's great grandfather to Rice himself, each generation had only one child, a son. And that son had been adopted.

About Rice there was next to nothing that he hadn't told me. He'd attended the prestigious Miskatonic University as his father had and his father before him. When he graduated he went to Turkmenistan to learn some ancient smithing practice. I had no idea what that meant or where Turkmenistan was. He returned and took the art world by storm with his sculptures, usually of some form of twisted serpent. After selling one to a collector for 1.2 million dollars, his next commission was from his father to design the sculptures for each of his twelve luxury suites. Then the video game, and then nothing else. He seemed like a usual rich kid with too much time on his hands trying to make up for the guilt he felt for being rich. His father, Kothar, was an entirely different matter.

This man ate countries for breakfast. The hotel business was his retirement money. He'd pulled himself up by his own bootstraps from what Kothar referred to as the "shit piles of Liverpool" in an interview forty years earlier. Rice Senior was more interested in building the hotels than running them. He went from domestic construction to military construction in three years. From there it was a quick jump to supplier of weapons and aircraft, first to the friends of Great Britain, and then to anyone who could afford it. He was still a young man then. By the '80s he'd gone deep into commodities, grains, arable lands, water. I didn't know someone could own water rights, but Kothar Montague did for half of South America. In the '90s he moved to pharmaceuticals. He bought up ten smaller companies, consolidated all of them and made an irresistible meal for Big Pharma. His take? An even 550 million dollars and a seat on the board of one of the biggest pharmaceutical companies ever. Two years earlier, he'd retired his seat and taken a profitable lobbying/consulting gig. Oh yeah, and he still owned twelve hotels, five of which he'd literally help built by hand. With three ex-wives dead, all rivals defeated, and a "Come fuck with me" glare that even made me nervous on the screen, Kothar was an obvious owner of the world.

But nothing in either man's past explained the loyalty of the staff. It hit me again the next night. I went down to the final basement to catch the show. I'd been so tense the past three days all I wanted to do was dance. One of the Samoan bouncers immediately left his position to serve as my personal protector. I was going to laugh at him until a leggy blonde literally flung herself on him to try to get at me.

"I have to talk to you! You know Rice, right? Please, I have to talk to you." She was screaming over the music. I let the bouncer know it was cool and pulled her into the bathroom.

Talk away, girl, I told her after she gathered herself together. She was barely legal, wearing enough wispy silks and light cotton material to guarantee hypothermia on the cold streets of San Francisco. She had Betty Boop pupils, and Daisy Dukes that looked like they were shrunk in the laundry.

"Great, this is great. So you know, Rice, right? Well, about a year and a half ago, I had some problems, right? And Rice, well, he kind of took me in and made me feel better." She lost herself in the memory for too long.

And then what happened? I asked.

"Well, he . . . I screwed up. I thought, he never said but I thought that what he and I had was exclusive. See, that was my bad for not asking the right questions. Anyway, I got really upset and mad. So I started cutting on myself. And Rice, he said I shouldn't do that. And I thought that he meant he didn't want to see it, not that like he really cared about me and didn't want me to hurt myself. So to show him how angry I was that he would just not care like that, I cut myself in his bed. I bled all over his furniture, I feel so bad about that . . . I bled on his sheets, his bed . . ."

What do you want? I asked her slowly, feeling nauseous.

"It's just that I've seen you with him, and I'm not mad. I've seen him with so many women over the past year and a half. I'm not mad, really. But if you could just let him know that I'm not the possessive bitch I was before. I can share now. Can you let him know that I still love him? That I want to be with him? And that I swear I won't let anything happen like that again? The cutting, I mean? I just need him in my life."

I left the bathroom panicked, not caring who saw. I should have. Poppy lounged in a corner with Shotgun, made up in skinny jeans, a retro herringbone button-up, and, I shit you not, black eye liner.

"Oh, Matt, look, it's your little Mongoloid friend." Poppy yawned.

What? I went in hot but Matt got between us.

"Matt tells me you're part Mongolian, aren't you? Weren't they the Mongoloids of old? Don't be so sensitive, girl. You're named after the Great Khan's daughter, aren't you?" I let my rage for her slide as I saw the worry in Matt's face. He knew that I could step by him if I wanted to and he was terrified that would mean the death of his girl.

Go home, Shotgun, I told him, holding his face with both hands. This ain't your place.

"Is it yours?" He asked the genuine question.

I left the club and went straight to my room. I woke the next morning with a clear plan. I had the head of the front office come see me. I asked him if he knew who I was and what my role was. He said that he was to give me unlimited access to whatever I wanted under the orders of Rice Montague Junior. I understood the distinction of those orders now. Rice Junior made the Suites fun and exciting. But Rice Senior had poured the foundation.

I want to see the cameras. The front office clerk looked confused then refused, but only for a second.

Behind the front desk, two faux doors and hanging plastic shielded an array of video cameras from the prying eyes of the public. The battery of screens when I walked in were innocuous enough— front lobby, every hallway of the thirty-story Suites, the kitchen, the bar, each of the restaurants, the elevators. All public places. I let the chief of the front office staff leave and hung out with the video operator for a minute.

How long you been working here? I asked in as friendly a voice as I could manage.

"About three years."

Like it?

"Love it. Mr. Montague Junior is the best . . ."

Yeah, I know. Hey, you work nights ever?

"Yeah, when the club is open I work nights."

I look familiar to you? I asked, hoping to take the interrogation to its final resting place sooner rather than later.

"No. Have we met before?"

I'm pretty sure I haven't seen you. But let me ask you something. You know Mr. Khan? He nodded his head, suddenly truly afraid. I made a gesture to the monitors and then asked him. You remember the last time you saw Mr. Khan?

"About a month ago. Maybe longer. At the club."

And do you remember who did that to him at the club? The video operator nodded his head. Good, because I don't do well repeating myself so I'm only going to make this request once. I want to see the footage of people's rooms.

It was up in twenty seconds. Any hotel that offers a hundred dollars of champagne in the wet bar and doesn't have a twenty-dollar webcam somewhere in their rooms is not the type of business that stays around for long. I knew they were there, probably audio as well. At first I didn't care about the audio until the video operator showed me the live feeds from the thirteenth floor. Most were pitch dark. But Poppy, oh Poppy. The only time she wasn't wearing nightclothes was when she was in her room. Then she wore nothing at all.

"I'll leave," the video tech said as Poppy chatted casually on the phone.

Like hell you will. If I've got to see this bony bitch naked, so do you. That was when he turned on the mic. Her weirdly accented voice resonated to us.

"It makes no sense. Rice thinks he can have his little minions say whatever they want and not get punished. I'm sick of it, brother." She complained like a child. "And then he's got this freak of a Mongoloid that he's grooming for who fucking knows what but it's the only interesting thing here. I want to smash it into bits and sup the marrow from its bones but, well, you heard what it did to Samovar. There's no way she can be the one that hurt you but the similarity is unsettling."

"I think she's talking about you," the tech said.

I know. Now shut up. Something happened in that moment. Poppy looked directly into the camera. She didn't move from her couch, she just stared directly at the fire alarm that held the camera.

"And that's not the worst part, brother. I think the Mongoloid is spying on me. I know. Even though I have one of her friends by his throat and can squeeze whenever I want to, the Mongoloid is retarded enough to try to invade my privacy. Is it wrong to call a retarded Asian a Mongoloid?"

She snapped her fingers and the camera went dead. I cursed at the surveillance operator with my eyes. His sweat said it all.

"I don't know. Sometimes heat, sometimes faulty wiring. A rat might have gnawed the wires."

Yeah, I barked, leaving the room. Fucking rats!

She'd heard me. Fourteen floors below through a one-way audio device she heard me tell the video tech to shut up. Well, if she heard that, I'd be sure she'd hear me yelling in the elevator.

You touch a hair of Matt's head and what I did to your boy Khan will seem like a slumber party compared to the nightmare I put you through, you pale-faced bony bitch!

I was exhausted by the time I got back to the penthouse. Not physically, just mentally. I kept looking for a bogeyman that wasn't there and couldn't do anything about the megabitch that stood out in front of me. I resolved that Rice was no threat. He was surrounded by people who cared about him, people he did good things for. Sure, there were some crazy chicks around but that comes with any dude that has a lot of money. If all I had to do for security was protect him from them, not a problem. No one in the hotel would even think of hurting him so he was safe enough here. Poppy would have to be taken care of. Not killed, but moved away from me, and more importantly Shotgun. But even that wasn't a major necessity so long as we stopped antagonizing each other.

When I woke the next day I could feel Rice only minutes away. I dressed in my best gear and ran down the stairs happy. As I passed the thirteenth floor, I could feel Poppy's grin.

"Go run," Rat Teeth said in my mind. "Go meet your master." But I ignored it. There would be time for her later. I reached the lobby just as he walked in the door. Everyone applauded for him. But Rice came up to me directly and gave me a big hug.

"Find anything interesting?" he said, his lips close enough to kiss mine.

They all love you.

"Then everything is as it should be." He smiled and took me by the hand into the elevator.

Three weeks later, Shotgun killed himself.

Chapter Ten
Shotgun

Three days before finals started Narayana appeared in my room, drunk.
I shouldn't have been surprised that he'd found a way to crawl
through the small porthole that pointed out across the water. It was
the scent of his liquor, dark and strong, that woke me.

What is it, Raj? I asked, sitting straight up.

"You play game smart," he stated and asked. More trashed than
I'd ever heard him. It took a second to remember the conversation
from years before.

Yeah, Raj?

"No one see you unless you want to be seen. You don't want to be
seen, you poke out eyes. You good, Chabi."

You too, Raj, I said, scared of him for the first time in a long
while.

"No. I am black sheep of black sheep family." I waited for more
but only heard him slump in a corner. I prayed to Gods I didn't
believe in that Mom didn't hear it as well.

Then forget the family if that's all they see you as, I said, rubbing
the sleep from my eyes. You're no black sheep to me. I looked your
name up. Raj is king, right? That's you, king of the badasses.

"Then you princess badass." I felt the smile in the darkness more
than I saw it. "I lay with many women. But you, you my only child."
The enormity of the statement choked me. I wanted to respond but I

knew in that moment of hesitation he'd left my room. I curse myself to this day for what I did next. I went to sleep. I allowed whatever self-doubt and confusion I was feeling to overwhelm me and I just closed my eyes.

In the morning Narayana disappeared.

There was maddening efficiency in his Houdini. There was no rubble, no measure of struggle on his boat, in his affairs, in the dammed air even. Had a hole opened in the middle of the sky and sucked him through there would have been more of a mark of his absence. Instead I got the insistent rocking of the tide against his hull, the familiar smell of his bourbon vanilla tea mixed with his favorite black rum from Nepal still perfuming his cabin. Nothing had changed except my mentor, my guide, was simply gone.

I sensed that absence as soon as I woke but ignored it, past my ten-mile swim to the Bay. Past my thirty-mile bike ride, past even swabbing his deck. I refuted the growing tension at the lack of his presence on the fringe of my senses. But when he didn't come up on deck at his usual 8:30, I raged. A quick survey of his boat and the dock revealed his car, his clothes, and all his weapons in their stored areas. Even his size three rice paddy shoes rested perfectly at the foot of his bed. Something about that image above all others triggered panic in me. I screamed.

Like I never screamed before, I shrieked with all my silent voice begging for some sort of sonic recognition.

Narayana!

Mom came running, shaken out of sleep if her robe was any indication. Out beyond the edge of where I cared, cars entering the freeway near the dock crashed into each other. Other houseboats woke violently and passing ship's captains would complain of headaches for days. But only Mom came running. I don't remember her ever being on the *Mansai*. But somehow she was in the cabin in under a minute.

He's gone. He's . . . he's gone, I told her, gasping for air as though I needed it to speak.

"Chabi, I don't understand. What . . ."

He's gone, Mommy. I don't know . . . I moaned, clawing her arm with no regard to my strength. Bless her for not flinching.

"He'll be back?" she said, taking in Narayana's simple cabin and my panic for the first time.

No! I snapped, my knees buckling as I tried to stand. He doesn't just go. If he does, he lets me know. The car is still here. All the clothes, the weapons . . . I crawled over to his stack of hundreds he hid in his coffee tin and showed it to Mom. See? He didn't even take his money.

"Ok. Calm down." Mom tried but it was no good. I flailed emotionally and physically. I tried so hard to scream with an actual human voice. I pushed and clenched with my stomach, locked my mouth open. But only saliva and pathetic defeat came out.

Don't ask how I got back to Mom's boat. How I disrobed, showered, and was placed in bed. I have vague memories of Mom propping me up in the shower, herself naked. All I'm sure of was my misery.

I could go days without eating, but no more than half an hour without breaking down bawling. Even when the dockmaster came by to inform us that Narayana had paid his dock fees for the next decade. Even when the Little Kid came by to my pitch-black room, filled with compassion and courage, to tell me he'd forged all my finals so I passed and graduated high school. Even when neighbors came by with vague complaints that they could "hear" silent cries that were keeping them up at night, I could not stop wailing.

I entertained no fantasy of Narayana returning the same way he left. In hindsight his departure that last night felt too much like a permanent good-bye. He was deliberate, grand at times, even demonstrative, but Raj was never dramatic. There would be no repeat performance of this act. This was a one-act misery play performed for me and me alone. I just didn't know what I'd done to earn admission. My agony had teeth. With no external source to feed it, the misery began devouring me. Every detail of each second I spent with Narayana I tilled and sifted like a keen-eyed prospector. All I found was dirt and shale. In each moment in all ways I had done exactly what he told me since that first day four years prior. That didn't help.

Finally it was the training, not my mother's threats to have me hospitalized, and not the Little Kid's constant calls I never returned that got me moving again. I'd been inconsolable for ten days straight, lying on my bed, eating only crackers and water in between embarrassing sobbing fits. The morning of the tenth day I left my 7 x 9 room and tried to make it to the bathroom. But my leg cramped. Understand, I'd swum across the Bay at dawn, run up Mount Tam in half an hour with an extra forty pounds on me, and biked down to Palo Alto and back without water, but I'd never had a leg cramp. I found the conflicting energies in the muscle with my fingers and deadened the combat in my thigh in under a minute by nerve-striking myself, but the message was clear. I was getting soft.

In the past I trained for the privilege of seeing the rare Narayana smile. Now I trained because I was angry. I ran from the houseboat to Petaluma. It took two hours. When I stopped, I realized I was still wearing the same clothes I'd lounged around in for the past ten days. A light-skinned young guy in desperate need of some post '90s fashion sense, maybe a little older than me, with an off smile, offered me some water, which I took before I realized I was thirsty. I was out of breath, sweating harder than I ever had with Narayana.

"Wanna smoke?" The bandanna-headed water guy offered a sweet smelling joint with a pulpy white mass that was not marijuana. I almost said yes.

Instead I smiled and kept running until I reached Napa. By the time I got there, I remembered the grief that was leaching out of me, in my stride, my breathing, my strength.

"No more crying." Those words came to me almost as quickly as the preceding "Fuck Narayana."

I was completely in Rice's thrall when the news came down. I'd almost forgotten about Shotgun if I'm honest. I hadn't been back to the junk in over a week. Hadn't spoken to Mom, hadn't practiced my katas, hadn't done any part of my exercises. I broke every piece of training equipment in the Suites gym just looking for some sort of challenge.

"I've got an idea," Rice said earnestly as we sat at the lobby bar late one night. He looked even better in the low light, his image reflecting off the wood-framed mirror that the thousand-dollar bottles of booze rested on in the back bar. "Let's give you some practice and me some money. What do you say to a bare-knuckle fighting event? Invitation only. Women only. Winner gets purse, of let's say ninety thousand dollars? We'll see who shows."

You serious? He was probing. If I didn't comment on my own past, would he know about me? I still hadn't told him about my private shame Narayana, more out of instinct than reason. But I felt that resistance slipping.

"Only if you are." He smiled, taking a bite out of an excessively stuffed portobello mushroom. "Look, I've got the contacts in the martial arts world, I'm sure I can get a one-night license from the California gaming commission, or screw that, let's just keep it illegal. Get a more exciting class of fighter that way. We do mixed disciplines, no gloves, no pads, all of it. Two hundred dollars, no four hundred dollars ticket price, clear out the dance floor for one night and we have capacity for twelve hundred easy. Two thousand if we're not caring about fire hazards."

Yeah. Sure. I was excited to see him so happy. I would've done anything to keep that smile going. Like I said, I was in his thrall. So were the employees and patrons that walked by all trying to gain a moment of his attention.

"Great." And then he overplayed his card. "I'll sponsor you. Or rather my family will. You're going to have to declare a discipline or a tradition you follow, you know that right?"

Freestyle. I tucked my chin like we were about to fight when a call came through on the burner Shotgun got for me months earlier. I'd forgotten I even had it until I put on a forgotten hoodie upstairs.

"He's dead," was all Dale would say on the phone. I knew who he meant. Rice demanded I take one of the corporate drivers up to the farm. We compromised and I just took one of the cars. The outside world shocked me. I hadn't seen the sky in days. It felt like what those gamblers in Vegas must feel like after they've woken up years after they've depleted themselves emotionally, financially, and physically. Only the frozen calm of Dale's voice announcing his nephew's death reminded me of another's suffering.

I arrived just as the police were leaving the main house, which sat a fair distance away from the more illegal side of the family business. They carted out a blood-splattered cadaver and a small pail, which I only assumed were the remnants of his head. I couldn't bring myself to look. As soon as I walked in, Roderick collapsed on me in tears. No doubt it was a sight, my tiny frame trying to support the bear. But Dale didn't try to stop him and he was the only one there. I held the big man as best I could and felt his soul break on me again and again. He mourned the way warriors of old did; he let it all out and left nothing to feel ashamed about. Dale sat in a small corner in their dining room and drank out of a big bottle.

After three hours, Roderick sat on a couch while Dale rolled two joints four fingers thick. I knew better than to ask any questions. They'd speak when they were ready. All Roderick had said so far was, "He didn't have to do that."

"Ok, big man. Time for a smoke," Dale said, nearly shoving the thing in his brother's hair-encrusted mouth.

"I can't . . ."

"Yes you can, big man. This is his favorite strain. It's got the red hairs and everything. Come on now." Dale lit it for Roderick. With one large inhale, the joint was gone. Roderick held it in so long I feared he was having some form of seizure.

"That's some good shit," he finally said, releasing an insane amount of smoke from his lungs.

"I like the idea of you and me stepping out on the porch for a second. What do you say?" Dale near whispered as Roderick's eyelids began to give way to fatigue. I nodded and we walked outside, Dale armed with another joint. "This one's for us.

"I know it's not your custom, but given the circumstances I'd take it as an extreme courtesy on your part if you'd light this one up with me," Dale offered gently after he'd taken a mannish-sized hit himself.

What happened? I said after I took my first dainty sampling of marijuana. Memories of the fungus rock came rushing back to me. Something in the taste.

"Honestly, I was hoping you could tell me. Ever since he started seeing that Poppy. . . . It was like he was addicted to her, couldn't go half an hour without talking to her, seeing her, something. I mean this girl was his screen saver, on his phone, everything. Got to the point that Roderick declared the fields and family time to be no Poppy time. I think that's part of why he's taking it so hard."

Poppy, was all I could get out. She seem weird to you, know what I mean?

"Wouldn't know. Never met her. Look, I've been in love. I know how it gets. I was trying to be supportive. Invite her into the family. We're not as rich and all that. But I figured if she liked him as much as he liked her. . . . But he wouldn't hear of it for a long time. It was only last week he agreed. Said we should go down to that hotel where both of you are staying and have dinner or something."

He's been staying at the Naga? It came out wrong. I meant for it to be a question but it sounded more like a statement. Dale was so wrapped up in his private grief he didn't even notice. I hadn't known he'd been there.

"Only times he's coming up lately is for the deliveries." Dale took another big puff before offering it to me again. I had to accept. "He'd been through so much. Maybe it's hard to tell just by looking at him, but he'd come a long way. I . . . I just don't see why . . . I've known guys who've taken their lives before. Tough guys, weak guys, loners, folks with friends. You see a lot of things. But I never saw this coming. He was happy. He was so fucking happy." Then it was Dale's turn to cry. Without saying a word he reached into his pocket and gave me Shotgun's suicide letter.

"I can't be the type of man that she needs me to be. I'll lose her to a better man someday. I can't carry that load. I love you, baby, and I'm sorry. Dale, Rod, give her everything. She deserves it and more."

I waited until I got home. My real home, the *Mansai*. In a ball I cried myself to sleep. The next morning I went over to Mom's and asked her to help me shop for a funeral dress. When she asked me who died, I started crying again.

At the Suites I could have gotten the most in-fashion misery dress of the year, but away from that place my head began to clear. There was something narcotic about the entire building. I'd be lying if I said I didn't enjoy it. But the medicinal flow of the Bay helped to clear my senses; the sight of my mom reminded me of my life before the Suites.

She was obviously the better choice for shopping. She knew me. Knew not to be in my face too much but also knew to be in earshot. She took time off of work just to be close. Work hours were such a precious commodity when I was growing up I didn't think I'd ever hear about her giving them up. Even when Narayana left and I was incoherent, she still went to work.

I spent the week before the funeral embarrassed and avoidant. Rice would get no response to his numerous texts, emails, and phone calls, despite how insistent each one became. He claimed he just wanted to make sure I was ok. But the want in his voice, the need, it unsettled me. Not his desire, but mine to make him feel ok.

I was more embarrassed by my own failings. Roderick and Dale didn't have to ask me to take care of their nephew; I knew that was my job. If they'd seen his reaction to the high life of the Naga Suites, they'd have pulled him out, let Dale run the weed trade with them. But he was so into Poppy. I recognized that unreasonable need and desire. It reeked of my high school feelings for Narayana. Pathetic and sad as it was, I couldn't condemn him for something I had done myself. But now he was dead and I couldn't shake the feeling that it was my fault. I was even robbed of my nickname for him. I could never think of him as Shotgun again.

Mom came to the funeral. She looked beautiful in her black church get-up, minus the hat, of course. She fitted me with a loose black blouse and a long black skirt, which gave my hips and legs room to breathe.

"It's going to be hard, little girl," she said when she saw my surprise at the wardrobe she picked for me. "No sense in being uncomfortable as well."

It was an impressive spread. Lots of food and booze. Two hundred people showed up easily, milling in and out of the formerly grand house. It was a collection of grape growers, weed dealers, bikers, locals, and family. People passed bottles of wine and whiskey, as well as joints, with a solemn abandon in the front yard. When anyone erupted in laughter over a Shotgun story, tears soon followed. Thirty people at the most were always with Matt at the closed casket in the living room of the family house. Roderick had pulled himself together a little better since I saw him last, but he still seemed distracted and infinitely mournful. Mostly he sat in the fireplace room. I couldn't see an end to his misery. Dale was less public with his grief. As his brother reclined in upholstered chairs fit for his size, Dale met everyone at the door and received visitors and ran the kitchen full of catered food, made sure there were enough chairs, all of it.

"This is my mom, Dale. Mom, this is Dale. Matt was his nephew." Dale moved so gracefully, he shocked us both. In the span of a breath he'd wiped his hands on his apron and gently took one of my mom's hands with both of his and bowed his head gracefully.

"This is truly an honor, ma'am. Chabi has been a great comfort to my family long before this . . . tragedy. I wish I had thought to extend an invitation before now. In any case, welcome to our home."

"I have nothing but sympathy for your loss, brother," Mom said gently as we walked into the house. "Your family has been a boon to my daughter, so please let me return the favor by helping with anything you need." Before Dale had time to reject the help, Mom was strutting to the kitchen with a determined look. Twenty minutes later, their laughter was the predominant sound coming from the kitchen. It was like they were both refugees from some unknown island of grief, who took solace in their shared common sad language.

I sat in the main living room, a palatial room, made for the times when extended families all sat around huge rectangular tables during holidays. Even with the mourners the room felt small. The coffin felt huge. I sat toward the back as Matt's friends from town and jail filled the front aisles. Some of the jail guys left envelopes on the coffin. Some people left flowers. Others left weed. There was so much love for someone now gone in such a selfish manner, I almost started crying again. Instead, I raged. I wanted to rush the coffin, pull Matt out of it. How dare he leave Roderick in such a state? How dare he let his uncles suffer just for a rich, entitled bitch? It was as though Poppy heard my thoughts because just as that idea entered my mind I got a text from her: "Can't make the funeral. Give my condolences to his brother, or aunts or whatever. TTYS. P.S. Rice misses u."

I rushed out the room to find water, ice, something to cool myself down. I locked myself in the third-floor bathroom. I was furious. Poppy didn't give a fuck about the funeral, Matt, or his family.

125

That text was letting me know that she was proud of the mess she'd made of his life, of how easy it was for her. When I came out, Mom was standing there waiting for me.

How'd you know I was here?

"I heard you calling," she said casually. My Voice had called for her without meaning to. "What's wrong?"

From his girlfriend. I'd kept Mom away from everyone and everything having to do with the Naga Suites. But I needed someone else to understand why it was hard to keep my breathing calm. Mom took more time than I thought necessary to read a simple text. Then she clucked her tongue.

"Fuck that whore," she said in her old pre-Christian voice. I smiled. Then her mouth puckered and she got stern. "No. Real talk. Women that can send that type of message to someone at a funeral ain't got no cause to be respected or listened to. On top of that, bitch seems cruel and hateful. I've dealt with enough of that in my life. You too. Dale and his brother don't need that bitch's mess in their heads right now. And fuck this Rice guy as well!"

I nodded, noticing for the first time where I got my temper. She calmed herself down, pulled out her copy of the serenity prayer, and chanted it to herself as she held it.

With a calm voice she spoke again. "You haven't always picked the best people to associate with, Chabi. Me neither. I can't judge you. I can only help. When you find good people like Dale and Roderick, you stand by them, protect them, and defend them against the shit we both know the world has to offer. Understood?"

Yes, Mom. And then, and I don't know why, I added, I love you Mommy.

She hugged me tight, and then excused herself to the bathroom. I couldn't deal with more grief so I went outside to the giant porch where all the smokers were. It'd been a while since I'd seen so many white guys with ponytails, but they were kind. They offered joints and swigs from their bottles. I was thinking about taking a hit from one when I saw a familiar face out of the corner of my eye. He stood away from everyone, almost around the corner of the porch. I went to him and saw his lazy smile.

"Sorry for your loss," he said gently.

Appreciated. I breathed hard then jumped in. You knew him?

"Only that he was close to you. You remember me?"

The infinitely forgettable rectal irritant.

"A.C. to most, but yeah." He lit his strange-smelling joint. "Forgive my directness but I've got to ask, what exactly are your feelings towards your current employer and his friend, the girlfriend of . . ."

Poppy was no friend to Shot . . . Matt. And I'm beginning to question whether or not she's even a girl.

"You're asking the right questions, Chabi. But still avoiding one of mine."

I don't owe you a thing, vanishing boy, so slow your roll. He looked dejected as he mumbled in some foreign language.

What do you want me to say? He's never done a thing against me, given me a job, and only wants my happiness. I can't explain why I don't want to see him, why that hotel creeps me out, why just wanting to make him happy fills me with dread. I don't even know how you know about him. I . . . I just. . . . Fuck. I was exhausted.

He's evil, isn't he? I asked finally.

"I wish!" A.C. laughed, coughing out a big hit. "If Rice were evil, his family would be of creation and subject to its rules. Rice, Poppy, all of them are etic creatures, children of entropy. They don't worship harm; they embody the end of all things. And if you want to stop them, you'll need my help."

Roderick stepped outside and announced the service would be starting soon. He looked my way, smiled, and did his best to pretend everything was ok by waving me over. The big man squinted for a second, looking more in depth for a second then went back inside.

Wait, I told the mystery boy.

"I don't have a lot of time to wait, Chabi."

You gonna put me on a time card, Mr. Forgettable? You really want me to choose between running off with you wherever and attending my boy's service? That really the best thing for your dental plan right now?

"It's not me putting the pressure on. It's the situation." He'd taken my threat seriously and prepped himself to guard against about half of my attacks.

Well, fuck the situation. I'm seeing Matt off. After that, I'll deal with those that got him in this position.

As soon as I walked in, Mom took me to the side.

"You're going to sing with me." I literally opened my mouth to say something, but Mom cut me off right away. "They were going to send him off with no music. You remember "Beautiful Hills of Galilee"? We're singing that at the end. Get over the shyness and be of service." Mom patted my hair and helped some of the more senior folks into the big living room.

Mom used to sing the song in the pre-Narayana days when she wasn't too drunk and I was having problems sleeping. It's a mournful and fatalistic slice of peace that probably wouldn't be approved by any therapist as an appropriate lullaby. But it worked for me.

Left to my own devices, I would have worried about singing for the entire service. Dale saved me from myself by sitting me next to a redheaded thick-boned blubbering wreck of a girl named Kate. In her mind she was supposed to marry Matt. They'd begun dating last year and Kate was convinced it was just a matter of time before they settled down. Her tears didn't get me, but her perfect match for Matt did. She was of his town, his folk. They should have been married, had kids, taken over the farm, given the uncles some little kids to play with. She felt like the thing that was interrupted, the dangling bit of life left from the snip taken from Matt.

Thick-boned Kate distracted me by demanding to be taken care of with her sniffles and whines as people got up in front of everyone and shared Matt stories. It wasn't coordinated. Whoever wanted to get up did. They spoke for however long they wanted, then sat back down. A lot of stories were about weed. Some were about prison. The most touching ones were about him as a kid. Roderick couldn't really get through this story. When it was Dale's turn, he mostly just thanked people for showing up. No one left while anyone else spoke. Finally, after some silent grief language cue between Dale and Mom, Mom got up and motioned for me to get in front of everyone. I'd fought men three times my size who openly professed a desire to rape me, but I'd never been more scared before.

"I never had the honor of meeting Matt," Mom said gently to everyone. "But he was a friend to my daughter and a good nephew to my friends Dale and Roderick. If it's ok with all assembled, my daughter and I will sing him off on his journey."

Mom started on the chorus and I joined in instinctively using my Voice. I left off as she hit the first verse. When I'd been a child she had sung the verses so softly that I hadn't realized the hymn was about death. But the realization hit me so hard that when I came in for the chorus, even I noticed my Voice changed. People sat up and felt smaller at the same time. Again, my mom killed the verse. But the third verse killed me with the line "For you I was slain." I almost lost the chorus but I came in with it almost as hard as Hazel Dickens. There was no intention in my sharing. I was just singing. As I was ending, I looked over to see my mom's eyes filled with tears. But behind her, A.C., the shadowy boy, leaned against the far wall and nodded gently at me.

I've . . . Mom, I'm so sorry but I've got to go, I whispered to her as soon as people started filing out the room.

"What are you talking about, Chabi?"

Mom. This, this isn't right. He shouldn't be dead. For once Mom didn't have anything else to say. She just looked at me and nodded. I've got to do something about it. I mean I can't bring him back, but maybe I can understand what's happened. Maybe I can make sure it doesn't happen again. I think . . . Mom, I think I might be able to be useful.

"You gonna use that kung fu Narayana taught you?" She smiled. How many times do I have to say it, Mom, it's not kung fu . . .

"Whatever, girl. If you can use any of that for something good, then maybe all that time wasn't a waste after all, is what I'm getting at." She took me in her arms, strong, but shaking a little. She was getting older, I realized, as I looked over her shoulder and saw the coffin. "You sang beautifully. You should do it more often."

Outside, A.C. leaned against the banister of the steps that led up to the house. He didn't bother looking at me as I walked toward him. But he did smile.

"Impressive voice."

Where to, ass ache? I snipped at him.

"Look, I'll answer every question you've got, swear it. But first I need to get anchored in the here and now."

Fuck, is it gonna be this much of a headache every time you speak? What do you need?

"Narayana left some entropy weapons behind for me."

Chapter Eleven
Entropy Weapons

I tore the Mansai *up looking for entropy weapons, totally unsure of* what they were even after A.C. explained it. There was a sense of violation I was trying to excise. Would Narayana truly have left something behind that I wasn't supposed to have access to? Would he have trusted this willow in the wind slouch more than me, his number one student? I had to know.

"This thing with forgetting me when you're not looking at me .. ." A.C. started as soon as we got back to the ship. The drive was faster than I expected and I knew he had something to do with that. He said something about synchronicity, but it was hard to drive and pay attention to him. I was having the same problem looking around the junk and listening to him. "It's not something I have control over. Get me? It's part of who I am, what I do."

Great at parties, I'm sure, I said below deck after looking under the bed. Mind telling me what these weapons look like?

"One is a sword made from the fang of the last three-footed dragon. The others are a set of six-shooters." A.C. walked up to the deck, probably to avoid me asking about a dragon. But he stumbled a bit. Not physically, but visually. Like he stuttered in my sight.

Dragons don't exist, I said, chasing him.

"Not anymore. That's why that sword is an entropy weapon. It exists as the end of a thing that was. Entropy writ small."

And the six-shooters? He did the stutter thing again. It was like I had blinked but my eyes were open.

"Long story which will only matter if we can find them. I can't hold on here much longer," A.C. said, his voice affected with the same strobe as his body. "Narayana never showed them to you?"

He said entropy weapons were too heavy to carry, I said, realizing their weight was exactly what this shadow of a man needed. Ok, eye checking is not gonna work. Tell me how they function.

"I don't understand . . ." he started.

I don't know what entropy weapons do. How do they differ from regular weapons? What's the point of them?

"The sword cuts things that can't usually be cut. The guns aim true and never have to be reloaded. They're cursed weapons, heavy burdens to hold."

He looked at me for answers. I silenced myself, stopped moving, stopped thinking, and tried to put myself in Narayana's headspace. He hid nothing from me on the *Mansai*. I'd been on it since I was twelve. What crevice hadn't I looked in? They were obviously powerful weapons, but he didn't want me handling them. Did he handle them? The only times I saw him with weapons was when he was showing me how to use them. I was getting nowhere.

"Fucking pirates! Never leave them with valuables!" A.C. did his best to shout, and although it sounded more like the third repeat of an echo, it was enough.

Yeah, and what do pirates do with treasure? I said, taking off my shoes and the skirt Mom dressed me in. Modesty had never been an issue for me.

"Bury it like damn dogs," A.C. said, smiling, though still flickering. I saw him fading slowly. "You ever seen this ship out of dock?"

Not since he docked for real. You said they ground you, right? I'm assuming they would keep anything that could drift still? I was barely talking to him, more to myself. It was the only way I could keep my mind on the task. I kept feeling myself forget A.C., forget what I was doing with him, why I was on the ship. So I kept a running external monologue until I dived overboard. Opening my eyes or mouth would have made me sicker than a dog. I thought of chopped snakes, Mom's discarded cigarettes and all the other things I'd seen people toss halfheartedly into our harbor. I wanted to go back up to air instantly, forgetting why I was underwater in the first place.

Instead I followed the anchor chain to the Bay bed and felt around until a long rectangular box made itself evident in my hands. Of course I forgot what was in it or why I was under my ship, but it didn't matter. When I came back up on deck, the flickering A.C. was present enough to jar my memory. With what little substance he had, he opened the clasp on the case that looked like hard leather but behaved like soft metal. Inside, an eighteen-inch soft curled bone white blade that smelled of fire and metal rested in a hilt of off-white polished gold. Beneath the sword two ancient black steel six-shooters lay snug in two holsters connected by a blood red belt.

"Feel better?" I asked, after A.C. cinched the belt round his waist and I toweled off. He did some weird trick with a thin swath of ash gray cloth that sheathed the sword and attached it to his back at the same time.

"Grounded if nothing else." He looked more . . . substantial. No more flickering, the dull contours of his body now came into sharp focus. "Can you remember who I am without looking at me?"

Colossal rectal irritant that needs to explain to me how he knows Narayana and why he's got freaky-ass weapons hidden under my ship? I said with my eyes closed. When I opened them, he had his same silly grin on. But after I take a shower.

I went to Mom's to shower and dress. With my full memory intact, the idea of A.C. on the boat didn't offend as much as if he was a total stranger. He'd been floating in the perimeter of my awareness for years and he'd never caused harm. At most he made me uncomfortable. But the promise of Narayana knowledge allowed me to face whatever tension might come.

"Ask away," A.C. said, now fully present and sitting on one of the fold-out chairs on deck when I came back. If the night air bugged him, he didn't care. The half moon cast partial shadows all around the deck, and A.C. seemed as comfortable in the light as the shadow. He smoked his strange smoke. Another mystery for another time.

Where's Narayana?

"I don't know."

Motherfucker, I will destroy you, I said, Salamander stepping toward him. In a second, a gust of wind spun him out of the chair, over my head, and into the opposite corner of the deck.

"Easy, Chabi." A.C. took a stance that seemed both passive and prepared. I couldn't tell if he was more ready to retreat or defend. "You want me to lie to you, I've got a thousand. But you want the truth . . ."

So he tells you where he's hidden what-the-fuck weapons then disappears from you?

"He stole them from me a few years ago. In the future he tells me where they are," A.C. said slowly. When I didn't stride toward him, he sat on the deck without the chair. I walked over to the chair he sat on, picked it up and brought it closer to him.

You're from the future? I said, sitting down.

"The future. A future, yeah. All that fluttering, snapping in and out of your life? That was me time jumping, trying to zero in on the right moment for us to meet."

And this is that moment? I asked.

"Close enough." He giggled. "A few years from now, for you at least, Narayana tells me where to find the weapons. And where to find you."

Why me?

"Are you serious?" He laughed genuinely. "Chabi, you're a liminal person. I need a cocktail," he told me.

You're joking.

"Oh, I'm sorry, you used to hanging out with non-drinkers? Is this the time in Narayana's past when he didn't drink? Oh, I forgot, that time never existed!"

There's a bottle of rum downstairs, I remembered vaguely.

"That's a start. Can you make a rum swizzle?"

I can make you eat your own foot!

"I'm not saying we spar, darling. I'm just saying Oakland is right there and I know a bomb-ass sake bar with the best Ika Sansai."

Man, you said you needed weapons. Now you're talking about sake in Oakland? You say you're here to help. Help me now. Give me something.

"Ok. I'm from a future where the soul of the planet is being fought over. On one side is the god of connections and its vassal, my friend Mico and his assembled hosts. On the other side are the relations of your friends Rice and Poppy. They have many names—Alter men, psychic vampires, children of Daru. They are the unborn, products of paradox, of entropy-creating life. The deciding factor in this contest is the decision of people like you: liminal people."

Where the hell is this sake bar?

"People, my people!" A.C. shouted as we entered the Korean restaurant in the Temescal neighborhood of Oakland. He walked in and started talking to everyone. They all responded, from the sushi chefs behind the small mini bamboo bar, to the Korean family of five we sat next to. It was small, no more than twelve tables, fit in a small alley in the neighborhood populated with small Victorian houses in the Oakland side of Telegraph. I assumed the food had to be great because it was small and packed. It reminded me of places Narayana would drag me to when I was . . . his. All the chairs were a dark wood with small-ass pillows on them. The tables were a well shellacked lighter wood. The fish butchers sat behind a half wall of Saran-wrapped rectangular cuts of bright white and deep orange fish meat.

They all knew him. He didn't even have to order his first large hot sake—it came with the table. A.C. ordered a yellowtail collar, marinated squid and vegetables, seaweed salad, and another large cold sake.

"You get all that?" he asked me after the waiter left the table.

What do you mean?

"You understood everything I said," he told me more than asked.

Yeah. What's your point?

"When did you learn Korean?" he asked, smiling.

Never. Something began to stick. Wait. You were speaking Korean?

"Yeah. A psychic Taoist paladin taught me ten Asian languages in ten days." The waiter came with the sake and two small wooden boxes to use as cups. A.C. chastised in jest. "You? You never learned it."

So how can I understand what they're saying?

"Liminal," the skinny anarchist said, taking a shot.

But wait. I called out to the waiter to ask how much the bottle of sake cost. He yelled back out twelve dollars, but A.C. is a friend of the owner so it's free. He can understand me.

"Well, he does speak English. But even if he didn't he'd understand you."

How?

"Liminal," he says again.

"I don't know what that word means."

"I barely do. Think on it like this. Let's say you want to give humanity, all of humanity, the spirit of it, a choice. All the people that ever lived and ever will live will be affected by the choice that's made. How do you figure out who gets to make that choice? Is it the best of humanity? The worst? The children? The imprisoned? The dead? The living?"

What kind of choice? What do you mean, the spirit of humanity?

"Humanity has always had options. And not that all humans have ever agreed on anything, but we veer, orient ourselves, as a species."

Whatever man. Ok, so all of humanity has to make a choice. You're saying I get to make that choice?

"You and about three hundred others scattered through space and time. You are the liminal people, the in-betweeners. Nowhere near gods but far from human. Your kind only comes from humanity and your task is to lead it."

When the yellowtail collar came—a big hunk of sizzling, tender fish neck charred from the grill—A.C. took it apart with his chopsticks like a surgeon. He poured some soy sauce out in a small dish and dipped a large chunk of fish in it. He caught me off guard when he offered it to me.

"I know it's a lot to take in." I didn't let him feed me, but I took the sticks from his hand. My fingers brushed against his. It was a new feeling, his flesh. Like he used far too much lotion.

You know a lot of liminals?

"More than most. Less than a few." He smiled then poured two wooden boxes of sake. "Your friend, the one whose funeral we were at. What name did his family call him?"

Matt. A.C. realized the place he'd taken me to as soon as I spoke. It wasn't that I'd forgotten about him, there was just a lot on my plate. But as the skinny anarchist spoke something into his hand as he held it tight to his mouth, I heard him say the words "Shotgun" and "Matt." He released his hand over the second wooden cup and even the people at the other table felt a rush of air. When I looked in the cup, it was empty. A.C. looked at me solemnly and said:

"For Matt. May he be kept safe from all other battles."

I nibbled on bits of seaweed salad and fish not saying anything for a while. A.C. respected my privacy. But it felt more awkward to be quiet in a restaurant than to speak so I tried to pretend the conversation we had to have made sense.

All the other liminals, they can do what I can do? The ones you've met, I mean.

"No!" he said, perking up, a little drunk. "No two liminals are even remotely the same. Taggert, he reads bodies the way psychics read minds. He can control other people's bodies as well. He's an all right dude. His daughter, Tamara, insane telekinetic, not too bad at reading people's thoughts either. Samantha's talent is tricky to explain. She can carry anyone through the unconscious realms and straight into the elusive realms. Prentis, she's an animal totem . . ."

You realize that when you talk like this I have no idea what you're saying, right? He nodded slowly then poured a bigger drink. I caught it in his body language then. He missed them all. They are your friends?

"They are. Along with the rest of Mico's inner circle." He stopped himself and gnawed on the marinated squid.

So all the liminals work for this Mico character?

"I wish." He looked serious, almost furious. "Some are wild. They have no knowledge of self. Some repress and hide their talent, content to live the lives of normal humans. Some are . . . twisted. They hurt and so they hurt everyone around them. There's one, Nordeen. He works for the other side." I gauged his eyes and noticed how they tried to parse me out. There was a moment of hesitation before he spoke again. Then he decided to change the subject.

"Tomorrow I need a ride." A.C. grabbed his jacket and stood.

I still have a world of questions! I snapped at him.

"All the more reason to get started early. Seven ok?"

It's two in the morning now, I question.

"Come on, I've traveled through time and space just to see you. I can't get a little bit of me time?"

He's out the door a half second before I am. I'm too busy worrying about the bill when I realize he's so far beyond such things that they don't even occur to him. But when I step outside, A.C. is gone.

I dreamt of Shotgun. It was a no-good dream. He was being tortured, bled, and burned. But then a cool wind lifted him from his tormentors and carried him out of sight. I didn't know where he went and that made me sad.

I woke, along with the sun, to near sub-audible grunts and flowing exhalations coming from on deck. The ship rocked not due to water, but wind. Never having heard it before, I was unfamiliar with the sound of A.C. training.

As A.C. danced his katas, I realized the gaps in my technique. In the time since Narayana, I'd found more secrets in my forms; hidden moves expressing emotion in one strike while subduing emotion in others. What I thought had been strikes were actually progressions to familiar postures. An overhead disarm which could just as easily be a choke. A check could be the beginning of an elbow. Here were hidden harms and additional traps I could lay depending on how I folded one kata into another. If the goal was perpetual movement and 360-degree awareness, then my main ally was flexibility in body and mind. I'd found sadness in the Descending Phoenix Choke and joy in the Weeping Salamander's Tail. Not that the movements themselves inspired the emotions, but when I was sad, my Descending Phoenix was perfect, as was the kick the Weeping Salamander's Tail produced when I was happy. But all my movements ended in strikes or sweeps.

Contact ended or altered the motion of my body. Mass, throats, arms, chests were always envisioned around me, countering or cooperating with my deadly intent.

But that morning I saw the enlightenment of the human form unbound by technique. A.C. jumped, swept, and parried across the deck, unconscious of proper stance or any style I could discern. A.C. danced, flowed in and out of both form and function. He struck at nothing, no imagined enemy was anywhere near his body, but when I put my forever phantasmal attackers anywhere in his circumference, I saw them being taken down and dominated almost as an afterthought. I went through opponents with straight lines. A.C. created rising circles of incapacitation that became more deadly the closer an opponent came to him. He looked haphazard, making up a string of random movements, all with martial capabilities, but linking them seamlessly. For ten minutes I just stared at him. When he was done, he looked at me and smiled.

"Wind style! What?"

In the Cutlass he lit one of his strange-smelling blunts. I tried to not let it get to me. The smoke in my nostrils wasn't offensive, but it was so familiar it was maddening.

"First stop San Jose," he pronounced.

For what?

"I'm fixed temporally, but not spatially . . ."

Use smaller words.

"The weapons ground me in the now. Now I've got to fix myself in the here." He told me like a college professor trying to explain physics to a member of the football team.

And that requires a trip to San Jose?

"Doubt my time here will require journeys further south. Do you?"

I'm driving, I said, giving up.

So child of the wind? I ask, after we moved clear of some South Bay traffic on the 101. He was about to light yet another blunt and I needed some air.

"Yup."

Meaning?

"If you wanted, you could say that one of four foundational energies or temperaments owns every human spirit." He tried it out, not sure if I'd accept what he was saying.

You could?

"If you wanted." He smiled. "Now if an individual was so inclined, he could learn the secrets of his own personal temperamental energy and sacrifice his life to it."

For what? I mean, why would you give yourself over to something that already has you?

"Sacrifice in this day and time emphasizes what's lost so much more than what's gained. When you go with your elemental force you're always operating from a place of power. Hesitation becomes a memory and power your birthright. To be truly inline with your element is to align yourself with your true nature."

I let the 92 highway roar by for a minute or two before I spoke again. If you're a child of the wind, that means there are children of fire, earth, and water?

"Yup. That's you, in fact."

What?

"Child of the water."

The fuck I am. I reacted more to the assertion that he knew me than to the association. I'm a liminal person, remember?

"Liminals are human to a point. And let's see. Where do you live? Are you a strong swimmer? Your moods likely to ebb and flow?"

You mean like every other woman on the planet? I snapped. The last part, I mean. I grew up on a houseboat, dummy. And it's more house than boat. My mom bought it, not me.

"Ok, but when you had a chance to move away, what happened? You decided to stay. Not only stay but to move on to the *Mansai* more boat than house. Stop here."

I pulled over next to a disheveled five-room Catholic church in a quiet Latino residential neighborhood. A community center in desperate need of a paint job and some community was across the street. While the scaffolding of the church was worn, the signpost in the front was bright, declaring, "You are not alone in the darkness. Your Father God loves you forever." In Spanish. I looked at it, realizing how often I'd taken in other languages, automatically known what they meant. It didn't bother me, it was just a given. Probably in the same way most people just heard my voice and never focused on my non-moving lips. A.C. got out and sat on the broken wooden front steps. Not even seven in the morning yet, the oppressive heat of the South Bay began to rise. He ignored the warmth and sat on the steps as he fished through his trench coat looking for who knows what.

"One gift of recognizing your principal agent is the ability to recognize it in others. Fight it as much as you want, but the waters have your head," he said, trying to beckon me out of the car.

What are we doing here? I yelled from the ride, refusing to get out until he started making sense.

"I told you, grounding myself to the here."

How?

"It's easy. I just have to let the guardians of this space know that I'm not here for any harm."

So what, you're gonna light candles? Hold a séance? Say some magical words? What? 'Cause from here it looks like you're just sitting in front of a janky-ass church.

"Calm yourself, Chabi. This will take ten minutes max." A.C.'s eyes sparkled with a bit of surprise as he pulled a knot of hundreds from deep within his coat. I waited in the car somewhat patiently until he said, "You can still ask me questions."

So if I don't speak Korean, what do I speak? I asked after a few minutes of serious reflection. That got to him. His smile wavered and his eyes went down for a second.

"You speak the first tongue. All other language is derived from the language that you speak inherently. What's more, it resonates with whoever hears it as their own language."

Where the hell did I learn that? I said, finally getting out of the car and stretching my legs. Old Mexican women walking with what looked like their "before" picture granddaughters walked by, silencing their chatter and making the sign of the cross when they saw me.

"Hell if I know. Mico thinks if all you liminals work together you'll be able to give every human being the choice about where to go next. Your skill would almost be proof positive of that."

Yeah, but he's in the future. So if I joined up with you, you'd know me already, wouldn't you? I laughed at him. I expected some form of snap back. Instead his sly smile returned.

"I wish. You know as well as me Narayana likes to bury his treasure."

So in the future he's alive? I say, trying not to think of myself as Narayana's booty.

"Yeah, but I don't trust him."

First smart thing you've said, I tell him. But A.C. was already distracted. He went to an old homeless man coming down the street. His overstuffed backpack and pale gray eyes let the world know he was alone. His sagging face was rough with spiky white beard hair. I could smell the urine and alcohol radiating off of him from over twenty feet away. A.C. went in undaunted, chatting and whispering to the man like they were old friends. He escorted the old man to the front door of the church, but refused to cross the threshold. Instead he put the knot of bills into the old man's hand and sent him in. Before he got back in the car, A.C. spit in one hand and made some form of occultation with the other over his closed fist, then cast that fist's content toward the church with an exaggerated flair.

You know, I'm kinda short of cash right now. Think I could borrow a few grand?

"Jokes!" He smiled. "A sign of a healthy mind. Next stop Livermore."

Out by the 84, I tried a different tack. Narayana spoke of his family.

"Alter men." Heat came from the child of the wind.

They pray a lot?

"No." He almost giggled. "Alter like alternative to men. In no way sacred. They could only pray to the void, the grand nothing, their power and protector."

I don't understand . . .

"Narayana comes from what are basically the opposite number of you liminal people. They are not born, they simply pop into creation as fully formed human-looking babies. No father. No mother. They grow and behave like humans in most ways, until they realize what they are. Then they become active. By themselves they are problematic. But when they are together, organized, they are dangerous. They disrupt all bonds around them. There are five thousand of them and they have an inborn hatred of humanity."

Narayana wasn't like that . . . I protested. But then I thought about what I had read about Kothar. About how he had been adopted, and how he in turn had adopted Rice.

"Narayana is the exception that proves the rule. And I'm not too sure about him right now."

I need gas, I told him, more to get off the road for a second than anything. But as I'm filling up, my phone rings. Two missed calls from Mom flash away as the new call comes in. Rice. Almost on instinct I picked up. But I felt the stillness in the air and looked across the car. A.C. is standing, tense, ready to fight.

"Please don't," he asked. That consistent smile gone. "Not right now. Please."

It was harder than it should have been to let it go to voice mail.

Fine. But I want some answers. I jammed the fuel spout into my car like it pissed me off.

"You're stronger than you look," the rectal irritant almost whispered once we were back in the car driving north.

Yeah, I get that a lot.

"I don't mean physically. You've resisted Rice's charm," he said a little louder, looking out the window. "A lot of people, strong folks, well trained, have fallen for him."

He's never done anything wrong to me, I let him know as I made the last exit for Livermore.

"Nothing that you've seen. He's like Narayana . . ."

Narayana never did . . . .

"Chabi, don't even try it," he said almost with pity. He pointed out a turn I was supposed to take before he spoke again. "You think it makes sense to turn a thirteen-year-old into a killing machine? He wasn't even cleared to train you. There's no way you should be as good as you are, liminal or not."

How did you know Narayana? I finally got out from my clenched teeth.

"We were trained together. Him in the ways of fire, me in the ways of wind."

You on some natural opposites–type beef? What, you guys always scrap or something?

"Far from it. Park here," A.C. said, pointing to the back alley of a grand Indian ashram. It was multicolored with floors seemingly made of nothing but smooth tile and marble. Somewhere close by, a dish of curry was being set to flame. The ashram seemed the entry point to a grand community of large houses built behind it. "Narayana and I were drinking buddies. Fire and air aren't opposites. That's fire and water. But it doesn't even matter. Narayana is an Alter. His nature is ash and dust."

I got out of the car this time and followed him to the steps of the ashram. It was wide and white. It seemed ornate almost to the point of excess, but the smell of incense calmed me and somehow made me feel grateful for the place. A.C. bowed gracefully to practitioners entering and leaving and they responded in kind. When people spoke to him, he responded in their language. I began to notice that now that he mentioned this other aspect of my ability. It felt more like noticing an accent than an entirely new language. When we reached the top of the stairs, he just sat.

So why did he practice fire if his nature was ash and dust?

"Because his nature is inert and fire was the closest he could get to redemption." A.C. pulled his sword. I had forgotten he was carrying it with him, just like I'd forgotten the guns were with him. Most likely because everyone else was ignoring them. A.C. spoke lightly into his hand again then ran his palm over the top part of the blade. I barely saw the blood before he let it slide off his palm and onto the steps.

Bit messy? I smiled, trying to make his tiny sacrifice less significant.

"Gets the job done." He was about to say more about Narayana but an old brown woman wrapped in an orange-and-purple sari came from out of an aged Audi running as fast as her plump legs could carry her.

"No, no, no, gentle spirit, please, you must come inside, let us welcome you properly." The woman dropped to her knees in front of him trying to clean his feet with her long, thick black and silver hair. She couldn't have been any younger than seventy.

"There's no need, little mother. Your house of worship called me as only a truly devout house could. I give thanks for this space," he said, pulling her up gently from his feet. She refused to meet his eyes with hers.

"But some food? Rest, perhaps? How will the rest of the wind spirits know that this is a refuge for them?" She tried to hit my feet with her hair at first, but when she caught sight of my eyes, she jumped back quickly.

"Let no one sweep these steps for three days. I've marked them with the blood of the wind. May it bring peace and prosperity to all who worship here. Let's bounce, Chabi."

What the fuck? I asked on the way back to the car.

"What? Can't handle my celebrity status?"

How did she know what you are? I asked.

"Every true believer, of any faith, gets to a point when they recognize the inherent qualities in another. She saw me for what I am because she knows herself for what she is."

Yeah, because that makes total sense.

"Drive, Jeeves. Next stop, Berkeley."

Don't think I won't choke you out, wind boy, I told him as I started the engine.

✳

When we hit Dublin, A.C. lit his weird joint again. I let out a sigh to let him know I was getting sick of it. His response was to open his window and generate a breeze that caught the smoke and pushed it outside without having too much air come into the car.

"Narayana is an Alter. They look like humans, sometimes act like us, but they aren't," he said slowly.

Ok, so what are they?

"Oxymorons. Creations of entropy. They exist . . . their sole purpose . . . is to hurry humanity to its eventual entropic end. To join with the cold of the universe," A.C. said.

But Narayana didn't do that. Rice hasn't done anything evil, I tried to argue.

"It's not evil I'm talking about. Evil exists to corrupt, pervert, transform. It can actually be useful in some cases. I'm talking entropy. The end of all things. Let's say you want to blow up a building. You've got an explosive. Do you throw it at the building or do you go to the foundation and let it go off there? Alters are not dumb. They want to hit where it will do the most damage."

In the middle, I whispered to myself, thinking of Rice's analogy. Still, I didn't want to believe it. But how? By throwing parties and building hotels? By teaching me how to fight?

"You know where every one of Kothar's hotels lies?" A.C. snapped back.

So Rice's dad is in on this as well?

"Look, I know you're new at all this and I'm dropping a lot on you, but I need you to pay attention."

You mean pay attention beyond driving you from one ass end of the Bay to the other, Ms. Daisy? That got a laugh out of him, though it wasn't my intent.

"Fair point. Ok, Kothar Montague is Rice's father. I'm using that term loosely, by the way. Rice has continued the tradition set out before him of building short circuits all across the ley lines on the world."

So people can't get laid?

"Narayana really taught you none of this?"

Taught me how to break bones.

"Ley lines are like the mystical veins of the planet. They are where all the free-floating thaumaturgic energy on the surface of the planet pools."

Ok now you're just making up words.

"The energy of miracle. Chabi, you've been to the hotel. You've seen how hard it is to leave. You saw what it did to your boy. Those places have power. And Kothar controls that power. Rice, at least in this time, isn't as powerful as his father but he extends his control in a different way."

The silver snake, I said, wishing I hadn't.

"Exactly. That's his totem. He brands anyone who walks into his club. Anyone who walks into those hotels has to pay homage to his totem. And each time they do, his charisma, his charm, his miracle-making ability gets more powerful."

Yeah, and he's developing a video game based on it as well. But so what? I said, almost shouting. I mean you're talking in these vague generalities, power, influence, so the fuck what? How does this all lead to worldwide entropy?

"Look," A.C. responded, almost exasperated. "Ok, psychopaths. You know how like you never hear about psychopaths in the middle of Virginia or some place like that?"

I guess.

"Right. Know why? Because they're always attracted to big cities. Serial killers and fringe folks are usually out in the cornfields and the like, trying to build up the courage to confront humanity. But true psychopaths, they love being around large groups of people. Now all your social scientists are convinced it's because they're trying to figure out how to act and feel more like normal human beings. But they're wrong. They're dead wrong. Psychopaths, sociopaths, their main issue is they're attracted to Alters. They want to be them. They aren't attracted to cities. They're attracted to the buildings Kothar and his line puts up. They're giant beacons of misery and pain for them. And it's been that way for over five hundred years."

He stays quiet until we get to the Ashby exit. I take it all the way up to MLK and make a right. Up a small street is a large temple with two golden dragons guarding the iron gates, packed to the gills with college students and semi-dirty hippies.

"This one is going to take a while," he tells me.

Blood or money? I ask.

"Time. Service. Feeding the hungry. It's a Thai cultural center. In a few years hipsters are going to make this place unbearable, but right now poor students and the near homeless use the weekend feast as a way to get a little flavor in their lives on the cheap. I've got to serve them all food."

I'll hang back. He's about to get out of the car when I grab the cuff of his sleeve. I hurt one of them. The Alters. Samovar, I think his name was.

"That was you?" He looked shocked. "Well, maybe we've got a shot in hell after all."

A shot at what?

"Stopping them, of course."

I walked around the grounds of the small temple. One part was an outdoor cultural center backed by a tool lending library. The inside was adorned with red and gold lions and dragons. One room had a large bowl filled with sand and sticks of incense stuck in it. A.C. most likely lent me some of his "invisible when you want" mojo because I wandered in parts of the temple no one else had permission to enter. It helped calm the confusion going on in me.

My reaction to A.C. was wrong-headed. He obviously knew more than I did. But he was assaulting the two men who had done the most for me in my life, telling me they were less than human. Worse, that they had designs on hurting me. How could the man who taught me how to defend myself have wanted to cause me pain? I remembered the riots not two miles from where I was standing. Narayana's voice, desperate and pleading in the night calling out to me as he scrapped with scores of SWAT. How could Narayana want me hurt? The worst part was how true it rang.

I remembered the pain of Narayana leaving. How it almost killed me. That was no normal pain. And only a few days earlier I found it nearly impossible to get out of the Suites. A.C. had called out my weakness for both men with such specificity I felt like a cliché. It was making me resent him. Then I caught him out of the corner of my eye. Not flickering, his sword and guns ignored by all. He stood behind the food line. People paid cash and got temple coins to pay for their food. They were supposed to give the coins when they received their hot bowl of fish ball soup or chicken curry. He wouldn't take coins from anyone. He smiled, giving the food away, infecting each person that went by him with his helpful smirk. I didn't want to like him but I did. It was different than with Rice. In this relationship, I knew I had a choice.

"Brought you some mango with red sticky rice," he said an hour and a half later. I'd occupied my time doing katas in the temple and just all-around people watching. I went outside and had a brief conversation with Mom. She wasn't too concerned, just told me people handle their grief in different ways. I thought I was too depressed about Shotgun, about all of it, to even try to eat despite what A.C. thought. But as I sat on the lawn the temple shared with the library, I realized his wisdom. I was hungry.

We done? I asked.

"Here? Yes. One more spot, though. The last, I promise. Come on, eat up. Your katas burn up energy quick. Bet you didn't know that's why you're so skinny." A.C. laid belly down on the grass next to me, slurping a noodled broth out of a large ceramic bowl.

I think I saw an . . . Alter . . . get hit by a car when I was younger.

"Didn't do much, did it? The car, I mean," he said, not at all surprised.

And when I hit Samovar . . . it was like hitting rocks . . . It all began coming back to me.

"Thank the asshole Narayana that he trained you the way he did. Because you sought the entropy of his bones you were able to do what bullets, knives, and all assorted other manner of weaponry couldn't."

You said before they only look human. Is that what you meant? The rice and mango were gone before I realized how much I ate. My belly began reminding me.

"Yup. It's like entropy couldn't just create. It had to create offensives to all of creation. Beautiful, powerful human-looking things totally devoid of souls committed to returning the planet to the void."

Shouldn't creation have some sort of response? Some kind of 'Fuck off, Entropy?'

"Yup. That's what I'm trying to be," he said, getting up and offering me a superfluous hand. I took it anyway. When we were eye level he spoke again. "And that's what you get to be by your nature."

Liminal, I said, beginning to understand.

"Liminal," he affirmed.

He got me going north, past Napa, through Mendocino County, all the way up to Ukiah. After speaking to the CD player gently, he got it to release the Sharon Jones and the Dap Kings EP that had been stuck in the machine since before Narayana left, so we had music going up. The only other CD I had was Sonny Rollins's Saxophone Colossus, a Christmas gift from Mom. But A.C. was into it and I didn't mind.

He kept quiet for a while but the wind got choppier. It started hitting the side of the car. His face was calm but the rest of his body tapped, swayed, and bopped. After a while I had enough.

Something on your mind you need to share?

"Sorry. Should've done this first. Tear the bandage off." As soon as he spoke, the winds began to calm down. "We're going to Pinoleville."

Never been. He kept quiet. What's up there?

151

"First Nations spot." A.C. pulled out one of his old-school six-shooters. It smelled of blood and iron. "My great-great-great-grandfather was a buffalo soldier. You know them?"

Black cowboys, yeah. I've heard the song.

"Black soldiers in the Indian wars," he said, cracking open the six-shooter to reveal blood red bullets. "My ancestor was a member of the Ninth Calvary. He was a crack shot, damn good tracker, and not the type to ever back down from a fight ever if the stories are to be believed."

Sounds righteous.

"He was a moron." A.C. surveyed the passing trees as he said it. "He was the first former slave to ever shoot a Native in a time of war."

Which means?

"The guns he used were cursed." He turned to look at me. His eyes were soft with regret. "So was his blood. The whole family line, me included, was cursed to bad luck and violent death because he couldn't see the similarity between himself and the Apache."

Were? I asked. You were cursed or you are cursed?

"Once I started getting into all of this, the wind and you liminals, I searched out the guns and made an arrangement with the spirits of the Apache and all the other tribes. I carry the burden of my ancestor's shame in these six-shooters and not in my blood. In return, I promise I am the last of my line."

Ok. Not to be a dick about it, but why the fuck are we going to an Indian reservation, given your family history?

"I make that deal with the spirits five years from now. In this time, my blood is still cursed. It's got to be dealt with."

Time travel, Indian curses, and magical bullets. Oh my . . . I can't help but laugh. Luckily he does as well.

A.C. directs me to a small one-story building that looks more like a broken-down mini mall than a Native American place of power. About twenty cars were parked in the lot; half of them were jeeps made fifteen years before I was born. All had bumper stickers about

Native Pride and the nature of the first residents of California. There must have been an open space in the middle of the center because I heard clear drumming and chanting from somewhere inside. The sun was well on its way to setting behind the building, giving the center an ominous feel. The entire day A.C. had been the model of going with the flow, living up to his connection with the wind in both form and function. But now, his resistance, fear even, was palpable. To his credit, he didn't rock the car with his wind.

"Fucking entropy weapons," he grumbled as he took the short sword from behind him and threw it in the backseat. "No sense in carrying in more than I have to."

Narayana told me they were a pain, I said, getting out on my side.

"He didn't lie about that. But, um, you're not coming in." A.C. tried to sound firm.

You gonna stop me? I tried not to laugh at him.

"I'm going to ask you. First and foremost, not a good idea to leave that sword alone. It has a tendency to find things to stab. But also, this is my mess, my drama. I'd rather not have you suffer for my crimes."

Sure you can handle this? I asked, nodding slowly.

"Hell no!" he said. "That's why I want you out here. We might have to make a quick getaway."

A.C. moved deliberately toward the center. Not slowly, but cautiously. I heard him swearing under his breath as he opened the door. I lay out on the roof of the car waiting for him, wondering if it was my lot in life to wait on weird dudes with bizarre powers. At the same time I was resisting the slowly building urge to play with A.C.'s sword. It wanted to be touched, and hungered for blood. It almost spoke to me, tempting me with the devastation we could wreak if only I would carry it. I looked in the backseat, expecting to see the damn thing had grown a mouth. But no, it sat sheathed and inanimate, but at the same time calling out for me.

Fucking entropy weapons, I parroted. I gained distance from the car, wanting A.C. to come back and take up his charge, then realizing what a weight it must be to carry three such weapons constantly. There was more behind that smile than he let on. I promised myself I would ask more about him, about where he came from, but then the drumming stopped.

Crashes, shouting, and a gunshot got me primed for action. The sword was near screaming in my ears, begging me to use it. I ran from it, toward the double-paned front doors. Halfway there, A.C.'s wind blew the doors open and me off my feet. He came running out half a second later.

"Go! Go! Go!" he barked, pointing toward the car as he ran. He couldn't see the five Native American dudes just at the door, chasing with rifles. I'd seen Indians around like this before at the range or in the pit fights. Northern California prideful Indians not willing to take any more shit from any more white people, or anyone else for that matter. Pissed-off Indians who had prison bodies, wilderness skills, and damn good aim. He'd never make the car in time. I went after the Native guys. A sharp "No!" came from him as I ran past him.

I didn't bother standing. Instead I spun my legs around and scrambled on all fours toward them. Not the angle they were used to shooting at. They made the mistake of letting me get close. I stood with Ashes Ascent—exhale, right knee into the opponent's left calf muscle while squatting, continue standing, right forearm into driving into the left side of the neck with a twist—and took the breath and balls from the biggest one. The smallest of them backed out the door trying to gain range to shoot, a pockmark-faced guy dropped his rifle and pulled his knife while the other two thought they could take me barehanded. They were good. Smart, quick to react, slow to panic. Still I had them in the doorway so they couldn't flank me. I chose not to worry about the gunman until I had to.

I Phoenix Palmed the knife man's defense guard—progressive strike from finger tip nerve shot, first knuckle cluster strike, third knuckle bone breaking shot—and used my right foot to Salamander Whip—fake low kick to full hip twist, hard high kick to the head of one of the barehanded guys. I sidestepped the flying elbow of the third man in order to obscure the range of the gunman I hadn't tracked. The hobbled Indian wasn't down either, just limping and scared for his friend with the knife. The man was holding his chest like he was suffering from a heart attack. The hobbled one grabbed his smaller blade from his shit kicker and threw it with blinding speed. I saw the set-up. He wanted me to dodge right, backing directly into his buddy's knee to the belly. He couldn't imagine I would be fast enough to catch the blade, break his buddy's nose with the butt of it, and then flip both the dude and the blade around in half a second.

Enough, I said, resting the blade lengthwise on my hostage's eyelid, securing him by the scruff of his neck.

"You sure you're fighting for the right side?" an old voice far more used to shouting than speaking asked me from farther inside the building. It was an old Native woman with a shotgun held at her waist, I learned as I turned my hostage to face her. She wore a complex necklace over an elaborately patterned green shirt and a pair of loose jeans.

"Leave her out of this!" A.C.'s voice shook the entire building, acting more as a force of nature than anything used for communication. I turned again to see him with a foot on the neck of the gunman I couldn't keep track of and one gun pointed past me toward the old woman.

"You got something I care about under your foot and I got something you care about in my sights, Wind boy. Don't see a problem here."

I do! I snapped.

"Difference is," A.C. barked, again speaking with the wind, "I start firing these weapons, you know I'm not missing. You sure your glaucoma isn't acting up, Spits with Dogs?"

"Right tool for the job, Wind boy. This shot will paint them all red. You're not threatening anything I'm not willing to do my own self."

As if on cue, they both grunted.

Can I make a suggestion here? I said slowly.

"Let's hear it, cursed girl," the Indian woman, Spits with Dogs, I guessed at her name.

This whole situation might better be resolved if everyone lowers their weapons and gives conversation a try. I let the blade off of my hostage's eyelid and gave him a firm but respectable push away from me. I understand you and yours might have reason to hate this man, but I can swear to you he's got no plans to hurt anyone here.

"No use, Chabi," A.C. barked, this time using his regular throat voice. "I told that miserable hag that when I came in. She's more interested in a scrap than words."

"Like I'd believe anything that came from your lying mouth." She paused for a second then lowered her shotgun, slightly. "But this one. She speaks the first tongue. Lies sound foul in that speak. What's the shit-stained warrior here for if not to start more shit?"

Forgiveness. I look over at A.C. and demanded he lower his pistol with my eyes. For a second I caught the torture in his eyes associated with not pulling the trigger. I imagined the guns speaking to him in the same way the sword was calling to me. But he was quicker about holstering the gun than I would have been.

Mrs. Spits with Dogs was actually Navajo. Anaba was her first name and she was pretty cool. She belonged to A.I.M. for longer than the American Indian Movement existed, and couldn't imagine activism without a gun at her side. She also came from long line of medicine women, the first of whom was the one who put the curse on A.C.'s great-great-granddad. Their hostility existed apparently at a cellular level. I liked her. The skin on her face looked like it had a crease for every month she'd been alive. But her hands were steady, her breathing calm. What animosity she had toward A.C. she never extended toward me. Mrs. Spits with Dogs only called me Sad Little Cursed Girl.

She took us into the center of the community center, her boys trailing tight behind us. Small offices and classrooms lined the hallways until we reached the center courtyard. A large teepee, as tall as the building, covered in deep red and tan hides, took up the whole space.

"Come on now," A.C. snapped. "You all aren't even plains Indians. What the hell are you doing with this damn thing?"

"I felt the bad wind rising," Spits with Dogs said with this malicious grin that showed her three cracked teeth. "Figured someone would need to sweat."

"I can't believe that at some point you and I become friends," A.C. said, taking his jacket and shoes off. Even from outside the teepee I could feel an infernal heat radiating outward from it.

"I can't believe it either," the old woman said, sitting on a bench. Her boys started disrobing as she pointed to them, assigning some to go in with A.C. and others to stand guard. When I went for my shoes, she stopped me. "Not for you, Cursed girl. Gender split sweats. Some of the old ways make sense, even if they are sexist." When I eye checked her for deception, I saw none.

There's no way I'm not keeping my eye on this damn thing while he's in there, I said, motioning over to the sword and guns A.C. left next to his pile of clothes.

"You think I'm leaving my grandsons at the mercy of the weapons that shot their ancestors?" she said with equal frankness. Down to his skivvies A.C. looked more like the Little Kid than the hero he played at.

"Don't know how long this will last," A.C. barked over to me as he opened the flap of the teepee. Both the heat and the monotonous drum sound became near intolerable when he did.

What the hell is going to happen in there? I asked.

"I'm gonna sweat." He smiled and was gone. Soon, four of Spits with Dog's six "boys" were in the teepee. The other two sat outside, similarly stripped down facing outward from opposite ends of the teepee.

For three hours I sat on the bench in silence, listening to the drumming, hearing occasional mumbles from inside, and eye-checking the weapons and Spits with Dogs; I saw her provide food and water for her sons; she left a bowl of something that smelled spicy and hot next to me. She got respectful and sampled a bit to let me know it hadn't been poisoned. Still, I didn't eat it. We were allies, not friends.

When the temperature dropped, Spits with Dogs brought her boys two large warm jackets. She put one for me next to the food. I nodded in appreciation but I didn't take it. I guess that was the straw for her.

"Trust me, it don't have smallpox in it or nothing."

I'm not cold.

"Not your flesh maybe," she gruffed. "No matter. Should get inside. Gonna rain soon."

You seeing clouds I can't see?

"I see lots you can't, Sad Little Cursed Girl." She said it sad, like she wished she couldn't.

Her other boy stayed outside while we moved inside the community center. I didn't take my eyes off the teepee, but Spits with Dogs was right. Not five minutes after we moved, the salty smell of rain and wet saturated the air. A minute after that rain started slapping the ground like it was owed money. Spits with Dogs had manners enough not to say I told you so with her mouth. Her eyes screamed it, though.

Why do you call me cursed girl? I asked her finally.

"Why do I call you it or why are you cursed?"

Who says I'm cursed?

"Anyone with eyes to see." She didn't take her eyes off the teepee. "It's the company you keep."

I don't think he's as bad as you . . .

"Him and his kind are ten times worse." And I understood how she got her name. "But I'm not talking about A.C. Something older, meaner, and more twisted marked you ages ago."

My mind immediately went to Narayana. An ancient memory long buried under spent rage and regret resurfaced slowly. A beautiful man doing terribly impossible things to a pretty car.

Where is it? The mark? I asked, feeling like I was asking where a body part was. Can you see it?

Spits with Dogs turned her gaze on me slowly. She drew a circle with her thumb in the air. Her way of asking me to turn around. I did a 360 and caught that wrinkled face return color to itself.

"It's on your back." She choked up. "It's big."

What does it look like? I ask. Afraid for the first time.

"I can't read it. It offends human eyes. I look at it for too long and I get . . ."

What does it say? I demand.

"I . . . can't . . . read . . . it. It's a name. The curse is a name."

Not two minutes past the witching hour, A.C. stepped out of the teepee. The sweat-smelling rain stopped at the exact same time. Drained, A.C.'s limbs shook and his jaw was slack. But his voice, his voice was strong.

"Getting fucking sick of paying for my ancestor's mistakes," he said, putting his pants back on.

What did Narayana put on me? I asked, keeping my eye on Spits with Dogs's trigger finger. She held her shotty until her boys started crawling out of the teepee looking more drawn out than A.C.

"His mark," A.C. says with a groan. "I'm not one to defend the asshole but I think he did it to protect you."

Explain.

"It's complicated."

"It's owed." Spits with Dogs moved quietly. I didn't know she was standing next to me. "The whole story. That's the price of the sweat." She took my hand in hers and squeezed hard. I understood. She could have asked anything from him as payment for the sweat. But she gave that debt to me.

Thanks.

"You won't thank me later," she said, letting go of my hand. She turned her back and walked away. "But not here, Bad Wind. Get out of here."

Chapter Twelve
Nordeen

*In the car, A.C. exhausted, me finally pissed—like the rain did some-*thing to wash the stupid out of my eyes so I could see what a fool I'd been for the entirety of my adolescent and adult life—and I noticed we were going fast. Like really fast. I took my foot off the gas and we were still pushing ninety.

"I've got fuller access to my skills now." A.C. answered my unasked question. "What? You don't want to move like the wind?"

You know what I want.

"I know what you think you want." He sighed. "Ok. Narayana Raj goes on the penitent path, the first of his kind, studies to find his liberated form. Only he doesn't have one. All he is is dust and ash. He is born of entropy and that's all he can create. But he still tries. Goes out on his own. Somehow, the dumbass runs across one of the only types of folks that can break his kind down, a liminal. You. But you're young and dumb . . ."

Eat a dick . . . I shout, watching how cars avoid us unconsciously as we weave past them.

"Dumb in terms of the way of this world. Don't get offended. Rather than leave you alone, he gets close to you. I have no fucking idea why. But he feels you. Trains you in what he knows. I'm sure the universe was scratching its head watching an Alter try to train a liminal in the ways of fire. But he gets so close that he actually gives a fuck whether or not you get hurt. So he gives you what he has, his mark."

A curse? He wants to protect me so he puts a curse on me?

"Spits with Dogs sees the world too distinctly. For her it's a curse. For him, it was his mark. It told other Alters that you were already claimed . . ."

By their one and only heretic, I said. How come they didn't chop me into pieces the second they saw me?

"The coding isn't that exact. It's not like he signed his name on you. He made a mark on your soul, something they all do. It says that you are his. The same way Poppy did to your boy. They know whoever marked you was old and powerful, but beyond that, he's a mystery."

So he basically pissed on me. My fury was getting the better of me. I was choking on the words.

"He's a dick," A.C. agreed. But then, almost under his breath, "He can't help it."

The fuck he can't!

"It's his nature. That dude could build a thousand orphanages with the best intent. They'd all burn down and take the kids with them. He doesn't have generativity in him, only entropy."

Then why do you fuck with him? I asked, barely noticing the coast on my left. Barely steering.

"I told Mico not to trust him, drew the entropy sword the second I saw him and went for his head! But Mico's a fucking redeemer. He believes everyone can be saved, even Alters." That was the first time I heard regret in his voice. "And Narayana is useful."

Good to know how the other side thinks? I asked, noticing the slowing as we approached recognizable landmarks of Marin County.

"More than just that. We . . . we weren't winning but we were holding our own. We had a base, started cultivating relationships with other liminals. But Mico . . . well, he did something stupid. He got into it with his God. It gave the Alters an opening."

To do what? I pulled into the parking lot of the dock. We'd made the hundred-plus-mile drive back down in less than twenty minutes, but nothing was surprising me anymore.

"Hah." It was forced from A.C.'s lips. "They had gotten the hint and went around us. They went back in time. To now. There's no entropy in Mico to take advantage of in my time. But now, he's vulnerable, young, dumb, and totally unaware of what he's capable of. They're trying to get their hands on him now . . ."

If he doesn't have any power now, why haven't they already killed him?

"They kill him, another takes his place. They don't want him dead. They want him perverted. Twisted to their side. Narayana read the ash and detritus in Mico's psychic wake and located the site and time of the entropy drain. It's San Francisco and it's within the next three days."

"You've got to go to work today," A.C. said as I emerged on deck early the next morning. We'd gotten back late. I'd stopped in and said hey to Mom. She hadn't seen me since the funeral, but she just took my face in her hands, kissed both my cheeks and told me I looked tired. A.C. did that peripheral thing he did so well, staying just outside of perception but being ever present until I fell out on Narayana's old bed belowdeck, truly tired for the first time in a while.

Why the fuck would I go back? I asked, practicing my kata from muscle memory. A.C. sat on the bow, his jacket off, no shoes, black T-shirt clinging tight to his bony ribs.

"Because they don't know what you know. Which makes you the best chance we've got to get more info. And to save Mico."

Oh, the Mico I don't know? I exhaled, stretching out for the Lion's Paw. Is he a friend of the cursing Narayana? I don't have to do shit, A.C. Get another idiot to follow your lead.

163

"I know how you feel," he said softly. My anger had already made me off balance, but when a small breeze at the back of my neck made me stiffen in the middle of the Peacock's Ascent I had to adjust my footing. No one else would have noticed, but I did. And so did A.C.

"When I first got into all of this, I thought it was so cool." He walked the length of the stern to the bow casually, doing his own kata, slowly, looking more like a dancer than a fighter. "I had super powers! I could kick ass. It was great. But that didn't last long. The forgetful thing, the whole not being able to remember me thing? It's not just because I'm out of my time frame. That's the debt I pay to the wind for these abilities. But I figured, who cares, right? There's always a trade-off in everything right? Then my teacher, the one creature on this planet that I felt ever truly had my back, disappears. Goes to places even I can't find. And I have to be the executor of his will. You ever try to settle the affairs of a djinn? Barely done with that and the rumors of the vassal of the lord of connections come on the wind and I have to track him down. It's nuts."

Take a break, then. Go to a beach somewhere. Some when. Why do you keep doing all this madness? I asked, fully engaged in the wonder of his moves.

A.C. stopped, jumped off the bow and landed silently in front of me. "They'll kill us all, Chabi. They'll start with humans, but animal, mineral, vegetable; the Alters want the end of all things. And those you love and cherish the most will be the first. I'll do my best to stop them. But if you're not with me, I don't think humanity is going to make it."

I hated him because I believed him. So I got dressed and ready for work. He stopped me again before I got in the car.

"You can't let them know." He leaned against the driver's side of the car.

I know.

"I mean you can't think it, you can't reference anything that's happened in the past few days, none of it. Remember what Spits with

Dogs said: lies sound different when you speak with the one true voice. You can't even think about me . . ."

I'll manage, I said, withholding as much venom as I could.

"Chabi, the only thing we have going for us right now is the element of surprise. They don't know I'm here or that we know each other."

We don't know each other, I said, going for the car door. The Wind Boy evaporated.

At the Naga Suites nothing had changed. It was as palatial and inviting as ever. Only a deep resonance in me paid attention more. I saw the twitching of the guests and suspected sociopaths. The ever pleasing staff, previously my peers, seemed more cowed and fearful than ever before, though their demeanor had not changed. The snakes all seemed to be moving.

I settled into the private office Rice had set up for me only a month earlier. My phone was filled with security concerns regarding the upcoming martial arts events. As usual, the event had the touch of antiquity and opulence Rice loved. He called it the Vish Kanya, and was apparently recruiting fighters from all around the world. Some only wanted to room with others of their martial arts discipline, others had strict dietary restrictions; one could only sleep on a bed of nails facing Mecca. For some reason all their queries were coming to my voice mail.

An hour and a half into responding via email, my video chat rang. It was Rice.

"How are you?" I almost started crying. His voice was so caring that for a second I simply couldn't believe the lies I believed about him.

It's been hard. I'm sorry, Rice. I needed time away . . . I said truthfully, pushing my Voice as much as I could through the screen.

"Chabi, come on now. You know me better than that. You take as much time as you need. I was just worried."

Thank you. My voice cracked as I spoke. I'm . . . I'm ok now.

"You don't have to be. Listen, when I didn't hear from you I had my father send over some help for the big fight. I didn't know how long you'd be out." He sounded almost apologetic.

It's ok. I'm here now. I'm ready to work.

"No worries, you're still in charge. But, you know, if you're still planning on fighting, you'll have to spend some of your time training." I felt the trap, but I kept stepping through it, wanting to feel the spring.

Makes sense.

"Great. His name is Nordeen. He's staying there. I'm in London but I'll be back in a few days, promise. In the meantime, let him take care of the logistics, ok?"

Poppy with you? He snorted with laughter before I'd even finished speaking.

"You wish." And then to twist the knife. "I'm thinking about you, lady."

The screen went dead before the name he used echoed in my mind. It was something, someone I wasn't allowed to think about. I had to let it go. I buried the connection deep in the place that still couldn't speak inside of me just before the phone rang again. This time it was the front lobby. I had a visitor.

What's up, Little Kid? I mustered my happy face as my old friend stood up from his seat at the bar. He looked like a typical poor student, shaggy shoulder-length mane, dirt piles of facial hair setting up encampments on his face, a dark green T-shirt ignorant of an iron's touch being held in place by a jacket that was owned by at least five other people before him. Only his skinny jeans revealed some of his previous fashion sense.

"We're the same age," he protested, but took my hand quick enough to shake. "This is my friend . . ."

THE ENTROPY OF BONES

"Jah Puba," the kid next to him said without looking my way. He was about four years younger than the Little Kid but even from his profile about three times more striking. His skin was sun kissed and smooth. His nose was round and small, his cheekbones were high, and his eyes were reddish brown, small and piercing.

"Jah Puba, is it? Let me guess, you're a DJ." I smiled. The bronze skinned boy almost turned to face me but chose instead to continue melting the ice in his drink with the power of his sullen glare.

"Not just a DJ, Chabi," the Little Kid interjected. "He does some great things with sound in general. He's like a RZA/Son House collaboration on the decks."

I don't know what that means, I said pulling the Little Kid away from his friend. But he seems moody as all hell. In any case, what do you need?

"I thought you could get him a gig here."

No! I said too harshly. I put too much on it and pushed Little Kid back a little bit. I haven't heard his stuff. Get me a demo.

"He won't record one!" Little Kid snapped back. "He's got this whole thing about the lived experience and not wanting it to be mitigated by technology."

For a second I had no words. I just stared at the stranger.

"Yeah, I know it sounds stupid," he finally came back. "But trust me, this guy is legit. Look, come down to 330 Ritch next week, ok? He's spinning there. Bring your boss, ok?"

I thought about Little Kid and what I owed him. I thought about the slippery slope of the Naga Suites, about how I'd been there less than two hours and already I felt myself missing Rice. For some reason I thought of Narayana and the manipulation game he'd put me in. And I got angry.

No, I told him plainly. I won't bring anyone to see you. I won't come. Don't come back here. You're not welcome.

"Chabi . . ." He looked utterly confused.

I will bloody my hands with anyone you bring here from now on. Understand? Leave and never come back. I mean it, Little Kid. It had never been so hard to use my Voice before.

He backed away, scared at first, then hurt. His friend hurried behind him, more confused than anything. They'd barely left the revolving doors when the bitch Poppy entered the lobby with an older man draped in thick blanket-like jackets colored amber and brown and a heavyweight-wrestler-sized blue-black-skinned man. Instantly the tone of the lobby changed. Those going about their business in their usual cowed manner became extra subservient. Residents averted their eyes from Poppy and her entourage. Even the temperature in the room seemed to drop.

Poppy's drink arrived from the bar without her ordering; she pretended to just notice I was sitting at the bar. She tried to beckon me with her eyes first. Then her hand. Finally, in frustration, she called out.

"Oh, don't be so obstinate, Chabi. Come say hi to a friend of Rice."

I made my way over slowly and felt the eyes once on me shift away. Whatever power the Naga Suites had to draw people in, I finally felt a milder version of that energy emanate from Poppy. In that dark secret place I pledged to see her die. In the meantime, I stood before her table.

"Chabi, meet Nordeen," Poppy requested with saccharine sweetness between her millions of teeth. Nordeen's deep green eyes seemed to glow from behind a pair of sunglasses. A wrinkled and tan hand reached out from a multilayered sleeve to meet mine. Whatever assumptions I had about his frail frame vanished when he shook my hand. His bones were reinforced by strong muscle. He may have been slight, but there was a deep strength in him.

"Charmed," he said, almost in my head, while continuing to hold my hand.

I understand you are here to make sure the Vish Kanya goes well? I reached down with my other hand to try to gently shake out of his grip.

"Among other reasons. Are you familiar with the origins of the term Vish Kanya? I will know if you are being mendacious." His accent was as thick and confusing as his SAT word.

Nope. I could feel him dancing around my brain, trying to find . . . the truth. About what? I don't think even he knew. But he kept holding my hand, somehow using that grip to reach into me.

"It means poison damsels. Sometimes it's a term meant to denote a woman who has a venereal disease." He took delight in saying that. "But it could also mean a woman who herself acts as a poison."

I don't know what you mean, I said, thinking of a proper defense, though not of the one who taught it to me. This man, more like an inappropriate mind slug, was rooting through my mind trying to find a truth that I was hiding. So I thought of a truth and hid it before he could observe it with whatever sensory organs he was using.

"In ancient India and Persia it was not uncommon to so saturate a fair woman, not unlike yourself, with poisons from the time of her birth that so she was immune from the toxic effects. Yet anyone who slept with her, or even breathed air from her lungs, would instantly die." He let his ancient tongue linger on the final word as he probed the candy-coated secret in my mind. Hard.

Smart girls, I said, finally removing my hands from his and scooting to a chair directly next to Poppy. I knew enough of this Nordeen's game to know physical contact wasn't necessary.

"How's that?" he voiced with genuine confusion, his face betraying nothing.

Your tales are only from the guy's perspective. The ladies had the perfect defense against rape and an almost unbeatable weapon. I let him thump hard against the secret knot in my mind, almost witnessing the struggle in the throbbing vein on his forehead.

"What about love?" he asked. I took offense at such a word coming from his mouth. And so I gave him my secret.

Love is for the lucky and the ignorant. I gave him my hidden image of me stabbing Poppy in the neck, from where I was sitting, over and over again. To anyone looking in on my thoughts it would have seemed like I was actually doing it as I placed all the power of my Voice behind the image. Both the big black guy and Poppy jumped as though they'd seen what Nordeen had uncovered. But the old man just laughed.

"I understand why Rice has chosen you as his Vish Kanya now." Nordeen smiled with impossibly clean and ordered teeth. "Do you know what this means for you?"

Not in the slightest, I answered honestly. The old man didn't bother to explain.

All day I felt Nordeen's meandering psychic hands like slug phalanges on the fringes of my consciousness. I never betrayed my awareness of it. Not to him as we discussed security for the poison damsels, not to Poppy as she tried once again to show her mock sympathy for Shotgun, and not to the big black guy, Fou-Fou. Anytime I left my office he was there. And not a peep out of him, not even the usual mental background chatter I usually felt from people. He was big, silent, and if the scar around his neck was any indication, used to getting into fights.

By the end of the day my exhaustion was my only tell in the silent poker face game I was playing. Sadly, the Wind Boy didn't do anything to chill me out when I got back to the *Mansai*. Not after he heard about Nordeen.

"That's it. You're out. I was wrong, you were right. Fuck it, you can't do it," A.C. tried to demand while serving me a hot bowl of grilled lemongrass chicken and rice on the deck. It tasted like an old recipe. Don't know why it surprised me that he knew how to cook.

Ah, come on, dad, I mocked. Who are you to tell me what I can and can't do? Besides, this morning you were all about me being your undercover agent behind enemy lines. What's so special about this Nordeen buster?

"Only total novices and absolute idiots underestimate him. He's AIDS with a fucked-up accent. Living death. And in this time, he knows more about liminals than anyone else on the planet. It sounds like he's taken an interest in you, which means you have to run."

Don't know how, I said, with a mouth full of turmeric-infused rice. Besides, the dude is like 150, what's he gonna do to me? If that bitch Poppy and her clan can't touch me, what can the senior citizen do?

"He knows when people are lying." A.C. sighed. "His knowledge is dangerous enough. But, Chabi, the Alters can't touch you out of fear of whoever made the mark on you. It pushes them off. Not humans, and definitely not liminals. Poppy brought him in to get a proper read on you. Plus you didn't tell me about the Vish Kanya before. It's a legendary blood fest. I should have realized this before. That's the mark Narayana put on you. It tells them that you are his Vish Kanya. His poisoned girl."

Some perverse sense of shame didn't let me tell him it was Rice that had called Nordeen in. Instead I ate my meal in peace, looking over the bow to the boats coming in. I knew the Nordeen business was serious but I couldn't help thinking of the Little Kid. The look on his face, his shame flowing, as he escorted his little DJ friend away from me, the biggest question mark in his life.

"I can train you," I heard the wind say, as the night proper was about to begin. A.C. sat next to me, his legs curled up, back against the mast. I didn't look at him, just felt his presence.

Had enough of strange men training me.

"You'll have to disguise your thoughts somehow. Nordeen is good but he still has to hunt down the truth. And he's got to be subtle about it. They're all probably still afraid that one of the old Elders is just waiting in the wings to fuck with them. The light touch is hard for that club-footed son of a bitch. He'll go slow, trying to pick through your thoughts."

He already tried today. Didn't go too well for him.

"Short term, yeah, no doubt you can take him. But this might be a distance game . . ." A.C. started.

You don't know me in the future, do you, Wind Boy? If it was possible for the wind to jump, A.C. would have.

"There's lots of people I don't know . . ."

Yeah, but you never even heard of me before you took this mission, right?

"What's your point?"

I know Narayana's alive somewhere. The only thing keeping me from searching the earth for him is this business right here. As soon as it's done, I'm going for the man. Now if you haven't met me, and Narayana's with your crew in your time, that means either I'm so crap at tracking people down that I can't find him, or . . .

"There are mountains of possibilities between then and now," he interrupts.

Fair point. All I'm saying is, I can see where this is headed. And, Wind Boy, it sure as hell doesn't look like a long game. I put my bowl of food down and flew off deck with a folding leap.

"Where are you going?" he called to me.

To the reason I'm doing this at all.

Mom's house was smaller. Or I was bigger. But I wasn't really. I stopped growing at sixteen and still had that body. Everything just seemed more compact, tinier. Smaller.

She was at work but I still had the key. I remembered how clothes, clean and dirty, used to conglomerate on the couches, over doors, wherever there was free space. Now there was nothing but clean surfaces. Everything was folded. The carpet had been vacuumed not two days earlier. The faint scent of incense hung in the air. The only thing I could find to occupy my time were a few dirty dishes. Mom had changed. Somehow, some way, she'd left the drink entirely and the church mostly. By her bed were books now. About healthy eating and the story of Hannibal. There was no TV. But her little radio and her CDs were still in the kitchen. I put on T-Bone Walker, made some tea, and waited for her to get home, wondering when it stopped feeling like mine.

She wasn't just surprised to see me, Mom was thankful. Her hug was strong and long. Instantly I felt guilty about eating and not bringing her over anything. But she looked happy and solid. In need of nothing. She sat with me, poured tea, and just gossiped. I tried to apologize again for leaving the funeral the way I did, but she wouldn't hear it. She just put on an old Bill Withers album and started singing with him. She held my hands and tried to get me to sing with her.

"Baby, come on. We sound good together when we sing, don't we?" she asked.

Better than when we scream. I smiled, and she nodded in agreement, not wanting to leave Mr. Withers alone in the harmony. What changed, Mom?

Her smile wavered but didn't fade. My hand instinctively tried to pull back to protect myself but she wouldn't let me. Not with strength, but with extension. Her hands went where mine did.

"I'm going to tell you, Chabi. I'm going to be honest. But . . . Ok, fuck it. When Narayana left, even before that, I saw how you followed him, how he dictated every move you made and it reminded me of that . . . of your father. I fell for him so hard. The truth of it is, Chabi, I saw you in me and I hated it. And when your father left I was as broken as you were when Narayana left, only I was pregnant. I had so much hate, so much anger . . . at him, at my heart for falling for him, at you, at the world. Don't get me wrong, love. I was so happy when you were born, but things just seemed so hard. I don't even know why . . ."

I wanted to tell her it was because I was mute, but I didn't know how to explain what that meant for right now. My "speaking" was just so commonplace to her despite the connotations A.C. was giving it. Instead of speaking, I listened.

"I drank because I didn't know how not to. Everybody tells you, husband or not, good job or not, you're supposed to be happy when you have a baby. The only time I was happy was when I was drunk. And I wanted to feel something other than angry. So I got drunk. And stayed drunk, until I saw you with the old man. But when I saw how you took to him, how he decreed when you ate, when you slept, how much you exercised, it brought me back to your charming-ass daddy. That gap-toothed Mongolian made pizzas for a living and couldn't string a full English sentence together when he was sober, which wasn't often. But I would have blown up a bus full of innocent children for that man. I stole for him, lied for him, and debased myself all so that I could hear his broken English version of 'I love you.' And when he found out I was pregnant, I only knew to be happy because his eyes rained tears on my face. He told me he loved me one hundred times every day that he saw me. He made a point of it. I knew he had other women, suspected even that he had other children, but my twenty-one-year-old dumbass self never even suspected he'd leave me. So when I saw Narayana's hold on you, I freaked. Somewhere deep in me, I knew he'd do what your father did."

To prove I was ready for more, I poured more tea. Mom checked me over good. She wasn't shaken by what she was saying and she needed to make sure I wasn't either. It was the first time I realized I wasn't hard because of Narayana. I was hard because of her.

"I started straightening up because I wanted to confront Narayana . . . but I was afraid. I'll admit that now, baby. I was so afraid of him I couldn't tell him to get away from my baby. I went to church. I told them I thought he was evil. I explained the whole situation. They told me the evil wasn't in Narayana, that it was in myself." I did my best to stifle a laugh.

"They said I couldn't claim you unless I first started claiming myself. Getting my mind back, my soul. So I quit drinking. Slowly. You know I can't mess with no meetings and all that. But the church had a band and you know how I feel about my music. You should come hear us play. It's not all hymns and praise Jesus stuff; it's good music with no fear of the Lord in it. It just . . . It felt good to feel something, Chabi, you know? Something other than rage and fear. That feeling took over for me when I felt like drinking. In the meantime I'd go to the parenting group at church. Never tried to make you go. Figured I wasn't strong enough to force you. But just listening to those other parents, they helped me get perspective. They got me to see that, drunk or not, by fifteen you had a mind of your own. I could only set the rules and follow through on consequences. Did it the best I could. And then . . . and then he left you. And as much as that old wrinkled man scared me to death, I'd bring him back in a second if it meant you didn't have to hurt that hard."

What did you fear in him, Mom? I asked, making sure she knew I was ok. What did you see that I still can't? was what I wanted to say.

"There are some people on this planet that are plain evil. In their core. Can't be changed, can't be helped. Best thing is to stay away from them. If you can't manage that, then you bury them six feet deep then forget to mark the grave. Your daddy, he was one of them. Narayana, he was about ten times worse."

Chapter Thirteen
The Flexibility of Bone

You don't train me, I told A.C. early the next morning as he stood on deck. I'd gotten used to him always being around when I woke up. *We spar.* He grinned.

I chased A.C. around the *Mansai* for a good two hours, him doing his wind tricks, me with my techniques, stamina, and speed before I was able to touch a single strand of his hair. Wherever I struck, he disappeared. Where I chased, he stood still. It was another hour before work and I was exhausted, a rare feeling for me.

"Don't feel bad. I've got more experience at this than you do," he said, taking a long swig off a bottle of orange juice.

You want to fight the Vish Kanya in two days' time? I sighed, resting my back against the stern of the *Mansai.*

"Trust, I've had my share of fights against those broads. Your technique will get you through the physical attacks easy enough. But Vish Kanya are clan-specific energetic sponges . . ."

They suck up energy? I asked, catching my second wind.

"Some may try to do that in combat. But I meant more that they gain their toxicity by being in constant contact with Alters. Imagine being in a house where you've got nothing but evil Narayanas around you all the time. Each Alter house has its own energies. The Alters form loose clans around totems to honor that energy. Not actual physical totems but energetic ones. They're like symbols that the Alters relate to."

The Silver Snake, I said.

"Exactly. Rice goes for the Silver Snake. His clan is reptilian. They appreciate the cold-blooded nature of the creatures. Without heat they don't move. Alters are entropy beasts that—"

Strive for the end of all heat in the universe. Yeah, got that. Poppy, she reptilian too? I asked, already suspecting the answer.

"No. She and her family are of the rat totem. In fact, she wants to be the rat queen." I don't bother speaking. "Alters are made when humans view or experience an authentic connection to the entropy of the universe. Some time, before any of us could write or speak beyond a grunt, someone witnesses a Rat King . . ."

A what now?

"It's when a bunch of rats get so intertwined by their tails that they can't loose themselves. It's a squealing, miserable hive of gross entropic failure. It is life growing into death."

That's nasty yo!

"I know, right? Well, this first witness of the Rat King was devoured by it both physically and symbolically. The energy of that person's life was converted into two Alters forever in love and at war. One half of that fight is Poppy; the other is her brother Galvin. Last time the two avatars of the Rat King were on the same continent, plague broke out in China and ended up killing millions. Even the other Alters don't like those two getting together. So this is the energy of her family. And they've trained a Vish Kanya, a human pet poisoned with their sickness to compete at this tournament."

Fine. I get back tonight; you show me some wind tricks. A.C. was about to protest but I was already belowdeck changing into work clothes.

"Rosa-Maria is dead," a note told me in Poppy's precious handwriting. The small scrap was waiting for me as soon as I entered the door. One of the blank-eyed receptionists handed me the note. I ran up the stairs to Poppy's suite refusing to cry. I hadn't spoken to her, hadn't even thought about her for weeks. But Rosa-Maria had been nice to me and had stood up against Poppy. I was tired of this rat queen bitch killing people I liked.

I kicked open the door to her floor and saw the big black Fou-Fou standing by her suite door. When he saw my gait, the Buick-sized man squared up.

"The lady is busy," he said.

You really gonna have those be your last words? I said, not altering my trajectory or speed.

"You overestimate your skill, girl." Just in range, Fou shot a hook at my head. I felt it coming, and the concussive blast of . . . something after it. But I didn't stop moving.

He was looking for a big movement, so I gave him a small side step. His eagerness to connect with my face made him overcommit and lose his balance. I found it. I trapped his arm between the top of my right shoulder and my left arm so tight that he winced. Before he could sound an alarm, I sent three fingers on my right hand into his neck with all my might. Once there I made sure what heat I could muster from the symbol in my back was sent directly into his trachea. Even before he dropped to the ground coughing blood and wheezing an unnatural sound, I knew he would never speak again. I didn't care.

I knocked on the door and Poppy and an angered Nordeen answered in under three seconds. He was flinching, snarling almost. His layers of sweaters were gone, leaving only a naked, bronzed, amazing chest in front of me. Bracing for an attack would've been a sign of the fear that I didn't know was building in me. Instead I spoke.

I think your boy has fallen. And he can't get up. Making sure not to touch me, Nordeen shifted past me and into the hallway. I walked into the bitch's suite to find her in deep red silk boxers, a black bra, and some thin, pale, pointless lace shirt. She lounged on her couch, both smiling and tearing in full fake sympathy.

"I'm just torn up, Chabi. Torn. Up. That Rosa-Maria girl was just so kind."

What. Happened? I said losing the calm in my Voice.

"Oh, don't worry about the details, Chabi. You've got enough to worry about now, with the Vish Kanya almost a day away. You don't need to hear the bloody details, what was done to her before she died; there's enough time for that later. I just don't understand who would want to hurt her so. She was always so polite, I mean except for that one time when I saw her in the hallway. Do you remember that, Chabi? Do you remember how rude she was? How disrespectful? She almost spoke to me as though I were a peer."

I took a step toward her and asked, Did you hurt her Poppy?

The bitch stood her skinny ass up, deliberately, still leaving one leg on the couch, as though the act of actually standing up would be too much for her. Her multilayered rat teeth appeared in her mouth. Her skin twitched like a million tortured creatures were fighting for freedom from it.

"Chabi, I do not hurt anyone. I never have. I didn't touch Matt; I didn't touch the maid. I don't have to touch anyone to hurt them. Do you understand that, pet? What changes I want to make to reality do not require my direct action. Others do the work for me. A point you're about to understand as you never have before."

"He's mute!" Nordeen rushed back in the room his eyes alight with a dark power.

"Now that is fitting." Poppy smirked.

I remember Nordeen saying something about showing me the birth of agony right before the black strobe light started working. That's what it felt like; like a strobe light that could project total and complete silent blackness around me—no, around the universe. Getting into a defensive stance made no sense, the blackout heartbeat scrambled every sense second by second. There would be nothing. Then the deafening noise of my own breathing. Nothing. Then the craven itching of my clothes. Nothing. Then the crushing weight of gravity on my body. I went to my knees grasping for balance but knowing no one would come to help. I flashed and reached out in my mind along the sensory lines where Nordeen had been creeping earlier. When I felt the faintest push back, I screamed, Stop!

My eyes were open but the vision only got clearer when Nordeen ended up on his ass. His nose was bleeding. Whatever language he cursed in, even my talent couldn't decipher. I hadn't touched him physically, but somewhere between my Voice and the imagination of my katas, I was able to strike back.

"Now, Nordeen, you stop." And there, Poppy again, sitting unhurt and casual in nightclothes. "I understand you're upset about your minion, but Chabi is going through a rough time right now. This aggression is unnecessary. Scales can be balanced at another time."

"My lady . . . ." Nordeen's attempt at civility was impressively inadequate as he stood wiping the blood from his nose. "This girl is a problem . . ."

"And you will find far greater problems if you step out of the circle of protection by continuing to engage her." The rebuke was harsh and complete, though Poppy's tone had not changed. To me, she gave the fake syrupy intonation again. "Now, Chabi, I am sorry for your loss. But please, Rice and his entire family are relying on you to be at your best during the Vish Kanya. Don't get distracted by minor conflicts and these rather tremendous tragedies."

I'd been standing for a while. Not re-establishing my balance but rather learning to trust it again. What comprehension I had about the previous five minutes I let go.

One day you're going to come for me directly, Poppy. No middlemen, no innocent victims. One day it's going to be me against you. When that day comes, don't blink.

"Chabi!" She laughed my name as I walked out the suite. Fou-Fou was gone but the bloodstain on the carpet remained.

✳

When I got back to the *Mansai* at the end of the day, A.C. was waiting for me.

"What happened?" he asked desperately.

Don't you have a home? I said, climbing on deck.

"Yeah, it's about four thousand miles and fifteen years in the future. In the meantime, I'm stuck with you. Now what happened?"

Why do you think anything happened? I asked, begging for one second of personal time.

"It's on the wind. Something about another liminal in debt to the Alters. Was it you? Did you . . . ?" he said slowly, realizing that I could be working for his enemy at that very moment.

Relax, Wind Boy. I don't owe them anything. I just got in a scrap with Nordeen's gorilla. I went downstairs to the galley and threw myself on the bed. I'd grown used to A.C.'s lack of footsteps. So when he started talking, I just rolled over to face the wall.

"You ok?" Genuine concern fell from his lips.

Yeah. Fou-Fou can't talk anymore but I'm fine. Nordeen did some weird thing to me, but I stopped him and Poppy put him back on leash. Like I said, scrap.

"So you're why Fou-Fou can't talk." A.C. said like it explained something. "You know the fight is tomorrow, right?"

. . . Not nearly enough time to teach me a whole new technique. I cut him off, knowing where he was heading way in advance.

"You don't have to know all two hundred and ten katas and eighty-nine blows to be effective, Chabi. That's what I've been trying to tell you. It's an extension of yourself, a combination of the old you with what's available in that moment."

You've got two hours to show me something useful. Then I'm eating food with my mom and getting some kind of sleep. I jumped up from the bed. I hated how easy it was to make him happy.

"Your whole technique is centered on striking, punching the movement of your energy into your enemies. Wind taps into the entirety of movement. All of it. Where there is movement there is wind. A strike ends movement or reverses it, in order to retain your fighting stance. Wind strives to constantly keep motion going. Hit me," he told me as we stood on deck after I'd changed into more comfortable fighting gear.

It was like I was waiting for it. I shot a high kick like a bullet. But as soon as I hit maximum extension, A.C.'s hand was there, holding my leg up and extended.

"Now if I was in full combat mode I'd be pushing up and sweeping your other foot at the same time to keep the motion going, understand?" I nodded but only after he'd let my foot go. The first twenty minutes felt like my first year with Narayana. I copied everything I saw A.C. do. And I failed at all of it. A.C. didn't get as frustrated as I did. He just kept laughing with his eyes. When I ended up on my ass for the tenth time, he finally had to say something.

"I know you can murder the hell out of whatever is in front of you. But how about just trying to move it?" he said, offering me a hand up.

All you're doing is moving, I said, flipping up from my back, refusing his hand. How does that put the hurt on folks?

"It's not always about you hurting them. Sometimes it's about letting them hurt themselves." He started his weird kata. I observed, not following literally or figuratively. I barked at him again.

I don't understand. Like even that kata there. There's no start, no stop. You just keep twirling, moving. I don't even see any clear blows in it. Just places where you throw your arms or legs up or down. It's like you're making it up as you go along.

"That's 'cause I am." He smiled, jumping from the deck to halfway up the mast and back to the deck behind me in under a second. The wind from all around me whipped up so hard the *Mansai* began to rock. "Look, I can teach you dance steps or I can teach you the spirit of the dance. What do you think is more important?"

I'm not trying to dance, A.C.! I snapped, not bothering to turn around. I'm trying to fight. I'm trying to survive.

"Sometimes in order to survive you've got to dance," the Wind Boy said, coming up behind me. "You try to murder everything that stands in front of you. That's a lot of expended energy. Granted, you've got heat to spare, but sometimes if you go with the motion of the world, you make your opponent's energy work against them."

I turned on him quick, expecting him to be a foot and a half behind me. Instead he was up close. I was about to find the entropy of his bones but I stuttered, unnerved by his proximity, his coolness, and his smile. He made me feel like a novice. Like my first day on the *Mansai* and Narayana getting frustrated with teaching me how to breathe while I move.

"I try to find the flexibility of bones. The porous nature of them. It's easier than their entropy. Strike me," he dared. His face was too close for a fist or a foot so I side-angled a head butt. I aimed for his chest but he twisted my target completely while shooting a thumb to the base of my neck so precisely that my neck extended against my will. The move threw me off balance and I began to fall. A.C. telegraphed my compensation and scooted under me, trapping my bracing hand behind my back as he sat with me. Again I was on the deck. Only this time, A.C. was under me.

"You could have kicked my shin, chopped my side with your elbow, even gone in for a kiss . . ." He started.

Why the hell would I kiss you?

" . . . But instead you went all out. With fury and anger. And absolutely no balance. When it comes to fire and rage, you are one of the best, Chabi. But if you're going to get through the Vish Kanya, you're going to need some of the inner art, the understanding of movement and balance." I threw all my weight into A.C.'s chest and felt him push back. I curled my stomach muscles and legs while reaching back with my free arm. Somehow I managed a perfect one-handed handstand on his shoulder. When A.C. stood, I flipped off him and landed on my feet.

"Beautiful!" he congratulated the move. When I smiled he said, "That too. You're always so serious when you fight. There's no joy in it. No freedom of movement or thought. You've got to be spontaneous. Like ODB . . ."

Old Dirty Bastard? I asked.

"Yeah, you know, no father to his style. It's not just pure fighting. It's also like fucking." He grinned.

Wouldn't know anything about that, I confessed, then immediately felt sheepish.

"Ah so," he said without judgment and sounding like an old Chinese man. "Well, that explains a lot."

Fuck you, I said lightly and turned to go downstairs. A.C. made a vault over my head and landed in front of me. In his form I began to see the joy in his movement. It started making sense. Given what he could do, what I could do, why wouldn't you flip jump, leap around the world?

"If you want." He smiled at me. "But seriously, I get why it's been hard for you to get where I'm coming from. The fight is the only way you've ever interacted with other bodies, other energies. I'm speaking a foreign language to you."

In a fucked-up accent as well, I said, trying to sidestep him. A.C. threw his body in the air and let the wind keep him aloft so it looked like he was lying on an invisible bed.

"But you do dance. I see that in you. You understand rhythm." I stopped moving, letting him know he looked ridiculous. "The rhythm will save you, Chabi. Rely on your tempo. See the tempo of others. You don't always have to interrupt that vibe. Sometimes you can participate in it. Those seeking combat will get unnerved, then you can contribute your fire. Fire isn't the opposite of wind. Added together they make a firestorm, understand?"

No, I said, pushing on his head, which righted him to a standing position.

"Yes, you do," the Wind Boy smiled.

Maybe. He stood on his legs and moved closer to me. His breath smelled like the sea. Without his jacket, he seemed more substantial, this man/boy I'd been seeing out of the corner of my eye for years. The guns that hung from his hip showed off his swagger. The sword almost permanently attached to his back accented a posture incapable of bending. I couldn't help but compare him to Narayana. But where Narayana was rigid, he was loose. Where Narayana burned, A.C. cooled and soothed. It was tempting to think of him as weak, but the reality was that he was more tantalizing than anything else. So inviting I would have fallen into him, on him, through him, had it not been for Mom showing up at that moment.

"Girl!" It was more the surprise of her voice coming through than the tone that made me jump back from A.C. For his part, he receded into the blind spot that he lived in.

Yeah, Mom? I went over to the bow to see her in her nightclothes.

"Roderick needs your help. I told you to call on them," she said, trying not to sound pissed. I could hear her Oakland accent coming through. It only did that when she was pissed or scared.

Been busy, Mom. What's the deal?

"Roderick's in a panic talking about how Dale is about to make some big noise at your work. Says he's got explosives and the like. Says he's talking about getting revenge for his nephew." What was I going to say? I had the same plan as him sans explosives. The man had more of a right to the plot than I did. But I knew Poppy and Rice. At least, I knew them more than Dale did. As competent as he was, they'd eat him alive. It took me a few seconds but I knew I had to stop him. Apparently so did Mom.

"How quick can you make it up there?" Mom demanded.

"Quicker than you think," A.C. answered.

Chapter Fourteen
A Return to Gringo's Last Chance

A.C.'s power worked like his martial art. He didn't generate movement but he added to it. All I had to do was start running and he added the power of the wind to my effort. A run that took hours ended up only taking fifteen minutes. A.C. was with me the whole way. Not in body, but in sentiment, feeling. In the wind, I felt his laughter and lightness. He was all around me and nowhere to be seen until I slowed down by the ranch, then suddenly, or rather not suddenly, as though he'd always been there, A.C. was right by my side, smiling.

I walked into the main house to see Roderick loading an arsenal into a black duffle bag in the middle of the living room. I made sure I had cover before I called out. Good move, as the big man looked up fierce and quick. When he saw it was me, he went back to loading.

"Hey, girl," he said pleasantly but briefly.

Roderick, I said closing the distance between us slowly.

"What's up, Roderick?" A.C. said and I was shocked by his voice.

"Hey, A.C.," he said after studying A.C.'s face for half a second. Then he went back to loading the guns.

"Quick question, man," A.C. said casually, motioning for me to slow down and be quiet. "Where's your brother?"

"Dumbass is out by Lamb's Tears putting together some

homemade shit he learned to make over in some war-torn land. Says it's time for those that fucked with our family to get fucked with," the big man recited almost as though he were in a trance.

"And you are . . . ?" A.C. continued.

"Well, I'll be damned if he thinks he's going in without backup. He's running on more anger than common sense but he's committed. You know what he's like, A.C.," Roderick said and kept loading his weapons.

"I can't tell him to stop," A.C. finally said to me. "But you can."

I knew what he meant. I summoned the inner Voice and told Roderick to look at me.

"Roderick. Go make yourself some tea. Stow the guns. Get some sleep." I felt him resisting so I added, "Your brother won't go. I promise."

When he went to the kitchen, I turned to A.C. What the hell was all that? I asked him.

"I'm on the fringes of consciousness for most people. Talking to me is like talking to yourself. People forget me almost as soon as they finish speaking. You can get lots of info that way." I nodded. "I'll keep an eye on him. Go get Dale."

Five minutes later I was at the shed. The weed plants were flowering. The nymph poo was growing everywhere, its scent daring me to take a nap. Everything the family had created was going to seed. But my focus was on Dale. I knocked on the door gently, being sure to let him know it was me with my Voice soon after. He told me to come in. Like his brother, he was prepping a mid-sized duffle bag. But he had small black vessels he was filling with two liquids, one green, the other clear. A thin line connected both of the containers to a sloped button. Before putting them in the bag, he pressed some lever on the top of the contraption hard.

"Hey, girl," he said coldly. He'd never been that cold to me in my life.

Dale. Your brother called me . . .

"Good. I'll need your help getting in," he said, offering me a .45, holding the barrel. "I know guns aren't your style. But we don't know what we're facing in there, so . . ."

No offense, but this ain't the move. If his eyes could have killed me, they would have. Instead he just put the gun down and went back to filling up his weird cartridges with liquid.

"I should wait, then? Until what? Bitch already took my nephew. Now she wants the farm? I should wait until she has her hands around my throat? Fuck that!" he said coolly, calmly.

I don't understand . . . I started.

"She got Matt to sign over his share of the farm to her. I don't even know this bitch! I've never met her. None of us have. And now she's moving in on us. Well, I don't know you, Ms. Poppy, but you don't know who the fuck I am, either."

I didn't know, I whispered.

"No, you didn't. You didn't know he was staying in the same place you were. You didn't know he was in love with her. You didn't know he was thinking about suicide. There's a lot you didn't know. Here's my question: how could you be so close to everything and not know anything?" He was shouting. I started crying when I tried to speak.

I stood still, unmoving, trying to find my balance, my answer for him. I couldn't. Not until he was fully loaded and had to push by me.

"We going to have a problem here, Chabi?" he asked. I was fortunate. Conflict is something I always know how to respond to.

Only if you try and walk out of here with those explosives, I said calmly, not bothering to wipe the tears from my face. He stood facing the door not looking at me. I looked into the darkness of what was once Matt's plant playland, both of us registering each other out the corner of our eyes.

I must seem like an ungrateful . . . I left the funeral and . . . I refused to let myself cry more as he started. I could force you, Dale. Fucking A, you know I could. But I'm asking you. Fuck it, I'm begging you. Let me handle this. I swear to you, on my mother, that bitch

188

will never own a pebble of this land and they will all pay for the suffering they've caused. That's my word.

"Contract said she's making a survey of the land next week," Dale said stoically.

Doubt she'll make it to the weekend.

"On your word?"

On my everything, I say, eye-locking him. Slowly, he put the bag down. I turned to leave but before I hit the door I felt possessed to speak again.

It may not seem like it, and I know I didn't deserve it, but I appreciate the trust and the friendship your family has always shown me. I've never had lots of friends. I'm glad to count you among them.

Outside the barn, A.C. sat on top of the mystery rock smoking his strange weed again. The scent lingered with the nymph poo and the weed. The half moon caught the mystery man in his best light.

You ready? I asked him.

"I was born ready. Question is, are you?" he asked back, opening his eyes slowly.

Enough with the challenges for today, ok? I half begged. I just need some peace. Just a little before tomorrow night. He gently stepped off the rock, almost floating down to my side. I let his strong and narrow fingers push casually into my neck and felt a measurable amount of my tension get carried off into the wind.

"When I have too much of it all, I like to find a nice quiet spot like this and find my bliss." He smiled smoking his weird joint. When I started singing "Pusherman," he came out and laughed. "Girl, your voice has so much power. Just remember, this place, this smoke is here for you."

Going up to the farm, it felt like I was running at the speed of the wind. Heading back to Sausalito, I was carried in the air by the wind. I didn't even give the conceit of pedaling my legs. I let A.C. do all the heavy lifting. If it was a bother for him, I wouldn't have known it. He carried me high above sight, leaving me with the divided moon as my only company. Of course I felt him around me, his smile, his casual courage keeping me up.

That night, just as I was about to crawl into bed, the Wind Boy showed up in the walkway to the lower deck, looking sheepish. I knew what he was thinking and had to stifle a laugh. Then, for reasons I can't figure, I blushed.

"I was thinking . . ." he started.

No, I said plainly.

"But, it's just that it might give you a better sense of how to . . ."

Dude, that is the worst pick-up line ever. Like ever, I said, threatening to get loud. Besides every fighter on the planet knows you don't get down right before a fight. Saps your energy.

"Ok, you're right. I see your point. I'm sorry. I was just trying to help. I wasn't trying to, I mean it wasn't just because I wanted to . . ." When his form started getting hazy I realized I didn't want him to leave.

Wait. He blinked back into full existence. If you want . . . I want you to crash out with me tonight. Just sleeping. But if you want, you can.

He jumped in the bed like a kid, like it was a sleepover. Not like a lover. That night the wind, warm and comforting, nuzzled against my neck, held my hand, caressed my back, and let me put my guard down for the first time in years.

I woke up early. The fights wouldn't start until midnight but I couldn't sleep. I'd never been nervous for a fight before. Surprising as it was to see A.C. snoring in my bed in full human form as I woke up, I couldn't stay there next to him. I had to move.

I did what I knew, what Narayana taught me. Despite the curse of it, it was my curse. It was all I still had of the man who put me on this path. I'd spent my whole life mastering the Downward Rooster block, Red Salamander strikes, Poor Dragon's Repose, the Ascendant Phoenix cry, Lion's Blighted bite, and seventy-two other strikes, blocks, counters, and techniques. And I was their master. Now that I knew to feel for it, the heat of the Vish Kanya mark on my back was white hot against the cold morning air.

I tried what A.C. taught me. But before I started, I put an old mix from the Little Kid on my headphones to get into the jungle vibe. With no skeleton in front of me, I practiced the entropy of bones. It had been a pinnacle for me. It was strong enough to take out Samovar. But now A.C. was saying it wouldn't be enough in the long run. And I only had hours to improve. I took to studying.

The issue wasn't technique, I knew that. My form was perfect and precise. I did my entropy of bones. Twenty or so times, going through the motions, feeling the beat of the universe, seeing that beat expressed in all matter around me. I joined with it, imagined the places in the fictitious skeleton in front of me where that rhythm would catch its breath, and then moved to add another beat, an off pattern tempo I could play through that imagined matter. There was barely any force from my fingers, but I knew whatever I struck in that moment would have been decimated. But A.C. was also right. In the practicing I felt off balance. Not greatly. If the skeleton had been there I'd have been fine, but I should have been able to practice the kata perfectly. The problem was not form, it was philosophy.

Whatever little sparring A.C. and I did never resulted in him touching me. I barely touched him. But somehow I always ended up on my ass. It wasn't just an aikido mindset of redirecting energy. I felt his energy, his vying for one-upmanship when we scrapped, but it was never through force. Slowly it began to make sense. Narayana taught me that the fist was the last refuge of the desperate fighter. He taught me that the force of a finger, an open palm, the side of a foot was like a surgical tool, capable of doing extreme amounts of damage when wielded properly. The entire interior force of a person could be interrupted with a well-placed finger. But maybe A.C.'s technique didn't even require touch. I had to get myself into a state to feel the beat of the universe—maybe A.C. always lived with it, and maybe he was always in line with that universal rhythm. When he struck, it wasn't at the entropy of bones but at their birth. Practicing on skeletons wouldn't work if that was the case. Practicing wouldn't be the issue at all. I would have to live it. But before I could do any more, I saw Mom waving at me from across the dock.

"You want some breakfast?"

I woke A.C. up and took him over as well. Mom made eyes at me. I was able to calm down after Wind Boy assured me she had no recollection of their previous meeting. It was almost like she knew something big was going to happen for me. She pulled out all the stops: blue corn waffles, turkey sausage, scrambled eggs with green onions, green and yellow bell peppers, tomato, and pepper jack cheese, and her famous fried potatoes. To drink she poured orange and cranberry juice and had sparkling water to make what she called her Miracle Mimosas, because it was a miracle it tasted so good with no alcohol. She was sweet with me and laughed at A.C. I was tempted to get bitter. To wonder why we couldn't have been this way my entire life. But it wasn't the time to look back.

Keep her safe, I told A.C. when she went to the bathroom.

"I'll do my best but . . ." he started.

Just for today. I'm going out. I want to try something.

"Sure you don't want me with you?"

Tonight? For sure. Today, my main concern is that they don't try and get me distracted by doing something to Mom. He nodded, trusting my logic. We said our good-byes when Mom came out but when I walked through the doorway I was alone. I looked back and saw A.C. present, but fading on the couch. She wouldn't see him, but if anyone came for her, they'd have a crazy-ass Wind Boy with extra-dimensional weapons to deal with.

I went to the site of my first fight; the place where I'd almost been raped. I pushed the Cutlass Royale into El Sobrante with ease. I hadn't realized how nervous heading over to Gringo's Last Chance at Heaven Bar and Grill would make me until I got off the freeway in Berkeley and let the streets carry me the rest of the way. Reflecting on it, I realized it probably wasn't just going, but also what I would attempt when I got there. I walked into a late afternoon crowd of drunks and degenerates doing pretty much the same things they were doing eight years earlier. I had to chill at the bar for a good twenty minutes before Marko recognized me. Then he got nervous.

"Tell me Narayana's not with you," he said, wiping down the bar surreptitiously, trying to avoid eye contact with me and the rest of his patrons. Marko looked older, fatter. I didn't think it was possible.

Haven't seen him in years, I said, continuing to fake drink my beer.

"Ok. Well, if I remember correctly you got your revenge on all those that had a hand in your misfortunes that night. And seeing as how you're just waiting for that beer to get warm . . ."

Baddest man or woman in here. I gave Marko my eyes to let him know the danger of not taking me seriously.

"Playing pool now," he said, resigned, pointing to a small black guy not yet forty with bullet marks where eyes should be. "Collects martial arts like fat kids collect bites of cake. But go easy on the bar, please."

I promise nothing. Now give me a name.

"Jeffery by birth. Tells people to call him Onyx. But look, girl, he's the real deal, ok? He's just as likely to come at you with that .50 he's got under his jacket as he is with his kung fu or whatever. He's a dealer. He's used to scraps."

I took my beer and tossed it perfectly on the felt pool top so that not a sip spilled until Onyx's eight-ball knocked it. The older man looked over at me quick. I smiled.

"I got money on this game, little bitch," he said, casually walking over to my bottle and slamming it.

Yeah, well, I heard a rumor about you and I wanted to know if it was true, I said. I broke out one of my headphones and put it in my ears.

"Seven inches limp." He laughed and his cronies now assembling laughed with him.

So your mom does have a dick. His boys had to stifle their laughs at that one. Nah, I'm just playing. No, see, the rumor I heard was that you can't take an ass whipping. I heard that as soon as someone starts taking your monkey ass apart for say, selling some dirty blow, you pull out the heat and start blasting. It was true enough of most so-called gangsters; I figured it would apply to him as well.

"Bitch, I don't know who you've been talking to but I'll put this heat down right now," he said, pulling his .50 cal with the serial number filed off and laying it down on the pool table so quickly even I almost jumped. Almost. "And I'll show you an ass-kicking. Might make some money off your ass after I'm done showing you . . ."

Hold up, hold up, I said, taking off my jacket then putting my other earbud in. Ok, keep talking that bullshit now. I'm ready whenever you are.

To his credit, he didn't rush in mad dog style. He put his guard up, maintained his stance and advanced on me. The first hard part was not attacking, ending the fight instantly, like I'd been trained to do. Narayana had taught me to take offense whenever anyone thought they could stand in front of me without getting struck. But this was practice, so I let him get in striking range. The second hard part was not closing my eyes and just swaying to the music. Listening and fighting were not my custom. But as I did I saw what I was looking for: the rhythm. I could literally see the tempo of Onyx's breath, his pulse, his heart rate, everything. He could only step at certain times, only swing at certain times, only inhale in concert with muscle relaxation. It was like listening to a symphony for years and only now understanding that there was a conductor in charge of the whole thing. I was so enamored with the beauty of the body that I almost let myself get kicked in the ribs just to see what it would look like with this new vision. Instead I spun out of the way, devoid of any martial arts form. I danced out of the way. It threw Onyx off. He barked something but I couldn't hear him. I laughed. Then he came in for real.

When he stepped in with his right foot to counterpunch with a left hook, a good set-up and fake, I wrapped his left arm behind my back with my right arm, Narayana's technique. But with my left I tried to feel, massage the energy in his chest that I was seeing. I played the orchestra of his body better than he did, not breaking or busting, but adding to, coordinating his own bio-rhythms to be more in tune with the universal sound I was hearing, feeling, seeing. Without meaning to, I sent some of the fire from the mark in my back through the man. It sent him flying backwards. I almost forgot to let go of his right arm. He went into the opposing wall. I took my headphones out.

Looks like I was wrong. He does know how to take an ass-whipping. My bad, I said. Marko had his hands below the bar, no doubt on a rifle. But one look from me and he assumed the same stance all of Onyx's friends did, pretending I hadn't just sent a patron of the bar into a wall. I smiled, paid an extra two hundred on my tab and left calmly.

I checked in with A.C., told him what happened, then took a long nap. At seven, I woke and dressed in all black. Not the black of the Naga Suites or even my mom's blacks. I wore my old black sleeveless T-shirt and the long black basketball shorts that went down past my knees. I braided my hair in two long ponytails and hid broken razor bits deep in the thickets. I Vaselined up my face with rubber gloves on so my hands wouldn't be slippery. A.C. was there, but he said nothing. I had to get my murder mask on and he knew well enough not to interrupt that process except for once.

"Look, I'm there. I'm with you every step of the way. But I've got to keep my presence on the under for as long as possible. With Nordeen in play they might have ways of getting to me. But if you need me, just call out my name. And I'll be there. We'll figure them out together."

Music, I said fifteen minutes after he spoke. I'll need music. That jungle, grimy type stuff, yeah? When I'm fighting. Can you handle that for me?

"Shouldn't be too hard," he said softly. "You got a plan?"

Yup. Kill them all.

Chapter Fifteen
Get Up and Find My Bliss

I left the Cutlass Royale at the house, the keys in an envelope slipped through Mom's mail slot. I did the quick run to the ferry as a warmup. The ride over to the city, with almost no one on it, gave me time to just be still. If I let my thoughts drift to A.C. he'd be there, right behind me, attentive. But I only did that once. He wasn't the one I wanted there. I wanted Narayana. I wanted to kill him. I wanted him to hold me. I wanted him to explain what he'd gotten me into and what my role was supposed to be. I just wanted to hear him call me good girl one more time.

I jumped off at the ferry building, wishing it was Pier 39. Saying good-bye to the tourists, being the stranger among the families would have been fitting. But I was late to my own execution.

Four blocks away, the Naga Suites began its pull on me. I felt the desperation of life without Rice again. It was only the absence of the calm the wind katas had taught me that showed me the subtle influence of the place. The impulse to reach out for A.C. got short-circuited by a small gust of wind against my face. I understood instantly. If he showed himself, Poppy and her ilk would be able to draw a bead on him. Better to save that reveal for the inevitable crisis. But the gust against my face was appreciated, a reminder that I wasn't alone.

The Suites had never been so threatening to me. That damn snake wrapped around the planet had its eye on me as I walked in.

The usual sociopaths and serial killers in training, the wannabe predators all turned to face me like I was a victim as I entered the lobby. I kept my relaxed posture, released all the tension from my face, and invited them to approach. None of them did, cowed by energies other than mine. Rice, beautiful Rice, wearing a pewter herringbone three button suit, walked toward me with his ever-present smile.

"Oh, Chabi, Chabi! I've missed you." The embrace was strong, combat strong, but somehow tender. I imagined the ever-present silver snakes taking the form of his arms and crushing me. I would have let him if he hadn't let go. "Are you ready?"

Of course, I smiled, wanting to give him everything. He chatted casually about the fighters and their sponsors as he escorted me downstairs on the elevator.

"There's a whole lot of pomp and ceremony involved with this fight. Nothing to worry about. They'll ask what house you're fighting for. They just mean what family. Just tell them you're fighting for the Montague line, ok?" I nodded just in time for him to give me a kiss on the cheek. "Kill them all, Chabi."

The only thing the basement of the fight shared with the basement of the dance party was dimensions. The psychic space was radically different, both more luxurious and brutal at the same time. A moderate sized platform raised a 30-x-40-foot ring that seemed to be suspended in the air. Black and red cords made the perimeter. Fighters, women big and small of all hues, roamed the flatlands of the room with their patrons. The patrons. If nothing else, they were proof of A.C.'s conspiracy theory. They all glowed and were gorgeous in nothing but the top fashion. They were accustomed to adoration from their lessers, their fighters, and those poor people that had to serve them. I fought to suppress the memory of Rosa-Maria as Rice guided me through the loose crowd of three hundred or so bodies. The patrons were well manicured and groomed. They seemed ready for modeling shoots, every one of them. But when I adjusted to my combat vision of them for a moment, I saw their bodies as polar opposites of human beings. Their hearts beat in reverse. They sucked in heat instead of exuding it. Their pulse rates felt like glass shards against sandpaper. They were life anathema.

"Here she is!" Poppy's voice shook me out of my vision state as she cleared the space between us with a tall Nordic fighter with John Lennon–style sunglasses on and thousands of small nicks on her face. Rice extended his hand to keep her at a safe distance, partially in jest, though his voice sounded more serious than I'd ever heard before. But just that damn smiling face. I wanted to say fuck my half-ass plan and just go on a killing spree. Starting with her.

"You know the rules, Poppy. What few there are," Rice said.

"Combat only in the ring, of course, silly. I just wanted to perform an introduction. Chabi, this is Pardu. You guys are going to fight," she said, like we were going to do each other's hair. Pardu grunted, looked at her patron/master, looked back at me and then extended her hand. I didn't even try to touch it.

"You should teach your . . . girl better manners, Rice," Poppy snipped.

"She's got all the manners she needs for the ring." He smiled, literally putting his body between us. He took Pardu's hand and I saw her weaken slightly toward him. "Hi, Pardu. My name is Rice. It's lovely to meet you."

"Enough of that!" Poppy snapped, breaking their hand connection. She was shuttling the larger woman off before Pardu could speak. But she managed to call over her shoulder, "See you in the thick of it, Rice."

"I know Poppy has been riding you hard since I've been gone, Chabi." He pulled me close, holding both of my hands to his chest. "There's a certain amount of . . . respect that she's owed. That her family affords. But, Chabi, I promise you, win this tournament and we can screw her up for a very long time. It's me and you against all of these guys, Chabi. You understand what I'm saying? You win this and we get to do whatever we want for as long as we want. Win this for me and I'll never ask you for anything else in your life, Chabi, understand?"

I'm sorry . . . I started not knowing why I was saying it, then remembering and wishing I didn't. I pushed it all out of my head, but he caught something.

"Sorry for what?" At that moment the sponsors in the crowd took on a formal pose, like military people coming to attention from a sound none of the fighters could hear. Rice tried to fight it then gave up, let my hands go and looked up at the DJ booth. A second and a half later bad techno competed with a lousy DJ announcer as he explained the rules of combat.

Any fighter could climb into the ring at any time. It was one-on-one fighting. You had to announce who your sponsor was. If you won a fight, you could call anyone out. If you lost, you couldn't fight again. If you won, you had to. Fighters' eyes surveyed each other trying to figure out who would go first. I figured I'd take the guesswork out of all of it. I sprinted to the ring, did a frontward somersault into the ring and opened my arms.

"Who do you fight for?" the voice overhead announced.

I shouted in my loudest Voice, Narayana Raj. The dead air proved why things can't grow in a vacuum. I felt the breath leave my chest for a second as most presences in the darkened floor did their version of gasping. I expected them to all rush me at once. But something in them demanded respect for the boundaries of the ring, as I was certain they had none for me.

"Go kill that bitch," an old but familiar voice rang out from the darkness. A bronze diminutive woman entered the ring from the other side. She stepped in already tired, her hands not wrapped, her hair everywhere, in tattered jeans and an old red V-neck shirt.

"Who do you fight for?" the overhead announcer asked with slight trepidation this time.

"Samovar Danu is my master," she said with such sadness that I almost felt pity for her. When she began to weep, I was totally thrown off.

You don't have to do this, I told her. For a second she stood waffling, looking out the ring and then looking at me. Finally she fell to her knees. I went to comfort her. Just as I got to her a small gust of wind pushed against my chest with a whisper of a word, Vish Kanya. It was enough. Poison Damsels. The creeping darkness of a man had told me about the multiple interpretations of the term. I cartwheeled off line just before the small woman took her hand wet with tears and flung the liquid at my face. I smelled the acridity of her tears. Those were secretions that burned.

I am not going to feel bad in the slightest about kicking your punk ass! I shouted. She spit at me. I moved quickly but saw the deadly phlegm eat through the ring where it landed. I thought I had her figured until I saw her sweating, a lot. It didn't burn through the ring. She didn't just have one type of poison. And the poison from her sweat was airborne. As far from her as I was, I could feel my head getting lighter.

"Nasty bitch," she cursed. She came in slowly, expecting me to retreat. Instead I circled, held my breath, and generated the fire from my back into my fist. When she was still out of reach I lashed out with my fist energy. I couldn't touch her physically but the force of the energy was enough to push her back across the ring. The good part was that she'd never been hit that hard before. The bad part was that now she was bleeding. She rubbed her fist with the blood from her mouth and came swinging. I didn't know what toxins her blood held, but I wasn't willing to find out.

With closed eyes I found the dubstep beat in her hard footsteps. For all her pollutants she was still human. In my private darkness I saw her tempo, the energies that controlled and informed her. I saw the source of her poison, a womb modified to produce illness instead of life. My pity almost got me killed. I didn't mean to let her get so close. I had to sidestep then send the venting energy I'd used to push Onyx into a wall directly into her womb. The crying damsel lay sprawled out on the mat unconscious, leaking out all her poisons.

Next? I demanded from the crowd, controlling my breathing. There was no cheering. No applause. Just more vacuums of silence and cold. Two bruisers, non-Alters, came up from the darkness of the crowd with gloves on and removed my opponent. I stood in the middle of the ring for a few minutes then got loud again. What? Is that all you've got? Are you all afraid? At least Samovar had the balls to put his girl against me. What? I've got to break all your bones to find someone to fight me via proxy?

Pardu looked even taller when she entered the ring. But I'd taken on bigger, stronger fighters. What I wasn't prepared for was her trick. By now I knew they all had one. I should have known.

Who do you fight for? the voice asked.

"The Rat Queen of the House of Barda sponsors me." She turned to face me.

You gonna sport those shades the whole time? I asked.

"No." She took them off and two orbs, one white, one black, sat in the sockets where her eyes should have been. The nausea was immediate. I imagined it to be what seasickness felt like for people who hadn't grown up on the water. This was her trick. I threw up hard. The blond behemoth was on me in a second. Now the crowd went wild. I spun under her and managed Ashes Nail Coffin to the back of her legs. Rolled to the other side of the ring, I focused through my sickness and was ready to go again when Pardu looked at my arm. It went limp. Even though I could move it, I didn't have full range of movement. But I knew this trick. If I focused on what I couldn't do, I'd be down. Again, Pardu used my confusion to close the distance, but this time my Yawning Rooster kick met her eyes.

Keep them closed and keep this fair, was the warning I gave her as the giant tried to clear her eyes, keeping one hand out for defense as she did.

"You're going to die tonight," the giant croaked.

Probably. But by hands worse than yours. The giant cleared her eyes. Keep them closed, woman! She stared at me.

I'd been stoking my internal fire. I used my hate, my frustration, my anger. It was white hot. I felt Pardu's effect, poisoning my lungs with her eyes. I just stopped breathing as I ran at her. She'd spent too much time on her eyes and not enough on looking. At the last minute I whipped my hair. It had only taken a second for me to move a razor blade to the tip of one of my ponytails. To hear her screams as my hair went across the all-black marble in her face was more punishing than even she could have known. To her credit, she didn't stop as her eyes deflated. She tried to punch and stare at me at the same time. I broke her arm and used my index finger to poke out the other eye. It bounced out of her face like a round stone on a bungee cord. She never screamed. The woman fell to her knees defeated, embarrassed, in pain.

"Enough of this!" Poppy shouted, coming into the ring. For the first time, I saw her rattled, upset. I loved it.

That's what I'm talking about. Let's handle this, I said, wiping eye guts off on my shorts.

"Let's," Poppy said and smiled. The bitch turned her back on me and spoke to the darkness. "By the first applications and the laws of the uncreated, I invoke equity."

The usual murmurs and noises I expected from a crowd finally rose. She spoke in her language. It was so intense that I didn't dare jump her from behind for fear of unseen consequences. Finally, after a full minute, Rice came into the ring. He stood with Poppy, confronting her, but still next to her. Nowhere near me.

"Where's the inequity?" Rice asked in their demented tongue.

"With no provocation, this ward of the forgotten traitor stole the only voice of one of my servants," Poppy said, pointing at me with full dramatic flair. I giggled about it until Rice looked at me with near apologetic eyes.

"Is this true?" he asked in English to me. "Did you take someone's voice?"

So what? I said, getting into a fighting stance. It was beginning to dawn on me what they would attempt. None of them could get close enough to touch me. I wasn't thinking clearly.

"You hear?" Poppy complained to the sympathetic darkness again, their cries becoming louder. "Without regret this . . . this liminal, yes, for those of you unable to discern, this is what an unheeled liminal looks like . . . this creature damages my property, wounds an Elder and threatens to disrupt one of our oldest ceremonies. I withheld the wrath of my family because I thought Clan Montague sponsored her. But by her own words she allied herself with the Traitor." Her patter, like ten thousand rat feet scraping across concrete, unnerved me almost as much as her full set of rat teeth. I caught her stare-down of Rice as she twisted her final blade. "Now, unless House Montague has allied itself with the traitor Narayana Raj, I demand equity!"

"I'm so sorry," Rice said gently as he reached out to me.

For what? I said. I tried to say. I whispered. My Voice was going. Don't you fucking dare! I shouted silently. Rice gave me a sheepish apologetic shrug as he opened his arms shoulder-length apart and played with a murky blue and gold energy between his palms. I'd never seen it before, but I knew, it was my Voice. Rice seemed more mournful than filled with regret; like he'd eaten the last cookie. How could I ever have loved him, wanted him? How did he have the ability to take my voice? These were the thoughts going through my head as my liminality was being taken from me. I looked in the corner and saw my blinded opponent and felt more kinship for her and the other Vish Kanya than I ever had before. Poppy wouldn't have been able to stop grinning if she tried.

"A.C.," I muttered with the last of my Voice. The Brooklyn dub guru Dr. Israel's song "Life in the Ghetto" instantly threatened to break all the speakers in the basement. My vindicating whirlwind coalesced into my favorite forgetful rectal irritant right next to me, six-shooters in hand. His first shot was perfectly aimed at Poppy. And as much as it pains me to give her any credit, the rat woman dodged the killing blow and managed to get a bullet in her clavicle for her trouble. Her shock that a bullet actually had the ability to hurt her was almost worth it.

"You get Rice. I've got Poppy. Don't hold back," A.C. said with a smile. I let the three steps it took me to get to the side of the ring fill me with the rhythm of life. Looking into the darkness of the crowd full of Alters, I didn't know fear or anger. Just challenge. It didn't matter that I didn't have a voice, I had a chance to just fight. To just let go.

Vish Kanya or Alter, it didn't matter, I struck, sometimes using the entropy of the bones, sometimes finding the generativity of the music. Some ran from me, others fell into me, others attacked head-on. I was quicker than usual, dispatching all comers in seconds. I thought I was just hyped until the gust of wind from the north side of the room reminded me who was on my side. A.C. was lending me some of his speed like he had on the way to the ranch.

That effect ended after about five minutes. While I had an impressive wounded and worried body count, I hadn't laid eyes on Poppy or Rice. But the dying extra speed had me worried. I couldn't see A.C., which meant I couldn't call out to him, without a voice. The music began to fade as well, and so did the lights. A Vish Kanya was able to land a blow on me. I started backpedaling. Two Vish Kanya and five Alters surrounded me. I breathed deep, but then was sucked into the air and dropped hard in the middle of the arena. A second later A.C. came falling back next to me from the darkness. He landed as though he'd been hit. I thought his sword had blood on it but I couldn't tell for sure. My vision and hearing began to degrade. But through the haze I heard familiar nonsense words.

"I truly do hate Nordeen!" A.C. said, trying to laugh. Alters and Vish Kanyas tried climbing into the ring but Wind Boy lived up to his name and generated a cyclone that kept them out and us safe in the middle. At least temporarily.

"Time to go." A.C. pantomimed grabbing the air about twelve times before he actually managed to catch what he was aiming for, a wisp of air. He circled it in his hands over and over again, rotating his hips as though he were spinning a hula-hoop. I barely understood what was going on, I was barely conscious, but I could tell it was taking all of his energy.

Just as a small hole in the middle of the air began to open and started making a sucking sound, the debilitating chanting of Nordeen got louder. He rose to the ring with Poppy and Rice behind him. The old man's chanting broke the cyclone in one place. A.C. raised one six-shooter at our enemies but a team of rats came from behind them, going for me. He shot them all in quick time. His other hand A.C. kept trained on the small portal. He threw one of the six-shooters through the portal and used the now free hand to push the trio back with his wind. What he did next scared and confused the hell out of me.

"Get up and find your bliss, girl!" he shouted as he picked me up. I tried to protest but I had no voice. I was too weak to fight back and I never realized how strong A.C. was. He actually threw me through the portal. Soon after, he must have thrown the other six-shooter and the sword because when I woke I was surrounded by the weapons at the weed brothers' ranch. Alone.

Chapter Sixteen
Akashic Records

I screamed. Nothing happened. Anywhere. Not in the real world, not in the invisible place where my voice usually echoed. I had no effect. Nothing. I threw myself on the ground, grabbed fistfuls of dirt, sobbed, and dug my face into the earth, screaming all the time. Nothing. I lost control of my breath, taking huge drags of air and still not feeling like I was getting enough. My heart started taking pot shots at my rib cage. I started shaking all over. I felt myself on fire one minute, then freezing the next. This was Narayana leaving all over again. Had I been poisoned? One of the Vish Kanya had gotten me. The world began to lose focus as I measured one other option.

Maybe you're just panicking like a little bitch. It was my own internal voice but it felt like a stranger's. And that annoyed me. Annoyed me that my own sense of self was compromised. Irritated me that I might be mistaking self-inflicted wounds for enemy fire. I was disgusted with myself for letting A.C.'s sword and guns lie languishing in the ground. The dirt caked on my shorts and my face began to embarrass me. But my body was still flipping out.

I demanded order from my lungs, steady breaths. I gave up my sight and focused on my balance. With eyes closed I sat on the ground with my back erect and relaxed. I let the heat flashes come and go as they wished. Same with the shivers. Soon I was convinced that I had been panicking and not poisoned. I let the embarrassment of that slide with last of the cold shivers. No time to be embarrassed. I had work to do.

No voice didn't mean I was helpless. I ran to Sheep Tears hoping I'd find Dale or Roderick. Both were gone. But the black sack was there. I grabbed it and was about to make my way back to the house when I went by the rock, right where I had landed. Despite the wind, A.C.'s joint and the lighter rested on the top of it, unmoving. I'd been so discombobulated I'd forgotten his words. He told me to find my bliss. He'd been lightweight pushing his smoke on me literally since we first met. And just as he's about to be captured by Rice and his ilk, he doesn't tell me to run and get weapons, doesn't send me as far away as possible and say "stay safe." He tells me to find my bliss.

It took a lot to get my action-oriented ass to not move. To think for a second. It took more to put the bag of bombs down. It took so much more to actually pick up that weirdly familiar smelling joint. It was only when I finally lit it that I remembered where I'd encountered its scent before. It was the smell of the fungus rock. Not the rock, the fungus itself. That was the last thing I thought before I took a hit and left my body.

It wasn't jarring or scary. More like I took off my clothes and slipped into a warm pool of water. I lost nothing in the transition. In fact, I felt like I gained. Like a million and one voices sang my body into being at once. I felt the unified effort of all creation in the formation of the moment and me. I was expanded outside of my body, and then reformed without physical limitations on a dark gray plain that had no horizon as far as I could see. My physique was made of a forever-moving ocean of fire, fed by a forever-blowing breeze. I was constantly churning but I wasn't agitated. It didn't hurt. It felt more like a natural consequence; an honest expression of who I was. Every move I made, every step, every self-explorative touching of this body made a sound, like low notes from an upright bass or cello. It came to me then that I was at the place where my Voice originated.

From my right hand side I heard a symphony and knew it was a new body. I couldn't help reveling in the coordination and rhythm in the movement of the body. My own movements had a pure representative beauty, like when you know a musician is putting everything they have into their music. But the approaching body played with subtleties, melodies, and harmonies with such casual ease, it screamed expertise. When I turned to look at him, he was as surprised as me.

"You are not who I was expecting," DJ Jah Puba, the Little Kid's friend, all grown up, said without a hint of malice. And far more attractive.

"Fair enough," I said, shocked not by the sudden appearance of my voice—somehow I knew I would be able to speak—but more at the reformation of my body into a semblance of flesh. "I sure as hell wasn't expecting you."

"It's been a while, Chabi." He smiled kindly at me, coming closer. He was taller, with broad shoulders, older than me, and barely recognizable as the sullen mop of a wannabe DJ. "Most people call me Mico now."

"You're Mico?" I shouted and heard the plane of existence echo out its version of hallelujah. "Ok, time out for a quick. Where are we? What is this place?"

"This is a location that rests in knowledge as opposed to time and space. You get expert enough in any discipline and you have access to everyone else who has had that level of expertise. It's called the Akashic record."

"Yeah, well, I'm not expert in anything . . ." As Mico was speaking, I felt my imagination literally change the landscape around us. I imagined a giant library and so a massive version of the Mill Valley Public Library formed in front of us. In reality it was the first library my mother ever took me to. It was a well-funded three-story building surrounded on three sides by redwoods. As a child I always imagined subbasements of books organized in antique stacks that went on for miles. But in the Akashic records, it was infinitely larger, stretching out in all directions farther than the eye could see. Mico didn't seem bothered by it.

"Yeah, me neither," he said, and formed a large sitting room with leather couches and paintings with impossible colors on the walls the same way I formed the library. "But all those experts need a common language. That's what your voice is. You speak with the voice of expertise. As a result you have access to this place."

"Ok, then how did you get here?"

"There's a woman named Samantha . . ." he started.

"Another liminal, like me?" The continuous chorus of voices harmonizes when I say liminal; it would be annoying if it weren't pitched perfectly. "A.C. said she could access the elusive realms. What does that mean? Is that where we are now?"

"Yes. This is like the reading room of the Akashic records. When you partook of the Manna Elohim, the joint, it told me you'd be here. Samantha has the ability to transport anyone she has sex with to these sorts of places . . ."

"Has sex with . . . ?" My body giggled but grown-up DJ Jah Puba ignored it.

"Chabi, where's my friend? Where's A.C.?"

My body resonated sadness before I could speak. I saw Mico's smooth, fine face so chisel-hard, bracing for bad news.

"He's alive," I managed to pull out without sobbing. "But Rice and the others. Poppy and the liminal guy . . ."

"Nordeen." For the first time I heard silence from all around.

"Yes. They caught him. I swear I didn't leave him. He pushed me out. I was going to get him." Instinctively I felt for A.C.'s guns and was surprised to find them on me. I pulled one out of the holster.

"I believe you. Now please put that thing back in its holster." I hadn't seen him move, but Mico was standing over me, his soft hand gently but firmly pushing down on my gun hand.

"I'm just saying he wouldn't have given these to me if . . ."

"Chabi, it's ok. I know you wouldn't hurt him." He sat back down, put his hand over his face and lay back. Spirit body or not, I could tell he was tired. And not from our conversation. I know combat fatigue when I see it. "But you're going to have to let him go."

"How's that now?" I shot up.

"A.C. went back in time, to your time, in order to save us. The Alters had gained power over us. We lost. I lost . . ."

"Yeah, A.C. told me. They had compromised you . . ."

"I broke from my truth." I didn't bother asking, but my body voice made it clear I was confused. He started again. "Tried to write a new truth. Tried to manipulate earlier versions of me. They found me . . ."

"At the Naga Suites," I said, beginning to understand. "The Little Kid wanted you to DJ for them."

"And if you weren't there, if A.C. hadn't reached out to you, let you know who they were . . ." He stopped for a second, and then smiled. "But it's more than that, isn't it? You took a risk for me. You broke character and scared us off from there."

"If I ask you about the Little Kid, will I be breaking a hole in the space-time continuum or something?" I was shocked how much I cared for that boy when I asked.

"He is one of the fortunate and the cared for," he tells me gently, and it's clear he can't tell me anymore. "If A.C. hadn't taken the chance to go back and meet you, I would have been in their box before I even knew what was going on, who I was."

"So you say thanks by leaving your best friend in their hands?" I shouted, and the chorus admonished me.

"They can't not break a child of the wind. He'll go to his nature, to the four winds, before they get anything from him. But if they get their hands on you . . ."

"Nordeen stopped him from doing that," I bark in my spirit body. "He was chanting something that kept messing with A.C.'s powers . . ."

"He'll get out of it. That's what he does."

"And maybe I'm the way he gets out of it now."

"You don't get it."

"Explain!"

"They can't have you," he said, just as pissed as I was. "Bad as it would have been for them to grab me when I was young, with you, if they completed your training at this age, you'd make Nordeen look like a tame house cat. You'd be worse than—" He stopped himself but I didn't let it drop.

"I'd be worse than Narayana." He nodded.

"More like Narayana times two. They'd find him through you and bind him to their cause with you."

"Don't trust him." My cold old hurt returned to my heart. "Narayana. If he tells you he loves you, that he'll never run, don't believe a word he says."

"I do," Mico responded simply. "I trust Narayana to be exactly what he is. I trust his actions, if not his words."

"So you stand by Narayana and will leave A.C. to die?"

"You can't kill the wind, Chabi."

"But you can torture it, can't you, Mico? And if that psycho Nordeen is an expert in anything, I can guess it's torture."

"This isn't easy on me, Chabi. If I had anyone in your time that I could call on to help grab him, believe me I'd send them. But I can't risk you. You've seen the influence they have. And that was them working in the shadows. If they've got A.C., if you've squared off against them, they've got no reason to be subtle anymore. This is when they are the most dangerous."

"Yeah, and they've got A.C. I get it. You're a general fighting a war. But I'm a grunt. Someone came back for me and now he's behind enemy lines. And you want me to do what now? Sit this one out? You act like you just met me."

"I did." He smiled. "This you, anyway. I don't want you going anywhere near the Naga Suites . . ."

"But you can't stop me, either. So you might as well help me." I stood.

"My ability to affect the past is limited." He stood to meet my eyes and I knew that he was happy I was going for A.C.

"I just need to get into the building with supplies."

"You'll be relying on the Manna Elohim."

"The what now?"

He sighed before he spoke. "What we're fighting for, what this is all about. It's what the Alters despise. It's how you got here. It's why they want your friend's land. It's an early outcropping of the Manna. They tasted it on the marijuana, now they want to source. But now you've smoked it you see. You've been in communion with it. If you utilize it to get into the Suites, they will all know you are there as soon as you enter."

"That's why I'm bringing supplies. And I'm not fighting for some weird plant fungus. I'm fighting for A.C." He nodded. Sad, but somehow proud.

"Narayana is . . . I can deliver a message to him in my time. If you'd like," Mico offered reluctantly.

"Tell him to pray I die in my time. 'Cause if I make it to yours, me and him are going to have words."

I probably should have asked Mico for my bodily voice back. Whatever. The fungus gave me the benefit of damn near instant transport but ten stories up from the basement in a hallway. I'd been gone a maximum of fifteen minutes. I didn't need my voice to kick ass. I pulled the two entropy pistols and made my way to the hallway. Their soul weight did make them hard to lift, but they didn't need reloading and gave me the clarity of sight to know where to shoot what Alters.

I pulled the fire alarm and watched all manner of people emptying rooms. Some were Alters and I showed them no mercy. To other people it seemed like some crazy quiet girl with a sword was shooting remarkably pretty folks at random. Thankfully, the human instinct to run away from trouble kept most civilians away. While everyone was flooding the stairs, I took the elevator. I remembered the emergency code from my time as security chief and made my way up to the thirteenth floor. I expected a lot more trouble than I got. Only ten Alters. When the door opened, I holstered the pistols and gave the sword the blood it wanted. Its entropic force made it lighter, not heavier, and it sang an awesome dirge as I swung it. It wanted to keep swinging, pushing me to go one floor down and clean out anyone there. But I restrained myself with thoughts of A.C. I just had to drop something off in Rice's apartment.

I pulled five explosives in the elevator and punched in the express code for the basement. Before I got down, I opened the emergency hatch in the roof and climbed up. Just to be safe I hopped on the maintenance ladder a floor above the basement. Jah Puba's God must have been looking out for me because that part worked out perfectly. The Alters lit the elevator up with lead as soon as it came down. When they walked in to investigate, the timers went off on the explosives. I caught a little heat and the emergency hatch blew up, but that was fine. Before the explosion was fully over, I jumped through the access door on the top of the elevator.

I forgot how strong the Alters were. Two jumped through the flames for me. I used the Red Salamander Rising strike to put one's balls where his throat was. The other came slicing through with a bladed weapon that extended from both sides of his hand. I took his hand off with my sword. I sheathed it then Dragon Rolled over the flames and into the former dance floor turned pit fight. Three came for me at once. One chick I'd already blinded in an eye, another favored his right leg majorly. I swept it with the Black Rooster's Peck before the one-eyed raving lunatic could release her blade at me. I shot back with two rounds. One for her other eye, the other for the Alter hanging back loading his piece.

Two more, working in unison, tried to disarm me, thinking the guns were my last line of defense and not my first. They darted around the room like cracked-out scorpions, lunging for me out of the shadows. I holstered the pistols and raised the sword. It sought them out for me. Then the rest came. Ten all at once. Bum rush. When it was done, I was the only one alive and unhurt.

Those on the stage didn't seem to care. Nordeen, Poppy, and Rice were the only ones standing. A.C. was flying, or rather being kept in the air by Nordeen's chanting. I let a bullet speak for me and sent it at Nordeen. He changed his focus and language to stop the bullet, but it only slowed it down enough to be dodgeable. At least it caused him to drop A.C. The Wind Boy was obviously hurt, but did his best not to show it.

"Now see, I go through all the trouble of getting you out of here," A.C. tried to joke. "And here you are, back in the game."

"She couldn't resist me." It was Rice. He said it, looked at me, and I almost believed him. With the gun still out, I waved all of them away from A.C. The rat bitch spoke.

"What was that, little liminal girl? I can't hear you. Speak up!"

I shot at her, but she scurried behind A.C., her talon-like fingers around his neck. "Do that again and I'll make a corpse of him, I promise."

"You've picked the losing side of a battle that's already won, girl," Nordeen said as I approached the stage, my aim switching between all three of them. "But there's still time. This is where our kind belongs."

"Ha!" A.C. coughed. "If liminals belong with Alters, then why are you the only one with them, Nordeen? Why do they spend all their time trying to kill liminals? Don't believe your own lies, old man."

"Shut your hole." Poppy made it sound sexy. Even to me. But I kept my focus on her as I entered the ring. So much so that I forgot about Rice.

"No lies then." He came up next to me, putting himself between the bullets meant for Poppy. "Here's my truth. You've destroyed an ancient ritual and cost millions in dollars and countless influence. But if you come with me, join me, be with me, like we've both always wanted, I swear, Chabi, it could all be worth it. We could end this stupid conflict before it gets out of hand. It could just be you and me. Forever. Chabi, look into my eyes, I'm not lying. Do this for me and I promise, I will never leave you."

What can I say? I bought it. I lowered my guns. I let him hug me; I let myself feel comforted by him. I couldn't help it. I saw the light go out of A.C.'s eyes and the joy in Poppy's face. But there was nothing I could do against his spell. And I knew it.

That's why I set the rest of the charges on a timer in Rice's apartment. They went off a second after he held me and the whole building shook. Instantly he knew what was going on. I would have apologized if I could have. But he had taken my voice.

"You fucking bitch!" That was all I needed from him. Just a glimpse of his true face. I broke his arm in four places before I threw him into Nordeen. Poppy tried running, but A.C. was on it, he flipped backwards the second she let him go and mule-kicked her ankle. Still, like the wounded rat she was, she kept scampering. I shot at her as she ran out some back door I'd never seen before. I knew I hit the bitch but not how bad. I whirled to try to get Nordeen but he was already gone. I saw Rice move quickly, gracefully, to the back room. It almost didn't matter; the sound of 155 tons of steel, glass, and concrete coming down on us was deafening.

"Chabi, quick, the weapons," A.C. demanded as he stood up. It hurt to let them go but it also felt lighter. He put them on. "Ok, now listen, Chabi. You've got to sing. I can get you out of here but you've got to sing."

I motioned to my throat. I could barely hear him. The ceiling was about to give in.

"Screw that noise. No one can take your voice. You can only give it. You broke Rice's hold over you. Your voice is your own. Come on, Chabi, there isn't much time!"

I started "Motherless Child." "Sometimes I feel like . . ." But I couldn't do it. The words came but I didn't want to disrespect my mother like that. Eight rebar beams from ten stories up tore me apart before I knew I was dead.

Epilogue
The Time I Died

I felt the Mansai *in a new way. The wind through the sails was the wind* in my hair. When the deck creaked so did my chest. What happens belowdeck is the closest I get to hunger, being dead and all. So when A.C. appeared on the deck, I knew instantly.

"So is this heaven or hell?" I asked. He looked apologetic already. It couldn't have been that long since I was in the basement of the Naga Suites; he still looked like shit.

"Guess that's up to you." He tried to smile. "I called in some favors. Compromised on some principles, begged some deities I swore I'd never talk to again, and got you this."

Rather than ask, I felt. "The *Mansai* and I are one. It lives as I do. But I can't get off it. I'm a ghost ship."

"I can end this if you want. It's not as simple as heaven or hell but you will move on."

"Can anyone see me?" I asked.

"If they step on board. Otherwise, they just see the ship." I stood, feeling the boat. It felt like when I met Mico, when my body was an ocean. "You'll have to go out to sea in order to experience the fullness of what you can do but your katas, now, shaped by the ship, will be truly powerful."

"Mom?" The thought came to me all at once as I looked over to her houseboat and saw her light not yet on.

217

"She's one of the fortunate and cared for. Rice and his crew won't get near her."

"There's a plan in all of this. Your buddy Mico wants something from me, doesn't he?" I smiled then got angry.

"Look, if you want to pass over I won't stop you. We all know you deserve the rest. But now you've seen the Alters. Seen what they can do. We need folks unafraid of them. Living or dead . . ."

"Or ghost ship, doesn't matter. You just need soldiers," I said slowly. "Narayana?"

"He's out there." A.C. pointed past the Golden Gate Bridge. "Right now, he's out in the sea somewhere. He hasn't told us, me, where. Maybe you run into him at some point before he links up with us. I don't know."

"He got all working parts when you guys meet up with him?" I ask.

"Yeah."

"Then he didn't meet up with me yet." I'm quiet for a minute. "Nordeen asked a valid question, you know. Who says you're on the right team?"

"One more hit," A.C. asks, showing one of his joints to me. His little smokeable God. "It will send me back to my time, and you back here to make your decision. But before it does, it'll show you what it is we're fighting for."

I take a drag, more to see if a ghost can take a hit than anything.

We're at a night spot in San Francisco. One of the ones I used to go to. It's not a club, it's a café turned club at night. Everyone is earnest, everyone is dubstepping their minds out, waiting for breakdowns, head bobbling, going nuts. The speakers are going to be as useless as half of the dancers' eardrums after tonight, but who cares? It's beautiful to behold. I'm about to ask if anyone can see me when the music changes.

It's all samples, but well looped and parsed. Not thrown together like someone with their first Casio. It's old school hip-hop, and Bhangra, and Cumbia . . . and something more. More than dubstep, more than the pastiche of post-hip-hop tunes. There's a generativity in the music, it's alive. There are Tamil traditional songs, Soca, Merengue; it's the music from all over the world. With a beat. I can't help it, I'm grinning and crying at the same time. It's wonderful. When I look up at the DJ, I'm only half surprised that its Jah Puba/Mico. It's not perfect yet, but he can hear the music I fought to, the rhythm of the universe. That's what he's trying to mix to, the universal sound.

"He wants to do the same with people's souls," A.C. whispers in my ear. I hear him fading, back to his time. "And he wants you to sing for him."

Acknowledgments

I wrote this at a low point in my life, after all that I thought was stable upended itself, and decided that security was a blanket meant to comfort someone else. I had to stretch. I had to rely on folks in ways I never thought I would. Those that came through I call family. I don't call the others.

To Nick, AKA the man on the boat: You are the best teacher I've ever had. My respect for you knows no bounds.

To Katy Franco: Because you treat my typos like misfit toys in need of care.

To Katie: Lil sis! Thanks for being an early reader and a forever honest voice.

To Jesse Powell: Writing brother for life!

To Chris Lane: Skinny man, you do big things.

To Nalo: For inspiring simply by being in the world.

To Tigress: Your support on and off the page made this possible. Thanks, pretty lady.

To John Jennings: Not just for the covers, but for all we will do next.

To Gavin and Kelly: Thanks for getting on board this Liminal train.

About the Author

Born in 1974, Ayize Jama-Everett hails from the Harlem of old. In his time on the planet, he's traveled extensively throughout the world—Malaysia, East and North Africa, Mexico, New Hampshire—before settling temporarily in Northern California. With master's degrees in psychology and divinity, he's taught at the graduate and high school level and worked as a therapist. He is the author of three novels, *The Liminal People*, *The Liminal War*, and *The Entropy of Bones*, as well as an upcoming graphic novel with illustrator John Jennings entitled *Box of Bones*. When he's not writing, teaching, or sermonizing, he's usually practicing his aim.

Taggert can heal and hurt with just a touch. When an ex calls for help, he risks his enigmatic master's wrath to try to save her daughter. But the daughter has more power than even he can imagine and in the end, Taggert will have to use more than just his power, he has to delve into his heart and soul to survive.

"A fast-paced story about superpowered people struggling for control. . . . a damn good read. It's a smart actioner that will entertain you while also enticing you to think about matters beyond the physical realm."—Annalee Newitz, io9

paper · $16 · 9781931520331 l ebook · $9.95 · 9781931520362

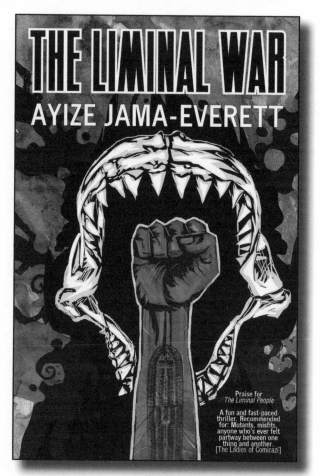

When Taggert's adopted daughter goes missing, he suspects an old enemy. With friends, family, and even those who don't quite trust that he's left his violent past behind, his search leads to an unexpected place: the past.

"A scrappy group of people with superpowers who careen through a criminal underground, the space-time continuum, and frequently outrageous battles to rescue a young woman who's gone missing. . . . The plot moves swiftly, cramming incident after incident into a novel that seems surprisingly slim for this breed of action-adventure. . . . An engaging sequel that sets its likable cast of characters against a fast-paced sequence of dangers." — *Kirkus Reviews*

paper · $16 · 9781618731012 | ebook · $9.95 · 9781618731029